I WILL MAKE YOU PAY

An absolutely gripping crime mystery with a massive twist

CAROLINE BALE

JOFFE BOOKS

First published 2019
Joffe Books, London
www.joffebooks.com

This book is a work of fiction. Names, characters, businesses, organizations, places and events are either the product of the author's imagination or are used fictitiously. Any resemblance to actual persons, living or dead, events or locales is entirely coincidental. The spelling used is British English except where fidelity to the author's rendering of accent or dialect supersedes this.

ISBN: 978-1-78931-139-6

To Declan for the daily support, encouragement and belief. To Ferdia Mac Anna and the three percenters without whom this book would not have happened. And finally to Cameron, Alexander and Imogen for always being there.

PART ONE

CHAPTER ONE

High Petergate, York

I watch Connie Taylor's lips move. They are daubed in a gaudy pink shade of lipstick, the same colour as her ridiculous hair. There is a string of saliva connecting her top and bottom lips. It stretches as she speaks but does not break. I stare at it with a mixture of fascination and disgust.

The skin above her mouth is etched with deep vertical lines, ridges which pay testament to her heavy smoking habit. Her teeth are crowded on the bottom, stained yellow with nicotine. I wonder if a cup of acid would make them white again. I imagine the lips burning away in the path of the acid to reveal a set of whiter, brighter teeth.

Connie is excited. "Did you hear me, Tom?"

I pull myself back from the daydream to find her eyes locked on mine.

"I know we're close to a payout. It's only a matter of time.".

We are sitting in Prufrock's, the café Connie works in. Its location next to York Minster makes it popular with tourists. The great cathedral is literally within spitting distance from my seat in front of a large window. A noisy Irish family have entered the café. The distraction shuts Connie up for a few moments. My thoughts drift again and I remember fondly how my fascination with acid began. I was twelve years old when a careless chemistry teacher left me unattended long enough to steal a bottle of sulphuric acid from the supplies cupboard. Shortly afterwards, I started my experiments on hamsters, which my mother unwittingly supplied as pets. Becoming bored, I soon graduated to cats — the neighbours' cats to be precise. That was a mistake. It's how I got caught. Three cats disappeared on our street in as many weeks and I had been seen with all of them.

I dislike the Irish. It was an Irish psychiatrist who had diagnosed me with Conduct Disorder. Dr Michael Daly. I have never forgiven him. He told my parents he feared I was a sociopath in the making. The diagnosis only served to give my father a label with which to further taunt me. Of course, when news of the diagnosis spread, I became a pariah, spurned by children and parents alike. But I learned two valuable lessons. First, I learned that wanting to be liked is futile. It's a weakness in others that can be exploited. Second, don't get caught.

I smile at Connie. "That's great. And do you know what? No one deserves it more than you."

Connie beams at me. She is truly pathetic.

I learned at a young age that everyone wants to be liked. Well, almost everyone. I couldn't care less what people think of me. That gives me a strength over others. Over the years I have perfected my technique. I form a bond with my target, make them think I like them. I put a lot of effort into creating a trusting connection.

Take Connie Taylor, for example, my present target. Why the owners of this place would hire someone like Connie is beyond me. Fat, middle-aged, ugly. The woman has no redeeming qualities. She is unfriendly to locals and tourists alike, and yet I have managed to befriend her. I noticed her reading the Daily Star *and the next day I made sure to bring along my own copy. Surprise, surprise! We share similar views on Brexit and refugees. Over the months that I have been coming to the café, we have discovered that we have many things in common. I too was brought up in care, or so I told her. I too watch* Coronation Street. *And I too love cats.*

She started joining me at my table during her morning break. I told her a few things about myself, mainly lies, but with a sprinkling of half-truths for authenticity. It didn't take her long to drop her guard. After all, I had worked hard to make her feel that I was someone with whom she could connect on a deeper level. And so, she shares her secrets with me. Her concern for her closest friend, Vicky. The abuse they both suffered. The shared trauma. And their quest for compensation. She worries that Vicky's love for her young daughter might get in the way of her finding justice. I am genuinely interested. Fascinated, in fact. I hang on her every word and she senses that. She is not used to such attention. It's addictive.

By now I know what car Connie drives, what her shift patterns are. Where she lives.

This will be our last coffee together, thank God. Her proximity makes my skin crawl. The smell of stale cigarette smoke and her vapid conversation leave me feeling sick.

I stand up. The more I get to know her, the more there is to despise. But she is a pawn in my game and I need her for my next move. I have forty hours left to find Vicky Richards. Tonight, I will make Connie tell me where Vicky lives. Then I will kill her.

"See you on Monday, then," Connie says.

I lean over and kiss her on the cheek.

"Not if I see you first."

CHAPTER TWO

New Earswick, York

Connie Taylor strained to listen. She had definitely heard something. It had sounded like someone knocking over a flower pot. It was dark outside, and all she could see was her own reflection in the kitchen window. She barely recognised the woman staring back at her. Decades of binge drinking and a thirty-a-day smoking habit had ravaged her good looks. Not yet forty-five, she could have passed for sixty. Deep lines scored her face. She was no longer working the streets, but her face told the story of those years.

She lit a cigarette and sucked the smoke deep into her lungs, feeling immediate relief sweep through her. She listened again. Silence. Just the ticking of the clock on the oven, and behind that the quiet of the empty fields surrounding the house. Connie had never been afraid of being on her own, not until recently. It was Vicky's fault she was so jumpy. The stream of texts warning her she wasn't safe, the midnight calls begging her to leave before it was too late. The two women had known each other for over thirty years, since meeting in care. They had both suffered back then, but, unlike her, Vicky had never been able to let go of what had happened.

Then, just five months ago, Harry Gascoyne's face had been splashed across the papers. The businessman who had dragged himself up by the bootstraps, the perfect rags-to-riches hero. How many millions had he made from selling his supermarket chain? A hundred million? More? Connie had warned Vicky that nothing good would come of going to the police after all this time, but she hadn't listened. Her therapist had told her that she needed closure. She said Gascoyne deserved to be exposed for what he had done to them, for ruining their lives. Vicky had suffered the most, but they both deserved compensation.

The more Connie had thought about it, the more she had liked the idea. Going to the police would let Gascoyne know they were serious, that they wouldn't be palmed off with a few grand. Vicky had marched into Harrogate police station and had given a statement. That was when the intimidation had started, the stalking, the phone calls. The last one had threatened Vicky's little daughter, Kallie, who was just five years old. The police didn't want to know. Vicky had gone into hiding.

Connie peeled the cling film off the meal she had brought back from the café and placed it in the microwave. Chicken curry and rice. She rarely cooked anymore. Why would she when there was always food left over after her shift? She sighed. This was her life now. Microwaved meals and nights in alone watching crap TV. Her days of hustling on street corners were over. She couldn't compete with the young foreign girls, and she would end up doing time if she got another conviction. Thankfully, she had the job at the café, part time, cash in hand. Between that and the social she could make ends meet.

Her phone pinged. It was Vicky.

Connie, please leave your place tonight. It's not safe. I'm not far, you can stay with me and Kallie until we sort something out.

Connie turned off the kitchen light and pressed her forehead up against the window, cupping her hands around her eyes to better see out into the dark. Snow was forecast, but there was no sign of it yet. She could see her back garden, a patch of grass just big enough for a small table and chairs. Beyond were the empty fields, through which the Westfield Beck flowed on its way to the River Foss. She could hear the wind in the trees, whipping itself up into a rage. A three-foot-high beech hedge, winter brown, was all that separated her from whatever might be out in those fields, looking in at her.

Connie jumped as the cat flap shot open with a crash and Shadow squeezed his fat body into the warmth of the kitchen. She sighed in relief. That's how rattled Vicky had made her. Terrified of her own bloody cat! She pulled down the kitchen blind, flicked the light back on and opened a can of Dutch Gold. The microwave pinged and she spooned the steaming curry onto her favourite IKEA plate, which she placed on a tray along with a jar of chutney. Shadow walked beside her into the lounge, purring loudly.

She turned on the television and slipped off her shoes. Shadow jumped up to sit in his usual place on the sofa. Her legs ached after another long day on her feet at the café and she rubbed at the veins which throbbed behind her knees.

The omnibus edition of *Coronation Street* had recorded and she felt the tension in her body begin to recede. The curry tasted good. She took a swig of lager to wash it down. When she was ready for bed, she washed her plate, knife and fork, and left them to dry on the draining board. She checked the locks on the front and back doors and went up the stairs carrying her cigarettes, phone, and another can of beer. In bed, she had her last and favourite smoke of the day. Finally, she replied to Vicky's text, telling her she was staying put.

* * *

Connie woke with a start as the room lit up. She turned to look at the bedside clock as a crash of thunder broke overhead — 3:30 a.m. The storm sounded as if it was right over the house. A minute or two later another streak of lightning lit up the room. It was followed by more thunder, but there was another sound from downstairs, like glass shattering. She sat up, straining to listen. Silence.

She knew immediately that he had come for her, just as Vicky had warned her he would. What should she do? She dared not turn on the light. If someone was downstairs, then he would know for sure where she was. She picked up her mobile with shaking hands. She would phone Vicky. She tapped the screen but her fingers were trembling and the phone slipped from her grip and thudded onto the floor. Downstairs, the kitchen door squeaked open. Connie knew that sound. Every day for the last few months she had made a mental note to buy some oil but had kept forgetting.

She scrambled onto the floor looking for the phone. Under her bed was a jumble of empty cigarette packets, shoes and pyjamas. A creak came from the top step of the staircase, right outside her bedroom door. She froze. Her chest was so tight that she could barely breathe. There was nowhere to hide and no one to hear her scream even if she did manage to reach the window. The handle turned silently and the door inched open.

CHAPTER THREE

Ferry Lane, Bishopthorpe

Ellen McClure could feel her phone vibrating in her back pocket. *Damn it!* She didn't want to stop now — there was only five feet of the galley floor left to sand. She flicked the sanding machine off and pulled the safety glasses and dust mask up onto her forehead. The shrill whine of the engine slowly died. It was her first weekend on duty as senior investigating officer with the North Yorkshire Serious Crime Team and she would be expected to answer any call from the team's HQ at Harrogate station immediately.

Her phone was still ringing, but it wasn't the station. It was Anthony. Ellen rolled her eyes in exasperation. *For God's sake!* An image of the two envelopes which lay unopened on the hall table sprung to mind. She knew they were from Anthony's solicitor. The firm's logo was on the front. There was no way she was talking to him, not right now.

Yes? she texted back.

The reply flashed onto her screen.

Please answer your phone. We need to talk.

Fat chance! she thought.

Ellen put her phone back in her back pocket, pulled on the safety glasses and dust mask, and resumed sanding. She didn't have time for Anthony's bullshit right now. Her new job was taking up all her energy, and any spare time she did have left she spent fixing up the boat which was to become her and her thirteen-year-old daughter Zoe's new home. There was maybe another two weekends' worth of work to be done before they could move on board, and that was only if she got the sanding finished today. In the meantime, they were living in a tiny flat over her sister Jackie's shop.

She focused once again on the sanding. She was just finishing the galley, an open-plan kitchen/living area with windows on four sides, overlooking the River Ouse. Three runs with the hired sanding machine, using finer grades of sandpaper each time, and now, at last, she was almost done.

Ten minutes later she turned off the machine and surveyed her work. There were blisters on the palms of both her hands, but she felt satisfied with the progress she had made. She could see a few scuffs on the skirting boards where she had let the machine get too close, but nothing that couldn't be covered up with a lick of paint.

Gypsy Queen, fondly known as *Gypsy*, was an eighty-foot wide-beam Dutch barge Ellen had inherited from her father, Paddy. Much larger than an average houseboat, it had two storeys over the waterline, with a large outdoor deck.

The inheritance had left her with a choice. Go against her father's wishes and sell *Gypsy* or sink everything she had into the project and turn the boat into a home for her and Zoe. She had chosen the latter.

From down in the hull she could hear Dan Dixon's gravelly voice. Dan, or Danny Boy as Paddy had called him, had joined the police force in the early 1970s, at the same time as her father. The two men had become firm friends and had remained so until Paddy's death the previous year. It was Dan who had introduced Paddy to his future wife, Brigid, another Irish immigrant. Today, Dan was supervising the installation of a fancy new diesel central heating system, the cost of which had depleted nearly all of Ellen's remaining funds.

Dan's shaggy grey hair emerged into the galley. He was carrying two mugs of tea in hands the size of shovels, which he carried out through the double doors that led to the deck.

He was angry. "That twat below doesn't know his arse from his elbow."

Ellen sighed and hung the safety glasses and mask on the handle of the sander. She followed Dan onto the deck, smacking at her overalls to get rid of some of the dust clinging to them. Outside, the air was crisp, the grey sky threatening snow. The bells of St Andrew's church were ringing. Sunday evening mass about to begin.

"I've only paid him a couple of hundred up front, Dan. He won't get the rest until you're fully satisfied and it's up and running."

Dan placed the steaming mugs of tea onto the deck table and sat down. On the river, a barge chugged slowly past.

"You know my thinking on it, Elly. The old stove did your dad just fine. There's other things you could have spent your money on, like paying someone to do that sanding."

Paddy had lived on board *Gypsy* for the last ten years of his life and would never have splashed out the kind of money Ellen just had on the heating system. Dan couldn't get his head around it.

"We've been through this, Dan. If there's one thing I can't stand, it's being cold, and the boat is freezing. Always has been."

Ellen figured that as long as she could get the place warm, then all the rest could be sorted in time. Her transfer and promotion to detective inspector at the elite North Yorkshire Serious Crimes Unit had come with a sizeable increase in salary. However, the decision to sink so much money into the heating now meant that she was having to do much of the heavy-duty work herself.

Dan frowned. "It was fine for your father. He just put on some extra clothes."

"Yeah, an anorak, and a hat and gloves, sometimes even in bed. You can see your breath inside for half the year, for God's sake. And it's not just me, it's Zoe too."

Dan handed Ellen a mug of tea. "It's your boat now lass, your decision."

Ellen raised an eyebrow. *Gypsy* was one of several houseboats moored along this stretch of the river, including Dan's live-aboard narrowboat, *Serendipity*. Dan and Paddy had worked together on each other's boats since retiring from the police force ten years ago. As a result, Dan sometimes acted as if *Gypsy* were half his. Still, Ellen could not do the project without him. And although she would never admit it, she needed Dan. It was to him that she had turned to for counsel when all of the trouble had blown up in Leeds.

She took a slurp of scalding tea. Dan liked to let the tea stew so that it was as tar-like as possible. She looked at her watch. Five past six already. Anthony was due to drop Zoe back at the flat at half past. He took Zoe most weekends, which gave Ellen the freedom to accept any overtime going or, if there was none, like this weekend, put in the hours on the boat.

She stood up. "I have to go. Zoe will be back at half past."

Dan looked at his watch.

"Stay where you are. You've time to have your tea. I'll clear up."

Ellen sat back down and lifted her mug, grateful for the few extra minutes' rest. A cruise boat passed by, sending waves lapping against the side of the boat from the wash. She shook some of the dust from her hair. When she looked up, Dan looked as if he was about to speak, hesitating in the way he often did before doling out advice he knew she didn't want to hear.

Here we go!

"You know what I'm going to say, Elly. You're working too hard. You need to ease back on the throttle. All this chasing here and there, it's no good for you."

She knew he meant well, but she was not in the mood for a lecture.

"I need to get this job done, Dan, get us on board. After that I'll relax, but right now I have no choice. It's only for another few weeks."

Ellen glanced at her watch again, not to check the time, which she already knew, but to give Dan the hint to leave it alone. He didn't take it.

"Look, I get it, you want to get on with the boat, get settled into your own place. But the move from Leeds, away from Zoe's dad . . ."

Ellen reached for her keys, but Dan grabbed them first. He wasn't finished.

"It's been hard on Zoe. She needs you around, even if it means you have to stay at the flat for a bit longer . . ."

The reference to Zoe stung like a slap. She snatched the keys from Dan's hand and stood up.

"Everything I do, I do for Zoe. The overtime, the time I spend out here, all of it. You of all people should know that."

Dan stood up and grasped her shoulders, forcing her to face him.

"I do know that, Elly. I'm not having a go at you. It's just the last year, especially the last few weeks . . . it's been hard on her too."

Ellen shrugged free of Dan's grasp. "I'm not having this conversation. I'm too tired and I'm late."

Was it too much to want a decent place for Zoe to live? A bedroom and a bed of her own to sleep in?

* * *

On the ten-minute drive into town she thought about what Dan had said. Since the move to York three weeks ago, both Dan and Jackie had been great, between them collecting Zoe from school and looking after her while Ellen juggled work and fixed up the boat. But deep down she knew that Dan was right. She had barely seen Zoe recently. She knew it wasn't ideal, but if she didn't get the boat ready, then who would?

When she arrived at the flat, she ordered a pizza. A few minutes later she heard the doorbell ring and ran down to open the front door, expecting to see Zoe. Instead, Anthony was standing at the door, holding their daughter by the hand. Born to Jamaican parents, he towered over her at six foot three inches tall. He had always been confident in his good looks, but now there was something else. Ellen ran her eyes over his outfit. His old anorak had been replaced with a trendy new parka. Around his neck he wore a bright-green knitted scarf. Designer. His runners had been replaced with expensive brown brogues. He had grown a goatee. Linda had obviously given him a makeover. Ellen bristled. It suited him.

Coming to the door with Zoe was new too. Up until now, Anthony had watched while Zoe ran in from the car on her own. Ellen clenched her jaw. She did not want to see him. If Zoe hadn't been there, she would have shut the door in his face.

She remembered the night she had told him she was leaving. Accusations had been hurled back and forth, followed by desperate pleas from Anthony to let Zoe stay. She had driven in the dark to a motel around the corner from the station in Leeds where she worked at the time. She and Zoe had lived there for a few months, before her transfer and move to York three weeks ago.

Anthony's tone was one of false friendliness. "Thought it was time I came to the door. See how you're doing."

Ellen reached over and pulled Zoe into a hug, releasing her from Anthony's grip. She could feel her anger rising. Of all the women he could have chosen to betray her with, he had chosen Linda. Not only had she lost a husband, but she had lost her best friend too. That was what had hurt the most, that and the rotten lies the two of them had fed her. She shook herself. Whatever had happened between her and Anthony, she wouldn't allow Zoe to be caught in the middle of it. She knew full well what it felt like to be caught in the firing line between two warring parents. Zoe dropped her overnight bag in the hallway and ran up the stairs to the first-floor flat.

Ellen glanced behind her to make sure Zoe was out of earshot. "I've nothing to say to you."

Anthony was going nowhere. "You're looking well, considering."

Like all of Anthony's compliments, it came with a barb attached. *Considering I'm covered in dust. Considering I work all hours of the day to give your daughter a nice place to live?*

"Can't say the same for you," Ellen replied, moving to close the door. She had said it to hurt him, but if anything, he was looking younger. He smiled at her in a way she had once thought charming. Now she looked at him with distaste.

"Look, I get it, you're still angry," said Anthony, holding up a hand to stop the door. "But you can't let that get in the way of doing what's right for Zoe."

Ellen felt a flush of heat rise up her neck.

"What do you want, Anthony?"

"I want to make sure you're going to turn up at the hearing."

"What hearing?"

"The custody hearing. You were sent notification. It's in two weeks' time. I'm not letting it slide again. This time the hearing goes ahead, with or without you."

Shit, he really means it. He's going to try and take Zoe off me.

"It's the first I've heard of any court date."

"For God's sake, I knew it. You didn't open the letters, did you? It's time you stopped thinking about yourself and started thinking about our daughter."

Ellen almost laughed at the irony of it. *Now you want to talk about what's right for Zoe? You weren't thinking about Zoe when you were fucking her mother's best friend, were you?*

She looked him straight in the eye. "Zoe is staying with me. I'm her mother, end of."

"You're never around for her, she would be better off with me. I work from home half the time, I can be there for her. The court will see that."

"Zoe is doing fine."

"Open your eyes, she's not doing fine. She's struggling with this move."

Now Ellen was furious. "Of course she's bloody struggling! We are all struggling because of you. Because of what *you* did. And now you think you can just take her off me?"

"Zoe has told me how little she sees of you. She needs to live with a parent who's not obsessed with their work. Let her come and live with us, even for a while?"

Us? Did he just say us?

"I'm her mother. She stays with me," Ellen said through gritted teeth and slammed the door in Anthony's face. Picking up Zoe's overnight bag, she climbed the stairs to the flat. She would have to go to court this time, although she hadn't booked the time off and Detective Superintendent Monroe would no doubt take a dim view. If she didn't show up, the judge could rule against her. She would have to talk to Zoe. Explain that life would settle down once they were on board *Gypsy*.

The pizza arrived and she and Zoe ate it together watching a recorded episode of *Strictly Come Dancing*. Ellen steeled herself not to ask Zoe if Linda had been at her dad's flat. When *Strictly* finished, she climbed into the bed she shared with Zoe, exhausted, even though it was not yet nine o'clock. Within a few minutes of turning out the light Zoe was asleep, her breath deep and steady. The wind battered against the old leaded windows, which somehow held the raging elements at bay. If Anthony thought he was going to take Zoe from her, he had another thing coming. She would fight him tooth and nail.

CHAPTER FOUR

Fossgate, York

Sleep for Ellen came reluctantly at one in the morning, but was broken some hours later by the sound of a bin blowing over in the street outside. Ellen sat up in bed, fully alert, her ears straining for the source of the sound. Outside a storm was raging. *Damn it, I'm awake now.* Zoe could sleep through any amount of noise. Ellen had once been the same. Not now, though, not after the things she had seen. Not knowing what she did about human nature. She sometimes wished she could un-know those things. She thought about what Anthony had said. She *had* been obsessed with her work, that much was true. Back in Leeds, the Ana Petrescu case had occupied her every waking thought. It haunted her still. The fourteen-year-old's body had been found a year and a half ago. The child had hung herself from a light fitting in the Leeds brothel where she had been kept.

The brothel had been one of a number on Ellen's watchlist when she worked in the Human Trafficking Unit of West Yorkshire Police. At the time, Ellen had been swamped with cases, and her boss, DCI John Parker, had specifically told her to drop her focus on that particular premises.

Now, a year and a half later, guilt and anger still kept her awake at night. Guilt that she had ignored her own misgivings about her boss's involvement with the brothel owner. Anger at the traffickers who had treated Ana so badly that she took her own life. Ellen had risked her career making sure that DCI Parker, who had been taking payments from the brothel owner, was exposed and prosecuted. In the end he had only served a few months, but his career was finished. He was dismissed without a pension barely a year before his retirement.

Over a period of six months, Ellen had managed to track down and prosecute almost all those responsible for the hell that Ana had lived through. Parker was finished. The brothel owner was currently serving five years in prison. By cross-referencing CCTV and car registration data, she had managed to hunt down and prosecute over a dozen men who had visited the premises. Most had got away with a fine or community service, but at least they had been outed to their families for the scum they were.

However, there was one individual she had not managed to find before her transfer came through. There was a video circulating on the darknet of Ana, which showed her being raped by a man Ellen had code-named Satan. In the video, Satan wore a black rubber face mask which hid his features from the camera, and which must have made him seem even more terrifying to the child he was raping. It was hard to be sure exactly, but he looked to be an older man, sixties maybe. His hair had the look of a bad dye job, blacker than black, and in stark contrast to the grey hair on his flaccid chest.

Ellen remembered the first time she had sat through that video. The rising nausea. Since then she had forced herself to watch it some fifty times. She knew every mole on that animal's body, every inch of his fat backside. She had pored over every detail of the room, concentrating on a small rectangular window set high above the bed. It was the only identifiable feature in an otherwise featureless room. From looking at the stills, it looked like the window in a basement. A car was barely visible through the window, so the room had to be below ground. The brothel had no basement and no such window, so the filming had taken place elsewhere. Ellen never got to track down the house, never got to apprehend Satan. The job with North Yorkshire Police had come through and she needed to take it, to get away from the poisonous atmosphere left behind by the trial. The search for Satan had died with her departure.

Watching her daughter sleep, Ellen moved the long braid of hair that had fallen over Zoe's cheek. Anthony's words were playing in her mind. *Zoe has told me how little she sees of you.*

The murder rate in North Yorkshire was one of the lowest in the country. That was one of the main reasons she had moved back here. Once the boat was finished then everything would settle down. She and Zoe would enjoy plenty of time together.

Zoe hadn't been planned. In fact, right up until the moment she had given birth and Zoe was placed in her arms, Ellen hadn't thought of herself as the mothering type. She had been unprepared for the intensity of love she felt for this little creature, with her shock of black hair and tiny clinging fingers. The fact that she looked just like Anthony and not the generic baby she had imagined had come as a shock. There was no way she was going to allow him to take her child. Not now, not ever.

Giving up on sleep, Ellen slid out of the bed and threw on her dad's old dressing gown. Paddy McClure's smell was still on it, a year after his passing. She couldn't bear to wash the plaid robe as the scent of him was such a comfort, especially on stormy nights like this one. She padded into the tiny kitchen and made herself a mug of tea, then took it into the living room and looked out through the window onto Fossgate below, its red-brick buildings and pretty wooden storefronts lit up by the occasional flash of lightning.

Her sister Jackie had let her move into the flat above the café she ran downstairs, at least until she got the boat fixed up. Both Ellen and Zoe loved the flat — all wooden beams and creaking floorboards — but it wasn't really big enough for the two of them. The living room was quite literally too small to swing a cat in, especially as it was now being used as a storage space for their belongings.

Although her new job was based at the police station in Harrogate, Ellen had never considered moving to the town. Not that she could even have afforded to. She preferred to add a thirty-five-minute commute each way rather than mingle with the yummy mummies in their four-by-fours ferrying privileged offspring to private schools. No. York, picture-postcard beautiful as it was, tolerated few airs and graces. That's what she'd always loved about the city. She had lived here for the first eight years of her life. Then, after her parents' divorce, her mother had taken her and her sister to live in Ireland. She and Jackie had lived for their summer holidays, when they would stay for a month with Paddy, living on and off the boat. At sixteen, after her mother's liver had finally succumbed to her love affair with the bottle, Ellen and Jackie had come back to York permanently. Those few years before leaving for university had been the best years, for all of them. The *Gypsy Queen*, once fixed up, would be perfect for her and Zoe, and bigger than any flat she could afford.

She slipped back into bed beside Zoe. The storm was in full swing now, with rain lashing in great torrents against the pitched roof above their heads. Ellen checked the time on her phone — 3:30 a.m. If she got back to sleep straight away, she would have three hours before she had to get up. But sleep continued to evade her, and her thoughts raced, and not just because of the delays with the boat or the confrontation with Anthony. She had seen the furtive looks around the office, heard the dropped conversations when she entered the room. They knew. Of course they did. She was the new DI who had broken the blue code of silence at her last station. Who had turned in one of their own. The whistle-blower. There was nothing she could do or say that would alter that first impression. She was not to be trusted.

Maybe she had deluded herself into thinking she could just walk away from what happened at Leeds. She had transferred with a promotion to the North Yorkshire Serious Crimes Team with an unparalleled track record. The elite unit at Harrogate was the obvious place for her. Why, then, did she feel so nervous? In just a few hours she would have to introduce herself at the first monthly team meeting since her arrival. Surely the past would be forgotten and she would be judged on her merits?

* * *

Her alarm sounded at exactly the same time that her mobile rang — 6:30 a.m.

She answered the call. "DI McClure speaking."

It was the station. The severed head of a woman had been found in Heworth Green.

CHAPTER FIVE

Walmgate, York

Ellen managed to shower, wake Zoe and leave the flat within twelve minutes. The forecasted cold snap had swept in on the tail of last night's storm and she flicked on the heater in the car. She dropped Zoe, who had her coat on over her pyjamas, at Jackie's place off Walmgate, her school uniform in a carrier bag, and then took a call from Detective Superintendent Alastair Monroe, who she put on speaker while she drove to the crime scene.

"Ellen? You've heard about the situation in Heworth Green?"

Ellen manoeuvred into the stream of rush-hour traffic.

"Yes, sir, I heard. I'm heading there now."

"It's a shocking scene, I'm afraid. There's no sign of the rest of the victim's body and the face has been obliterated with acid."

Ellen shuddered. She also knew that with no body and damaged facial features they would be lucky to get an ID on the victim before the press weighed in with headlines about police incompetence.

Monroe continued. "Listen, I'm ringing you because I've decided to give you the lead on this case, for now at least . . ."

Ellen's jaw dropped open. Monroe was appointing her as senior investigating officer. She mouthed a silent "Yes!" and slapped the steering wheel with her open palm. Being appointed SIO on a major murder inquiry was a huge opportunity, and one she had not expected to come so soon. There were any number of officers in Harrogate who would rightly have their noses put out of joint as a result of her selection. Her excitement quickly cooled. Something didn't feel right. Why had he said "for now"?

"That's great," she said, crawling slowly through the pedestrians crossing at Walmgate and turning left along the old city walls on Foss Islands Road.

"It's a major opportunity for you, Ellen, but I won't hesitate to take it off you if I feel you're struggling. You have an unparalleled track record as a detective, but this will require more of you."

"I understand, sir," Ellen said. "I won't let you down."

"You also have a record of running your mouth, of being a renegade, and that won't wash here. I want this investigation to run like clockwork. I want proper procedures followed — to the letter."

A sense of unease trickled through Ellen's body. She had never been accused of being a renegade before. Obsessive, sure, and she would be the first to admit that she did run her mouth at times. But she would never jeopardise the validity of evidence by unnecessarily flaunting procedure.

Monroe continued. "I have to warn you, there are certain members of the team who will not be happy. The whole Parker thing is still at the forefront of some minds. If you can manage to win over those people, you might keep the position, if not . . ."

Ellen bit her lip to stop herself saying that she didn't give a shit whose noses were out of joint. Particularly not DI Matt Jackson, whom she suspected Monroe was referring to.

She had only known Jackson for a short time, but she already didn't like him. The feeling was probably mutual. Over the previous weeks, she had looked up from her desk on several occasions to find him glowering at her across the squad room. John Parker had been a friend of Jackson's from many years before, when both men had worked in Bradford. If there was one person in the squad room who reminded her of her old boss, it was Matt Jackson. Both were arrogant loudmouths.

She took a breath. Alastair Monroe was a straight talker, and she respected him for that. He had taken a risk giving her the lead.

"I appreciate it, sir. You won't regret it."

Ellen ended the call and pulled right into Layerthorpe. The euphoria of moments ago was gone. A woman had lost her life in brutal circumstances. A monster was at large in the community, and the responsibility for catching him lay squarely on her shoulders. She had every intention of hitting the ground running.

As she drove she phoned several key people she wanted on her team, including DC Sarika Kaur. Ellen had come to know the young detective when she was with West Yorkshire Police. Although Sarika had been based in Bradford and Ellen in Leeds, the two had liaised closely on several cases involving human trafficking and had become friends. Sarika had even invited Ellen to her wedding the previous month. Third-generation British Sikh, intelligent, and with a strong work ethic, Sarika had been head-hunted for the Serious Crimes Unit only six months before.

Sarika picked up on the first ring. She was, in fact, almost at the crime scene — the duty sergeant at Harrogate had tipped her off twenty minutes ago. Ellen felt a sense of relief. She had done the right thing in ringing Sarika. A law graduate, Sarika was methodical and disciplined, preferring to weigh up all available options before taking a considered position. Ellen, on the other hand, had a propensity to act first and think later.

She didn't need Monroe to warn her that there were snakes waiting for her in the long grass. She trusted Sarika to have her back, and had a feeling she was going to need her before too long.

CHAPTER SIX

Heworth Green, York

Ellen arrived at the crime scene just twenty-two minutes after receiving the call from the station. She was acutely aware of the 'Golden Hour' — the critical period at the start of any criminal investigation. Effective early action by police officers helps to secure and preserve material that may otherwise be lost. The more time that passes following an offence, the more likely that crucial evidence could be lost or destroyed. Witnesses will have forgotten or misremembered vital information. CCTV footage may be deleted. With a live case like this, it was vital to get police and forensics officers to the scene as quickly as possible, capturing evidence and talking to potential witnesses while memories were still fresh.

Six or seven doors down from the Shoulder of Mutton pub was Lockton House, a four-storey Georgian villa, part of an impressive terrace set back from the tree-lined pavement. An ambulance and two police cars, their blue lights flashing, were parked directly in front of the house.

A throng of reporters, photographers, and gawkers had gathered on the pavement. A line of cars and vans were parked illegally along the double yellow lines, the deterrent of a parking fine rendered irrelevant by a potential scoop.

Ellen parked around the corner and pushed her way through the crowd, holding up her badge.

"DI Ellen McClure." Her breath left behind a white mist in the freezing air and she ducked under the police tape to the sound of clicking cameras and shouted questions. The crime scene manager, DC Glenn Halford, signed her in. Ellen recognised Halford from Harrogate. He had shown her an app on his phone which was counting down the days to his retirement: thirty-four days, five hours, and eleven minutes.

She looked up at the house and noticed a cornerstone under the eaves with the date 1825. Below it, over the front door, was a well-preserved sign which read 'Lockton House'.

"What have we got?" Ellen asked, pulling on the plastic suit, gloves and shoe covers Halford handed her.

The DC indicated a white tent which had been erected over the front steps. "A proper house of horrors. The head was found at five thirty on the top step over there. The owner of the house left early to catch the five fifty-five to King's Cross and almost sent it flying."

An image of the victim's head bouncing down the path like a football flashed unbidden into Ellen's mind.

Halford continued. "She and her husband are currently being interviewed by DI Jackson inside. From what I understand, neither are considered suspects."

For God's sake! It was usual practice for the on-call SIO to be the first called to the scene. Monroe was a political animal, so he no doubt had his reasons for calling Jackson before her, but now she felt on the back foot.

DC Halford held open the flap of the tent and stood back to let Ellen enter.

"Hope you haven't just had your breakfast. I almost chucked mine up. Scrambled eggs on toast. It's not so much the smell as the . . . well, you'll see for yourself."

Ellen took a deep breath before stepping into the tent. Halford followed her in. There were two SOCOs at work, obscuring her view.

"I don't need to tell you to use the stepping plates," Halford said, pointing at the metal plates which had been placed for walking around the remains. When the SOCOs saw Ellen, they stood back to let her take a quick look. "Careful," one of them said. "We think acid has been used."

At the sight, Ellen felt as though all the air had been sucked out of her body. "Fuck me!"

A woman's head, complete with pink-coloured hair, was sitting on the top step. Bloodshot eyes bulged out of their sockets, capturing the terror the victim must have felt in her last moments. The nose and upper lip had been completely burnt away, exposing the teeth and gums. An enlarged tongue protruded out of what remained of the mouth.

This was no spur-of-the-moment killing. Whoever killed this woman had taken his time. He had wanted to make an impact.

Ellen heard footsteps and looked round to see Sarika Kaur enter the tent behind her. She stopped short when she saw the head.

"Bloody hell!"

Ellen moved forward onto a stepping plate and looked around the top step.

"There's very little blood."

She looked up around the walls and inside the small porch roof. No signs of arterial spray, no spatters of blood. Ellen beckoned to Sarika to step carefully forward onto an adjoining metal plate.

She indicated the walls. "She wasn't killed here. It's too clean."

Sarika bent closer to the head, without moving her feet. "Are we sure she's a she?"

Ellen leaned forward. The face had been so badly burnt it was indeed difficult to determine the sex.

Sarika pointed with the tip of a pen at the hair. "The pink hair would suggest a woman, but that doesn't mean she definitely is."

Ellen gestured towards the jaw, which was slack but slender.

"Look at the jaw — it's too soft for a man. Too smooth as well."

The sound of raucous laughter preceded the tent flap being thrown open and DI Matt Jackson appeared. He stepped heavily onto the metal plates, half on, half off them.

"You took your time," he said.

"I came as soon as I was called," Ellen replied, trying and failing to keep the irritation out of her voice.

"Good one for you." Jackson turned to face Halford. "A guy goes into a boozer and says to his mate, 'You won't believe what just happened! I was taking a shortcut along the railway track, and I found a girl tied to the rails. I untied her, and we had sex over and over again. All the positions — everything!' His friend replies, 'That's great! Did you get a blowjob?'" Jackson paused before revealing the punchline. "'No, I couldn't find her head!'"

Halford gave an awkward laugh. Sarika threw her eyes up to heaven. Ellen wasn't the only one who thought Jackson was an arsehole.

"I couldn't find her head?" Jackson repeated, as if surrounded by imbeciles.

Ellen shook her head in a gesture of disbelief. Jackson reminded Ellen of a pit bull terrier, with a bullet-shaped bald head and the thickest neck she had ever seen. She and Jackson had reached the rank of detective inspector via very different routes. Ellen, at thirty-eight, had completed the Graduate Fast Track Programme, which had facilitated her rapid advancement from police constable to detective inspector in just seven years. Jackson, at forty-eight, had come the traditional route, twenty-five years' hard slog, climbing rung by rung to reach the role of DI. His resentment of her was only too obvious.

Jackson looked from Ellen to Sarika. "Jesus. Lighten up, will you?"

Ellen clenched her fists. Gallows humour came with the job. It was a tool in the emotional survival kit of most emergency personnel. She had no problem with it, but something about Jackson's tone pissed her off. Perhaps it was his general aggressive demeanour, the offhand way she had seen him treat those junior to him. Monroe's words were playing in her mind. *There are certain members of the team who will not be happy.* She was stuck with him, at least for the time being, but she would try to keep things as professional as possible.

"You've interviewed the residents, I believe?"

"Yeah. I've just finished taking a statement from the woman who found our friend here. Neither she nor her husband recognise the victim, but, given there's not much of her to see . . ."

Ellen looked at her watch.

"I'd like to have a word with them."

Jackson's tone was combative. "I've just told you, they know nothing. Why do you need to talk to them?"

Ellen chose to ignore his question.

"How long have you been here?" she asked.

"About forty-five minutes," he answered, all trace of false hilarity gone. "Why?"

"I'm wondering why I wasn't called earlier." Ellen made no attempt to mask her irritation. "I'm sure Superintendent Monroe has informed you, Matt, that I've been appointed SIO for this investigation. I should have been called first."

Jackson looked at her for several moments before replying. "Word to the wise, McClure. If I were you, I wouldn't be getting my knickers in a twist about who was called when. You're hardly in a position to throw your weight around."

So much for keeping things professional.

Ellen pulled herself up to her full height of five feet five inches and faced Jackson.

"I'm the on-call SIO. If you don't like it, you can ask to be moved onto something else."

Behind them, Halford and Sarika quietly exited the tent. She didn't blame them. Matt Jackson was a bully. Anyone who witnessed him being confronted like this risked a backlash later on. The two SOCOs were hovering. Jackson moved closer and spoke to Ellen in a low voice. His thin lips articulating each word with intensity.

"You happened to be on call last night, good for you. And for whatever reason, Monroe is letting you run with this for the time being. But it won't last, right? So don't go making any more enemies than you already have."

Ellen wanted to punch him in his smug face. But it would suit him down to the ground for her to lose her cool. It would allow him to paint her in a bad light to her new team. To Monroe. She had no intention of letting that happen.

Ellen held his gaze. "Monroe will do what he sees fit, but like it or not, I'm the SIO right now, so I suggest we get back to what we're paid to do."

Jackson turned his back on her and exited the tent. Ellen breathed out and reflected on how her life could have been had she chosen a different career. She could have gone into any number of jobs. Why would any sane person have chosen this? The dead she could cope with, it was the living she struggled to handle. Neanderthal morons like John Parker and Matt Jackson.

She turned back to the step. The next time she would see the victim would be at the post-mortem examination. The SOCO team and the photographer had priority now. It was time to leave them to it. She wanted to speak with the residents of the house.

* * *

Halford directed Ellen and Sarika through a side gate which led around to the back of the house. Jackson had said the couple knew nothing, but there had to be some reason why the killer picked this house to flaunt his grisly trophy.

Ellen suddenly remembered that she had forgotten to get Sarika a wedding present the previous month. It had been a spectacular occasion. A full-colour Sikh ceremony in the gurdwara in Bradford. It had been a revelation to see Sarika dressed in a red sari, her hands painted with henna. Her husband, Jaspreet, a lawyer Sarika had met at law school, had been equally spectacularly dressed with a beautiful white turban. Hundreds of people had attended the celebration, all of whom seemed to be related to the bride and groom. Ellen had slunk off early. Weddings were not her thing. Her own ill-fated nuptials had taken place with just a handful of people at the registry office in Leeds.

She glanced at the DC. "By the way, I'm definitely going to get you guys a wedding present. It's just that, with the move and everything, I didn't get time."

Sarika stopped and faced Ellen. "I told you, boss, forget it. I was just glad you came. Look, I'd be careful with Jackson. Humiliating him like that will only make him worse."

Ellen shrugged. "Maybe." But she knew Sarika was right. Bullies like Jackson put great store on being seen to be powerful. Demeaning him in front of his subordinates would only inflame his pathetic ego. She grinned at Sarika. "But it felt good."

CHAPTER SEVEN

Lockton House, Heworth Green

Ellen and Sarika took a quick tour of the house before talking to the occupants. It was a large property with six bedrooms, more like a small hotel than a family home.

The owners were a professional couple in their early forties. Sarah Clarkson, a solicitor who worked in Leeds, was usually the first to leave in the morning, while her husband Tim, an architect who worked from home, dropped their two children at the primary school around the corner a little later on.

The couple were in the kitchen. The kitchen itself was twice as big as Jackie's entire flat on Fossgate. Everything was stainless steel, shiny and efficient. At its centre was a battered refectory table, complete with a series of carefully mismatched chairs. It was big enough to seat twenty. Mr and Mrs Clarkson were seated at one end of the table, each nursing a mug of tea provided by the family liaison officer. Sarah Clarkson wore an elegant trouser suit. She looked pale, her manicured fingers visibly trembling. Their two young boys were chasing each other around a black granite kitchen island in their school blazers. Fighting an urge to shoo the boys out of the room, Ellen introduced Sarika and herself.

"Beautiful house you have here."

Sarah smiled weakly. "We've just finished the renovations."

The two boys were hollering now, their parents not in the least bit put out by the noise.

"Must be, what, six bedrooms?" Sarika said, who knew full well how many bedrooms there were.

"Yes. There were eleven when we bought it. We've knocked some of them together, so we've six now. We've not been here that long. Three years. We've just got it the way we want it, and now this."

"The house was a care home for fifty years." Tim Clarkson spoke for the first time. "It needed a lot of work to turn it back into a family home. The table came with the house."

The two boys were properly shouting now and Ellen felt her patience failing. She indicated for the family liaison officer to take the children upstairs. She closed the door after them, relieved that the racket was over. It always amazed her how people seemed immune to the noise of their own children.

"I have a few more questions, if you're up to it. We need to know if you know anyone with the same hair colour as the victim." Ellen nodded towards the front door. "I appreciate it's difficult, but please think carefully."

Tim shook his head. "We both only saw it . . . her . . . for a few seconds, but neither of us know anyone with pink hair."

"And neither of you heard or saw anything suspicious last night, or in recent weeks?" Sarika asked, her tone soft. "Any strange cars parked outside or anyone calling to the door?"

"As I already told the other detective, I came in from a function at one in the morning and it — the head — was not on the step then."

"And you are absolutely sure of that?" Ellen asked.

Tim frowned. "I think I'd have noticed a severed head sitting directly in my path, even with a few drinks on board."

Ellen's phone had been vibrating in her pocket, but before she could answer it the door opened from the garden and DC Halford approached. He whispered in her ear.

"We've found the victim's driving licence, ma'am."

"Where?" Ellen whispered back.

"You'd better follow me."

Ellen excused herself and followed Halford into the garden, where Jackson was waiting. Sarika brought up the rear, closing the kitchen door behind her. Jackson handed the driver's licence, encased in a clear plastic evidence bag, to Ellen. The ID belonged to forty-four-year-old Connie Taylor.

Jackson smirked. "Connie Taylor. Prostitute and drug addict. Used to work the streets down by Holbeck Lane in Leeds. Didn't have the pink hair then. Rough as a badger's arse."

The name was not one Ellen recognised. In recent years she had come to know many of the prostitutes working that area, but she had never come across Connie Taylor.

"Where was it found?" Ellen asked, noting that the address on the driving licence was in New Earswick, a pretty village two or three miles away. Ellen knew it well, having lived there for a few unhappy months as a child.

"One of the SOCOs noticed it, tucked in under the head."

Ellen looked up sharply. "You're kidding me?"

"Nope. She was taking a blood sample and there it was."

The woman in the photo had the same short-cut bob. But it was impossible to tell if it was her — the acid had rendered her face unrecognisable.

"So, the killer placed his victim's ID directly under her head," Sarika said.

Something didn't add up here. Ellen had assumed that the killer had used acid on the face of his victim to make identification difficult. Over the years she had learnt, however, never to assume anything.

"He wanted us to identify her quickly," said Ellen. "The question is, why?"

CHAPTER EIGHT

New Earswick, York

Sarika drove the short distance to New Earswick, during which time Ellen made several calls. She wanted a local Murder Investigation Room to be set up at Fulford Road police station, which was only a five-minute drive from Heworth Green. Monroe would not be happy. The station in Harrogate was state of the art. It had been built just a few years previously at huge cost, but it was a forty minutes' drive away without traffic. Fulford Road, the main station in York, was the obvious choice.

Next she called Jackie and asked if she would collect Zoe from school, supervise her homework, and put her to bed. There was no way she would be back before Zoe's bedtime. Being appointed SIO was a major opportunity to prove herself. This case could make her career, ensure that she and Zoe could be comfortable and secure. Anthony would no doubt make a big deal about it. The timing couldn't be worse, what with the custody hearing coming up in just a few weeks. This would play right into his hands, make it look like she was never at home. But she didn't have time to think about that now.

Ellen clicked into a text from Monroe, then glanced across at Sarika.

"Hope you've no plans for a normal life for the next few weeks. All leave's been cancelled, effective immediately."

Sarika shrugged. "Only another wedding next weekend. Jaspreet's cousin."

"I could put in a word with Monroe," Ellen suggested. "But if I'm honest, I'd rather you were here. I'd really value your backup."

"I cancelled it already. Jaspreet's mother is on my case to start a family. I'll let him deal with her."

Number one Pear Tree Field was the last cottage at the far end of the L-shaped lane, which came to a dead end just past it. Beyond a hedge, brown fields bordered by tall trees stretched as far as the eye could see. Fallen branches were a reminder of last night's storm. Ellen had a vague memory of playing hide-and-seek around here. She had lived with her mother and Jackie two streets across for six months or so after her parents had split up, when she was eight years old. It wasn't a happy time, and she pushed the memories to the back of her mind.

New Earswick was a model village with some 900 cottages built by the Rowntree family 100 years before. Many of the cottages had kept their external ornamental woodwork and decorative gates. There was an atmosphere of pride in the community evident in the general standard of upkeep of the houses. Number one Pear Tree Field was the exception, conspicuous in its disarray. Various items of rubbish were piled up in front of the house, including overflowing bin bags and the rusted wheel of a bicycle. It reminded Ellen of the house she and Jackie had lived in around the corner. A memory flashed through her mind of her mother lying half-conscious in front of the television, empty wine bottles stacked up behind the curtains. The fridge empty, dishes lying unwashed. Their father knocking on the window and Brigid refusing to let her daughters open the door. She wondered if Jackie remembered but knew she wouldn't ask her. Their time in New Earswick had ended suddenly when Brigid's sister had come and taken the three of them back to live in Ireland, away from Paddy and everything they knew.

The front gate was open and the drive empty. The unlined curtains at the front of the house were drawn, upstairs and down. Ellen pulled on a plastic suit, shoe covers, and gloves, and tried the front door. It was unlocked. She inched it open and called out. There was no reply, so she entered.

The hallway was cold. The heating had been off for at least several hours.

"Sarika and I will take upstairs," Ellen told Jackson and a DS named Paul Benton, who had just arrived. Both were suiting up.

The staircase was narrow and creaked noisily on the top step. The upstairs landing, like the stairs, was covered in a stained red carpet. A door on the right was open, revealing two single beds. Sarika indicated silently to Ellen that it was clear. Ellen turned the handle on the door to the left.

The first thing that struck her was the smell of stale cigarette smoke — that and a heavier odour, like an old-fashioned butcher's shop. The floor, like the landing, was covered in red carpet. Sarika flicked on the light switch, which threw a yellowish pall over the room and illuminated a double bed with a white duvet cover. Except it wasn't white anymore. It was splattered with blood. There were two lengths of rope, one tied to the ironwork bedhead, the other attached to the foot of the bed. Ellen flinched at the thought of what had happened here. On the bedside table was an overflowing ashtray and a can of beer.

Ellen stared at the bed. "She was tied here, tortured maybe. But this wasn't where he decapitated her."

She looked around to see if there was an en suite — there wasn't. Only then did she notice drag marks on the carpet leading from the bed out onto the landing. Because the carpet was red, she had missed the marks. She only hoped she hadn't walked on them.

Sarika was leaning in to examine the lengths of rope more closely. "How can you be so sure?" she asked.

"There isn't enough blood in here." Ellen pointed to the drag marks and made sure to walk around them. "See these marks? He moved the body. Let's check the bathroom."

Back out on the landing, Ellen turned to Sarika.

"Take a deep breath, you'll remember this sight for a long time."

Ellen pushed open the door. Blood covered every surface. It was pooled on the tiled floor, with splashes on the toilet and sink. To the right stood a bathtub with the shower curtain pulled closed across it. Ellen eased back the plastic curtain with a gloved finger, certain now of what must lie behind. In the bath lay the naked, headless body of a woman, the severed neck bone looking up at her like the eye of a cyclops.

"Jesus!" Ellen recoiled backwards. From behind her, she heard a moan escape from Sarika.

She yelled down to Jackson and Benton, who she could hear on the stairs.

"Body's in the bathroom. Watch where you walk."

She turned to Sarika, aware that she only had a few seconds before Jackson descended on them.

"Are you okay? It's fine if you need some air."

Sarika flapped her hand in front of her face.

"I'm fine. At least, I will be. Thanks."

The body was covered in a series of long cuts and stab wounds. On her right forearm was a tattoo of a dolphin swimming into a sunset. There were also cigarette burns, at least twenty, covering the chest. Ellen pointed to them with her gloved finger.

"With any luck there'll be DNA on some of those cigarette butts next door."

Connie Taylor's last hours must have been excruciating. She had been systematically and deliberately tortured. But for what reason?

Sarika moved down the body, examining the various wounds.

"He spent a long time with her, so it makes it more likely that he'll have left some trace of himself behind," the DC said.

Jackson and Benton appeared at the bathroom door.

"Fuck me!" said Benton. "It's far too early for this."

"Don't come any closer," Ellen said, standing up. "Same goes for the bedroom. Looks like she was bound to the bed, tortured, possibly killed there, then dragged in here and decapitated. We need to get a SOCO team here right now."

Ellen's instinct was to cover the body up, but it was necessary to leave it in situ for the pathologist. It was a horrible insult to this woman's dignity to have the likes of Jackson leering at her. She had suffered a horrible end and deserved to be treated with dignity.

"I think there's more to this than an argument with a punter that went too far," Ellen said.

"Maybe, maybe not."

"Oh, come on, Matt. This guy was on a mission — revenge, looking for information, whatever. This was not done on the spur of the moment."

Jackson took his mobile phone out of his pocket and speed-dialled a number.

"First rule of a good detective, McClure, rule nothing in or out at the beginning of an investigation. You should know that."

He headed down the stairs, followed closely by Benton. He would be phoning Monroe.

"Just found the body, guv . . ."

Ellen returned to the landing, thankful to have a few moments to pull her thoughts together.

"He broke in after dark. Tortured, killed, and decapitated her. It's what happened next that I can't work out."

"Why risk moving the head, being caught on CCTV?" Sarika asked.

"Exactly. And why leave the head on the doorstep of that particular house?"

Sarika looked thoughtful. "Sarah Clarkson works with the Crown Prosecution Service. Maybe it's someone with a grudge, or they're trying to send her a message."

Ellen's phone rang. It was the pathologist, Giles Featherstone. He was at the scene at Heworth Green. He would be there for at least another hour, but would have the head moved to York Hospital and would arrive at Pear Tree Field no later than 10 a.m. Until the photographer had taken his photos and the SOCOs had gathered any and all evidence, Ellen would not be able to search the bedroom. She headed downstairs.

Outside, she spoke to the uniformed police who had now arrived at the scene, instructing them to knock on the neighbours' doors and take statements. If someone had seen anyone so much as move in the past twenty-four hours, she wanted to know about it. In particular, she wanted to know if Connie Taylor had had any visitors the night before.

Ellen looked around the small kitchen, taking care not to touch anything. The place was a tip. The bin was overflowing. A bowl sat on the floor, presumably belonging to a dog or a cat. Dirty plates covered every surface. On the kitchen table an ashtray spilled its contents. Next to it was an empty cigarette packet, a lighter, several empty beer cans and a bottle of wine, also empty. Two shelves held various ornaments — Spanish flamenco dancers, a gondola from Venice, teddy bears, old postcards, unopened bills, empty crisp packets. The woman had been a slob.

A small stained-glass pane in the door to the garden had been broken from the outside. The killer had entered here. Green glass lay shattered on the floor. The killer must have reached his hand in and turned the key, which was still sitting in the lock on the inside. With any luck there might be a print, but Ellen knew it was unlikely.

Her eye was drawn to a single plate with a green leaf design, which stood on a plastic draining board by the sink.

Ellen had bought two identical plates from IKEA, egged on by Zoe, who loved the large but delicate green leaf, like a fossil freshly uncovered from a rock. The plates were sitting on her own draining board in the flat at Fossgate. She imagined the victim eating her last meal off that plate at the same time that she and Zoe had been eating their pizza. She shook her head to dispel the unpleasant thought. The plates would have to go.

Ellen walked into the living room. It was sparsely furnished, with a well-worn red leatherette sofa in front of a three-bar electric fire. Another ashtray overflowed with cigarette butts on a once-white melamine coffee table. There was no sign of a struggle. Several framed photos sat on the shelves of a bookcase. One, a selfie of two women in their forties, held Ellen's attention. She recognised one of the women from her driving licence. Connie Taylor had her arm around an attractive brunette, pulling her in for the selfie she was taking of the two of them. On Connie's forearm, which was extended to hold the camera, was a small tattoo of a dolphin. In the photo, Connie Taylor looked happy, with a smile that lit up her whole face. The other woman was smiling too, but it didn't quite reach her eyes.

Sarika appeared in the room. "Nothing much so far from the neighbours, according to uniform. No one saw anything suspicious last night."

"Anyone speak with Connie lately? See her coming or going?"

"The next-door neighbour says she saw her arrive home from work at about nine. Says Connie worked in a café beside the Minster, Prufrock's. She was single, no kids."

"Any record?"

Sarika's phone rang and she took the call, holding up a finger to Ellen to indicate the information was at hand. She finished the call.

"Three convictions for solicitation, here and in Leeds. The last one was four years ago."

There was a crash from the kitchen and a black cat appeared in the living room.

"Who have we got here?" Sarika lifted the cat up into her arms. "Shall we find you something to eat?"

As Sarika headed for the kitchen, the enormity of what lay ahead was now starting to dawn on Ellen. At eleven o'clock, she would have to brief a room full of people on what information she had so far. She would have to have set the parameters for the investigation by then, have tasks ready for the various teams. She needed to get over to Fulford Road straight away.

Sarika came back into the living room. "We've set up a barrier at the end of the lane. You won't believe the amount of press down there."

"Good. Let's keep them as far away as possible. And call the RSPCA to take the moggie."

Sarika reached into her breast pocket and pulled out a business card.

"Here. A reporter from the *York Press*, name of Lewis Samuels, asked me to tell you he has information regarding the victim. Some story he's been working on. Said he won't talk to anyone but you."

Ellen took the card and looked at it.

"He's not bad looking. You should go talk to him." Sarika flashed her a devilish smile.

Ellen shook her head in mock disbelief. Sarika knew Ellen's view on journalists.

The *York Press* was a reputable local paper and she recognised the name Lewis Samuels from his byline. She texted him with a message to meet straight away in a café she had passed down the road. The canteen at Fulford Road nick might not be open, so she might as well stop and grab something to eat, and Samuels might have something useful. Sarika could go on ahead and get things started at Fulford Road.

CHAPTER NINE

Lazy Days Café, Haxby Road, York

Ellen pulled into a space outside the Lazy Days Café, fifty yards past the Nestlé factory on Haxby Road. A man leaning against the bonnet of a vintage, orange-coloured Mercedes waved at her. This, she assumed correctly, was Lewis Samuels. He was tall, early thirties maybe, dressed casual but smart. She didn't trust journalists. In her experience, every journalist she had ever worked with had one priority and one priority only — to land a story. If there was no hope of a scoop, few of them would miss an opportunity to unfairly criticise the police. Bent coppers, inept coppers, lazy coppers — the public couldn't get enough of them. It was demoralising.

Samuels looked intelligent, but she knew from experience he was just the kind to be wary of. She would give this guy two minutes, see if he had something. Otherwise she was out of there.

At the counter she ordered a flat white from a girl with a tongue piercing. Samuels ordered an Americano and insisted on paying for both. Ellen picked out a seat to the side of the window, where she had a full view of the road outside but couldn't be seen. She wasn't about to be spotted having a clandestine meeting with a journalist, and from her vantage point she could see any police cars pulling off the main road. Before Leeds, she wouldn't have hesitated to have a quick coffee with a potential source. But now, she had to be on her guard.

The girl with the tongue piercing arrived with the coffees, slopping some of Ellen's flat white onto the table. Samuels smiled benignly at her. He dropped three sugar cubes into his mug and stirred slowly. He spoke carefully, articulating his words.

"What you did in Leeds, the case, I followed the whole thing. It took guts, and I respect that. It's why I approached you."

Ellen's jaw clenched. That period in her life had been traumatic. She had found herself ostracised by her colleagues. The openly hostile ones, the Matt Jacksons of the world, weren't the problem, at least with them she knew where she stood. It was the more subtle forms of rejection that had been the hardest to deal with, the polite avoidance of any mention of the case, the lack of acknowledgement from those she thought should care about what she had gone through.

She snatched a look at her watch. "What do you have for me, Mr Samuels?"

"Your victim, Connie Taylor, contacted me over two months ago. She thought I might be interested in her story. She and a friend of hers were in care together thirty years ago and she claimed both were sexually abused when they were maybe thirteen or fourteen by some big-name local businessman."

He had her attention. "Why did she come to you instead of the police?"

"They had already been to the police. Her friend, Vicky Richards, had spoken with a therapist, who persuaded her to report the entire thing. Vicky gave a full statement. Named the abuser, named Connie as a witness. Nothing came of it, nothing was followed up. That's when Connie came to me."

Ellen's antennae were up for Samuels' angle. What was he looking for? A story on police incompetence? She wasn't about to give him any printable quotes, not even a "No comment." He was looking at her now.

"Listen, I appreciate the information," she said in a way which communicated the opposite. "If you think this is somehow related to Connie's murder, tell me now, otherwise I have an investigation to get back to."

Samuels rummaged in a leather satchel hanging on the back of his seat. He pulled out a manila file and placed it on the table.

"I met with Connie Taylor. She told me she and her friend Vicky had been subject to serious intimidation since Vicky gave her statement."

Ellen stared at Samuels.

"Intimidation from whom?"

Samuels hesitated and she wished now that she hadn't asked the question. She wasn't sure she wanted to hear the answer.

"They couldn't say for sure, but the intimidation started after Vicky gave her statement at Harrogate station."

Ellen felt her heartbeat quicken. "Hold on. Are you suggesting someone from Harrogate nick was intimidating these women?"

"Connie said the very night after Vicky gave her statement, both she and Vicky started getting hang-up calls in the middle of the night. There were threatening notes left both on Vicky's car and in Connie's letterbox."

Samuels flipped opened the manila file and pulled out three sheets of A4 paper, each with a single sentence in large font. He pushed them across the table for Ellen to read.

Watch your back.

Keep your mouth shut, whore.

We are watching you.

Ellen read the notes. It was very likely this woman's statement had been leaked by someone at the police station. If that was true, then she would have to get involved. However, right now she was not about to be drawn into acknowledging anything to Lewis Samuels.

"What makes you think it was a police officer?"

Samuels held her gaze.

"Vicky gives her statement and the same night she and Connie start getting hang-up calls? No one follows up? Come on!"

Ellen gulped down her coffee and moved to stand up. It was time to go. "There could be any number of reasons it wasn't followed up. This Vicky Richards might not have been a credible witness for starters."

Samuels reached over and put his hand on her arm, which she shrugged off.

"I'm sorry," Samuels said, raising both hands in the air. "Just give me another minute to explain. The notes were only the start. There's a child caught up in the middle of this. I think she might be in danger. Just hear me out. Please."

Ellen hesitated for a moment. *Fuck!* She sat back down.

Samuels pulled out a photo from the file and placed it on the table in front of her. The blown-up photo was a selfie of two smiling women in their forties. Ellen recognised the photo as the one she had seen at Pear Tree Field. Samuels pointed to the pretty brunette.

"That's Vicky Richards on the right. A few weeks ago, Vicky got back to her flat in Clifton to find her dog lying in a pool of blood, his head bashed in. There was another note."

From the manila file he pulled out another A4 sheet of paper. The same large font: *Keep your mouth shut or your daughter will be next.*

Ellen sighed. She needed this like a hole in the head. "Did she report it? The dog? The threats?"

Samuels shook his head. "No. She was too afraid to. As far as she knew, it was someone in the police who was intimidating her, or someone the police had tipped off. She took off, and according to Connie she's been hiding out ever since, moving from one rented room to another."

Ellen was momentarily distracted by a blue Honda which had pulled up outside. It's occupant, an overweight man with bushy eyebrows, entered the café and ordered a takeaway latte. He looked across as if he recognised her. She couldn't place him.

Samuels was still talking. "Look, you need to find Vicky and her child, make sure they are safe. What if Connie was killed by the same person who killed Vicky's dog? What if Vicky was his real target?"

The journalist wrote a name on a piece of paper and handed it to her. "If you want to check out the story, you could contact Vicky's therapist. Her name is Dr Maggie James. She wouldn't speak to me, but she might speak to you."

Ellen knew Maggie James from university. Knew she worked for the National Probation Service. After leaving Samuels, she walked to her car and waited for the man with the takeaway latte in the blue Honda to pull away. She placed the notes and the photo Samuels had handed her into her bag.

* * *

On the drive to Fulford Road, Ellen was aware of a deep need for a cigarette, a gnawing craving she hadn't felt in weeks. Monroe had given her a chance when so many others had shied away. In truth, she owed him a debt of gratitude, and poking around looking for evidence of police collusion was not the way to repay him. Especially not on the word of some random journalist.

At the next red light she reached into the glove compartment and retrieved the emergency pack of cigarettes she kept there, lighting up and inhaling deeply. She had managed three weeks without smoking but she needed one now. From the first drag she felt sick and lightheaded but instantly calmer.

Her phone rang. It was Sarika, who had just arrived at Fulford Road. The SOCO team were at Pear Tree Field and had found Connie Taylor's phone straight away, down behind the bed. It had been sent away for immediate analysis.

Yes! This was just the break they needed.

"Great work, Sarika. Listen, if you have a minute, I need you to run a check against the name Vicky Richards. See what, if anything, is on the system about her."

"Okay. Oh, you mean now? Before the team briefing?"

"Yeah. It's important. I'll fill you in when I get there, in about ten. Just see what you can find out."

"Vicky Richards . . ." Sarika was clearly writing the name down. "Am I looking for some connection with Connie Taylor?"

"Yes. There should be a statement given at Harrogate nick in the last month or two. Connie Taylor should be mentioned in that statement. Look through the incident reports as well, see if there is anything there."

Ellen took a final drag and blew the smoke out of the window, followed by the half-smoked cigarette.

"And Sarika, keep this strictly between ourselves. No one else is to know."

Ellen's mind was racing. A large group of people would be waiting for her to brief them, to give them preliminary lines of enquiry to follow. The information Lewis Samuels had given her could be key to the investigation. Vicky Richards' statement had to be examined, and someone at Harrogate would have to detail why no action had been taken over the allegations she had made. Someone inside Harrogate nick knew something, had at best leaked Vicky's statement, and at worst . . .? Ellen heaved a sigh. This was not the fresh start she had been hoping for.

CHAPTER TEN

Fulford Road station, York

Ellen arrived at Fulford Road station ten minutes later, happy with her decision to set up the Murder Investigation Room there. The Harrogate station with its state-of-the-art equipment and resources was only forty minutes away, but you could easily add another forty minutes with rush-hour traffic. Fulford Road couldn't be more different. Built on the site of an old army barracks, the station was housed in one of a number of red-brick buildings on the compound. It looked like the set of a Second World War movie.

Ellen quickly found Sarika, who directed her to her temporary office. She needed to change into her grey trouser suit, which she kept for public engagements and high-level meetings. There would be a short press conference after the team briefing, and Monroe might ask her to handle it.

The press conference would be straightforward. She would say something about following several lines of enquiry, how the police were confident the perpetrator would be caught very soon. The sinking feeling in her stomach reminded her it would be her first meeting with the press since Leeds, and she wondered if the same media lowlifes who had written those lies about her would be there, poking at the old wound, baiting her to get a reaction.

She remembered that day at the court, the pavement thronged with reporters and photographers, all jostling to get a look at the whistle-blower, the copper who had just given evidence against her own boss. Her father, Paddy, had come along to support her. After the hearing had finished, he had whispered, "You did the right thing, love, that's all that matters." For him, she had ignored the intrusive questions, the veiled insults. She had been pushing firmly but calmly towards the waiting taxi, but then her father was jostled and almost knocked off his feet by a determined photographer trying to get a clearer shot. Ellen had acted instinctively to protect Paddy and shoved the cameraman — hard. He had fallen. There was damage to his camera, which Ellen still maintained was accidental. The whole sorry incident had been filmed, eventually making its way onto the local nine o'clock news. She had come off looking like a lunatic. She had let her father down, and let herself down too. She shook herself as if to throw off the memory.

Sarika pointed tentatively at the shirt Ellen had just put on, which was gaping at the bust. *Damn.* It had fitted fine the last time she wore it. The last few weeks living on pizzas and Chinese takeaways were to blame. When this case was through, she would lose half a stone. Pulling on her suit jacket, she buttoned it up over the offending bulge, feeling pinched and stiff.

"Anything on Vicky Richards?" She pulled out a pair of flat black shoes from her kit bag. At least they were better than her trainers.

"I only had a few minutes, but I ran a search through the system for the names Connie Taylor and Vicky Richards, like you asked. There was nothing against Connie's name except for the solicitation convictions. Vicky Richards has four convictions for solicitation and possession, the last one six years ago."

Sarika walked over to the door and looked up and down the corridor to make sure there was no one listening.

"There was something else. An incident report was logged for Vicky Richards two months ago. The code is for sexual assault of a minor. Looks like Vicky spoke to Matt Jackson, but there was no file opened."

Ellen's stomach tightened.

"Matt Jackson? You're sure?"

"Yeah, definitely Jackson. Why?"

"And you're sure there was no file opened?"

Sarika shook her head. "Doesn't look like it."

The incident report would have been logged by whoever had been on the desk. If there was no file opened then no further action had been deemed appropriate, and no statement would have been taken.

"There's something not right here. That journalist from the *York Press* just told me that Vicky Richards came into Harrogate and made a statement. So why was there no file opened?"

Sarika stared at her. "Shit. You think Matt Jackson buried it?"

"I'm just saying, any allegation of sexual abuse, even from thirty years ago, should at least have resulted in a file being opened."

Sarika's phone pinged with an email. It was a friend on the intel team whom she had persuaded to send over an advance of Connie Taylor's most recent text messages. Everything, including her texts, emails, Instagram, WhatsApp, browsing history, and Facebook page, would be examined in detail, along with bank statements and online shopping. Anything which might offer information on who Connie Taylor was interacting with. The full printout would not be available for several days, but Sarika had used her initiative.

On her screen was a series of texts from Connie's phone from two nights ago, which she read out.

10:15 p.m.

Connie, please come and stay with me and Kallie until we sort something out.

11:32 p.m.

I don't scare that easy, Vicky.

11:36 p.m.

You should be scared, remember what he did to poor Rocky?

11:38 p.m.

I'm staying here in my own house. You do what you have to. Turning off my phone now. Talk tomorrow.

There was a knock on the door and Sarika opened it to find DS Paul Benton, somewhat out of breath. Monroe had sent him to tell Ellen the team were waiting in the Major Incident Room and to get a move on.

They took the lift and Benton pressed the button for the second floor. He was dressed for comfort in tracksuit bottoms and a hoodie. He had recently returned from four months' sick leave after being stabbed at the end of the summer. This was his first full day back. He was on light duties while he continued to recuperate under DI Jackson's wing.

"How's the leg?"

"It's fine thanks, ma'am."

His tone was polite but his eyes were guarded. Jackson had clearly painted her in the worst possible light, that much was obvious. How many others assembled in the MIR felt the same as Benton?

She felt a rising sense of unease. Looking down, she saw her right heel was badly scuffed so she licked her finger and rubbed at the marks. She had to clear her head and focus on the team briefing. The lift doors opened and they entered the MIR. At least sixty people looked in her direction, civilian staff, uniformed officers, and detectives. Monroe was there, waiting at the top of the room, but she couldn't see Jackson.

Sarika whispered in her ear as they exited the lift.

"I'm assuming you are going to sit on that information for the time being?"

She looked worried and Ellen could not blame her. Sarika was up for promotion to DS in the next few months.

Once she got that and her probation period was up, she could consider getting pregnant. Time was ticking and the last thing she needed was Ellen dragging her into a shit storm with her boss and her colleagues.

"Give me some credit!" Ellen said, sounding more confident than she felt.

CHAPTER ELEVEN

"Okay, let's get started." Alastair Monroe's tone was commanding. The background murmur of conversation dropped as everyone busied themselves finding seats, some dragging chairs, others perching on empty desks towards the back of the room. Although hitting sixty, Monroe cut an imposing figure. He was a man confident with his position of authority.

Ellen had used the word 'assertive' to describe herself in the interview for DI. She *was* assertive, pushy some might say. She would expect something to be done by those under her, but she often got people's backs up in the process. Monroe was assertive in a different way. People *wanted* to give him what he asked for. It was said he would go to any lengths to defend his own, an old-fashioned value appreciated by every officer under his command. But if you crossed him, there was no going back.

It was a credit to Monroe's reputation that he had managed to draft in as many DCs as were here. There were five DCs and a DS from Cleveland alone, who he had managed to sequester in record time. While Ellen had been introduced to most of the detectives in the unit, she hadn't so much as laid eyes on many of the civilian staff or the uniformed officers.

Sarika placed a mug of coffee and a pastry from the refreshment table in front of her.

"You're a star," Ellen said, remembering that she'd forgotten to pick up a roll at the café. She was ravenous. She hadn't eaten anything since the pizza the night before. She took a large bite of the apricot Danish and washed it down with a slug of coffee.

Jackson arrived and strolled to the front of the room, indicating to one of the Cleveland DCs to vacate his seat. The young DC sprang up immediately. Ellen saw Sarika raise an eyebrow. She vaguely recognised the officer Jackson had sat down next to, but she couldn't quite place him.

Monroe was speaking. "As you will know, the head of forty-four-year-old sex worker Connie Taylor was found in Heworth Green at five thirty this morning. Her body was found just after eight o'clock in New Earswick."

Ellen pursed her lips. What made Connie Taylor a sex worker first and a human being second? The designation of her as a 'sex worker' was undoubtedly a calculated one. A prostitute was a less sympathetic victim, someone who had been courting violence. Those two words 'sex worker' would ensure that Connie Taylor's name would not be on the lips of the public for too long, and that would suit Monroe and his superiors just fine. The papers prioritised 'people like us' stories. The 'it could have been me' element was what sold papers, got people to tune in to news bulletins. A sex worker meeting a sticky end would draw intense but short-term interest only.

Monroe was speaking again. "We have a press conference after this briefing. As of this morning all leave is cancelled. I want to emphasise that every single person in this room is needed to make the system we have work. I know I don't need to ask for your full commitment. Together, we can get this sick bastard before he or she goes on to kill someone else."

Monroe next introduced Ellen as the SIO for the investigation. As Monroe was speaking, DS Benton was placing photos on a whiteboard which ran the entire length of one wall. Photos from the Lockton House crime scene were grouped to the left and those from New Earswick to the right. Everyone in the room, including the civilian staff, had heard the grisly details, which had led to a heightened atmosphere. However, as each photo was placed on the board, the mood became progressively sombre. This wasn't just a mutilated body. Connie Taylor was a real person whose life had been brutally stolen from her.

When Monroe had finished, Ellen stood up and took his place. The room went silent. Everyone had heard about Leeds, that was clear from the curious looks on most of the faces staring back at her — some benign, some less so. She wondered how many of those assembled had seen the video from the courthouse and were re-running it in their mind's eye right now.

The first team briefing was always going to be tough. Giving that briefing to sixty-odd people piled on the pressure, but she could do it. She took a breath and introduced herself, making eye contact with as many of those gathered as she could. It was important to show the room she would not be intimidated by gossip.

"At five thirty this morning, the head of a woman was discovered on the doorstep of a house in Heworth Green. Under the head was a driver's licence, which led us to a search of a house in New Earswick. There we found the remains of Connie Taylor.

"There is no known connection with the residents of the house at Heworth Green. Connie was not killed there. Rather, the scene of the murder was at her residence at New Earswick, some two and a half miles away. You can see from the pictures that the victim was subjected to a horrific death. We need to find whoever did this, and we need to find them quickly."

In her peripheral vision, Jackson was whispering to the officer next to him.

"Connie was a sex worker, at least she had been in the past, so that will be an important area of her life to look at.

But don't let that fact get in the way of your compassion for this woman."

Jackson and the officer beside him were looking at her now, sniggering at some joke made at her expense. She could feel sweat gathering under her arms beneath the tight blouse.

"There will be some significance to the killer around the placing of the head, so I want everyone joining the dots when interviewing witnesses or collating information. We need to find out why this particular house was chosen to place the head."

"Any preliminary on how the victim was killed?" asked Monroe.

"The head and body will be moved to York Hospital for a post-mortem later this afternoon. The victim had been tortured, and obviously her head removed, but cause of death is not fully known at this point. We won't know for sure until we hear from Professor Featherstone." Giles Featherstone was the senior pathologist attached to York Hospital.

Reading from a list she had prepared before the meeting, Ellen started to assign jobs to the detectives present.

"DS Robinson will take charge of getting HOLMES 2 up and running. I've ordered twenty screens, which should be here within the hour from Harrogate. There's going to be a lot of information and I want it entered as soon as it comes in. We need to get that data working for us."

The Home Office Large Major Enquiry System, known as HOLMES, was a ridiculously laborious name for the computer database used in the investigation of major crimes where large amounts of data have to be processed. The name had produced a snappy acronym, conjuring up images of Sherlock Holmes. As with any system, HOLMES was only as good as the information entered into it, and the next stage was to gather that information.

"Four teams will start gathering information on the victim. I want our priority to be finding out who Connie Taylor was and what happened in her life in the period leading up to her murder. The intel team will be looking into her phone and computer records to see who she's been communicating with. There is some interesting stuff emerging there."

"She was a prostitute," Jackson said, his voice impatient. "We need to look at her johns, that's the obvious place to start."

"Yes, that angle needs to be covered, Matt, but by all accounts, Connie wasn't working the streets anymore and had few, if any, visitors to the house in New Earswick. We need to keep our investigation as broad as possible at this point. She worked part time in a café in town, Prufrock's. I'll be assigning one team there and another to interview known sex workers in the area."

As Ellen assigned the various teams, those who had already been assigned tasks started splitting off to talk among themselves. There was an urge to get going, and the noise level had risen. Ellen rapped her pen against the incident board to get everyone's attention.

"Okay, everyone's attention please!" she shouted above the din. "I want you all to listen to the entire briefing, and not just tune out once your own job has been assigned. We need joined-up thinking here."

The room went quiet again except for Jackson, who was still talking with the officers directly around him. His voice was loud, intrusively so. Ellen forced herself to stay calm. *Stay professional.* She stared at Jackson as she spoke.

"I need everyone to focus on the big picture — that includes you, Matt. You need to be able to spot connections between what you are doing and what everyone else is doing too. It might be one small detail which makes all the difference."

There were nods of approval around the room but also awkward glances towards Jackson, who snorted loudly now in response to some joke he had just made. He was deliberately trying to undermine her.

Ellen reached into her bag and retrieved the blown-up photo she had been given by Lewis Samuels. She placed it in the middle of the incident board. As she turned back round to face the room, she locked eyes with Sarika, who was shaking her head as if to say, "Don't do it." Too late.

"This is a recent photo of Connie Taylor, taken with her friend Vicky Richards."

Ellen glanced at Jackson, wanting to gauge his reaction. The DI was staring at the photo.

"One line of enquiry suggests that there may be some connection with this friend, Vicky Richards," Ellen said, drawing a large circle with a red marker around Vicky in the photo, with a question mark above.

Ellen caught Benton exchanging a look with Jackson. She was on to something, that was for sure.

"It appears that Vicky has been in fear of her life for the last few weeks, and has gone into hiding with her child. She apparently gave a statement to police at Harrogate naming a local businessman as having abused both her and Connie Taylor some thirty years ago, and she warned Connie in a text message that this man is coming after her and Connie, to silence them."

Ellen turned to Matt Jackson. *Not so cocky now, are you?*

"Sorry to spring this on you, Matt, but I just had a quick look and the incident report indicates that you saw her, at Harrogate, two months back. Ring any bells? Only I can't access the statement on the system and there doesn't appear to be a file opened."

Jackson was no longer smirking. "Vicky Richards? Yeah, I think . . . yeah . . ."

Ellen kept her face neutral.

"Maybe take a closer look." She pulled the photo off the board and held it in front of Jackson. "Recognise her?"

A rumble of excited chatter ran around the room. She had him on the ropes now and it felt good.

Ellen's satisfaction was short-lived. Monroe jumped to his feet and demanded she and Jackson see him in the corridor outside. He was angry.

CHAPTER TWELVE

Monroe's face was thunderous. "Look, Ellen, I don't know how things are run in Leeds, but that in there — that's not how we do things."

Ellen pressed her nails into her palms.

"Apologies, sir, I appreciate I should have run it by you first."

Ambushing Jackson had been a mistake. If he was Monroe's lackey, then embarrassing him — and especially doing it so publicly — would reflect badly on the boss man himself.

Jackson was chomping at the bit. "Rubbish! She saw her opportunity to take a cheap shot at me by bringing up that crap and she took it."

"That kind of thing won't earn you any favours here, Ellen. We work as a team," Monroe said.

"I do appreciate that, sir, but I have new information—"

"Which is a pile of shit," Jackson interrupted.

Ellen pressed on. "I have new information that this as-yet-unknown man was also accused by Connie Taylor of sexual abuse. That makes him a person of interest in this case."

Jackson was working hard to contain his rage.

"Not true. It was a complete try on. His accuser was Vicky Richards, a prostitute and a junkie. She was deemed an unreliable witness."

"By who? You?" Ellen asked.

Jackson brought his face right up to hers.

"Yes, by me."

Ellen stood her ground.

"So you remember her now, do you?"

"I've heard quite enough," Monroe said, his voice loud enough for the entire room behind to hear. "From both of you." He paused, then turned to Ellen. "Where did this new information come from?"

Ellen swallowed. She was sure she had not been seen talking to Lewis Samuels, but if she had been, then not revealing that fact might look bad.

"I can answer that, boss," said Jackson, his eyes triumphant. "It was a great friend of ours, a journalist, you might remember him . . . Lewis Samuels."

Shit. Someone must have seen her. That guy in the café. Now she realised why she recognised the officer seated beside Jackson in the briefing room. The bushy eyebrows. How had she not spotted it was blue Honda guy. *Shit, shit, shit.*

"Is this true?" asked Monroe. "Lewis Samuels from the *York Press*? Have you lost your mind?"

"She was seen sipping cappuccino with him not an hour ago in a café near the victim's house."

"Lewis Samuels was your source?" Monroe was in total disbelief.

Ellen's mind was racing. It looked bad. Speaking with a journalist, one who was clearly unpopular with the police, was one thing. Undermining a colleague on the basis of what that journalist had told her was a whole other thing.

She took a deep breath and looked Monroe in the eye.

"I said it was a preliminary line of enquiry, sir, that's all. It tied in with the information from Connie's texts."

Sensing his chance, Jackson jumped in.

"Give the lead to me, boss. I'll have the guy who did this locked up before tomorrow night. It will be one of her johns or a pimp. I'll find him."

Ellen was desperate. "Look, my mistake. I didn't intend to cast any aspersions, I just wanted to establish if this was a useful angle to follow up."

"I've heard enough," Monroe said. "I'll leave you as SIO for now, Ellen, but I want full focus where it belongs, on her johns and on interviewing the girls she worked the streets with."

Ellen breathed a sigh of relief.

"Agreed, but if we could also make it a priority to find Vicky Richards, just to make sure she's safe?" If Samuels had been right about Vicky, then she needed to be found. Her and her child.

Monroe's expression hardened.

"Let me be very clear, DI McClure. You are not pursuing this line of enquiry. Do you understand?"

Ellen felt her jaw tighten.

"Yes, sir."

Monroe clapped his hands together to indicate that the dressing-down was over.

"Good. Now get back in there and finish the briefing. I want everyone focused on the johns and the pimps."

Ellen chewed on her inner lip. Now was not the time to argue her point further. Monroe pressed the button for the lift.

"Matt and I will handle the press conference."

Jackson gave her a smug grin.

The doors opened and Monroe stepped into the lift, followed by Jackson.

"And Ellen, I hardly need to say, you are not to speak with Lewis Samuels. In fact, you are not to speak with the press, full stop."

The lift door closed. Ellen was left standing alone in the corridor. The briefing room behind her was completely silent and she knew that meant the entire group were listening to every word. Her shoulders slumped. As she entered the room to finish the briefing, she could sense a change in atmosphere. She had crossed a line. Spoken to a journalist known for his open criticism of the police, and this on the back of what happened in Leeds. She could see the hostility writ large on the sea of faces staring at her. The only friendly face was Sarika's, and even she looked ready to snap.

* * *

Ellen walked back to her office with Sarika at the end of the briefing and slumped into the chair behind her desk.

"Could you hear what went on outside with Monroe?"

"The whole squad heard," said Sarika, taking a seat herself. "Let's just say it didn't go down too well."

Ellen ran a hand over her face. "Yeah, I got that. It was like I'd suddenly developed the plague."

"Lewis Samuels is not well liked, and maybe for good reason."

Ellen didn't answer. She was googling Dr Maggie James on her phone.

Sarika raised an eyebrow. "Why am I getting the impression you're not going to drop it?"

Ellen could understand Sarika's reluctance, but if Lewis Samuels was right, then Vicky Richards and her daughter could be in real danger. Before she could change her mind, she had dialled the number for the Department of Psychology at the University of York.

CHAPTER THIRTEEN

Heworth Green, York

Vicky Richards saw the blue flashing lights as she approached Heworth Green. There was a long tailback and traffic was being detoured down Mill Lane, along East Parade, before joining back in at Stockton Lane.

She tapped her fingers nervously on the steering wheel. The detour would take her off the main road and add maybe ten minutes to her journey. Ten minutes more that she and Kallie would be exposed on the open road. The trip had been a mistake, she realised that now. Looking in the rear-view mirror, she saw her daughter's face beaming back at her. Kallie was holding on for dear life to the box containing Edith's birthday cake. They had bought the cake in Tesco, already iced with pink and white frosting, but Kallie had helped her jazz it up, sprinkling green and yellow hundreds and thousands over it, and placing the '9' and the '0' candles they had bought on the top. Kallie would be so disappointed if she didn't get to see Edith blow out her candles.

Turning off Heworth Green and onto Mill Lane, she switched on the local radio for the traffic news. The newsreader said that the remains of a woman had been found outside a house in Heworth Green. *Remains.* She didn't like that word. What did it mean, anyway? That explained why there was a detour, why all those police cars were there. She switched the radio off. Imagine saying that on the radio in the middle of the morning? *Remains.* Luckily, Kallie hadn't heard. If she had she would have asked, "What does 'remains' mean, Mummy?" She glanced in the rear-view mirror again. Kallie definitely hadn't heard.

It was the first time in nearly thirty years that she had been down these back roads behind Heworth Green. As she drove past a small park on the right, she felt her heart beating faster and was aware her fingertips were starting to tingle. That was where he had taken her, that first day. It had been her twelfth birthday. She tried to push the image back down, down where she held all her memories from that time. He had come for her, had suggested they take a stroll, alone. He had been so kind, making sure she was well wrapped up in her coat and scarf. Matron had smiled at her.

"Can't have you catching cold now, can we?" he had whispered. It had made her so happy, that this important man wanted her to go with him. No adult had spoken to her like that before, had made her feel wanted. Vicky swallowed.

The traffic was moving slowly. She just wanted to get past that park as quickly as possible. He had led her through it and over behind some trees. She remembered the shock as, without warning, he had leaned over and thrust his huge old tongue into her mouth, moving it back and forth inside in a stabbing motion. She hadn't known what to do, how to react. All she had felt was shock and confusion. They had walked back in silence in time for her afternoon classes. He spoke then: "Good girl."

She hadn't said anything to anyone. She hadn't even been sure it was wrong. He had seemed so pleased with her. It had been a test, to find out if she would tell. She passed the test. That was before the car trips with Connie.

Connie was in a mardy with her. She said Vicky was making her frightened, that she was overreacting. But Connie hadn't seen Rocky's body. All that blood. That was real, and if someone could do that to a poor defenceless dog, then they could do it to a five-year-old child. If only she would agree to come away from York, make a new life with her and Kallie in London, where no one would be able to find them. Connie was stubborn as hell, but Vicky really believed she would come round eventually.

The traffic moved quickly enough once she was back on the main road and ten minutes later Vicky pulled into the car park of Stockton Nursing Home. Until a few weeks ago, she had been working here as a care assistant. It was the first job she had really loved. Her Probation Service therapist had encouraged her to take the courses in care work. She had been afraid she would not be able to do it, but with Dr James's encouragement she had stuck with it. When Kallie started in nursery last year, she had been able to take the job here. She felt a pang of guilt when she thought of Maggie James. Vicky hadn't shown up for her session on Thursday and she knew Dr James was worried. Dr James had called and texted, but Vicky hadn't answered.

She had never imagined herself working alongside nurses and doctors. They treated her like an important part of the team. The residents liked her too. She took several of them out to the shop every day for ice cream, just to give them a change of scene. It was fun. They always had a bit of a laugh. A few of them in particular she had become really close with. Bill and Edith, Ken, Annie, and Mavis. They were like family. She even took Kallie in to see them sometimes on the weekend, much to everyone's delight. Kallie didn't have grandparents of her own and she loved visiting the old folk at the care home. The residents bought sweets and kept them for when she came in. Just like real grandparents.

What happened to Rocky had ended all that. Poor Rocky. She had rescued him from the pound. He was a white fur ball with weirdly short legs and the cutest face you had ever seen. Whoever had killed him had left a note saying Kallie would be next.

She had had to leave her flat. Whoever had killed Rocky would easily be able to find out where Kallie went to nursery or where Vicky worked. She couldn't take the risk. For the last few weeks she had been moving about, staying in the cheapest accommodation she could find. Her meagre savings were nearly gone and she would have to move away, to London maybe, somewhere she would not be found. Away from York, away from Connie. She couldn't bear the thought, but she would have to leave soon. The only reason she hadn't yet left was the hope that Connie would change her mind and go with them.

Vicky walked across the gravel car park to the front door, holding Kallie by the hand. She was glad she hadn't let Edith down. She was not only wishing Edith a happy birthday, she was saying goodbye to all her friends.

Edith had blown out her candles and everyone was singing happy birthday when Vicky spotted Connie's face on the TV in the corner of the room. The sound had been turned down, so she grabbed the remote and turned it back up. *Please God no! Don't make it true.*

The reporter was talking.

"The head found today in Heworth Green belonged to forty-four-year-old Connie Taylor, whose body has been found in New Earswick."

Shock hit Vicky, and for several moments she could neither speak nor move. Half sitting, half falling into a chair, she willed herself to stay calm. She couldn't afford to panic. Kallie's life depended on her staying in control.

After a brief goodbye to Edith, she bundled Kallie into the car, her hand trembling as she clipped her daughter into her seat. She started the car but didn't drive off. Where should she go? Not to a police station, that was for sure. Was it safe to drive back into York, to pick up their things? Her passport was in the Airbnb they'd been staying at. She felt like a rabbit caught in the headlights. *Where do I go?* She felt angry now. Why hadn't Connie listened to her. She'd warned Connie for weeks that something bad would happen.

But Connie hadn't listened. He would be coming for her and Kallie now. She felt her stomach lurch. Panic threatened to take over. *Do something!*

No one knew where she was staying, not even Connie. She would go back to the Airbnb with Kallie and lie low until the morning, then she would head to London first thing. No one would find her in London. But there was one problem. She was nearly out of money. She didn't even have enough for the petrol, let alone to rent somewhere. Dr James had said once that if there was ever a real emergency, if she was ever really desperate, then she would sort it out with the social. Well, she needed help now. That's where she would go.

CHAPTER FOURTEEN

The University of York

Ellen and Sarika parked up and walked across the open green area in front of the Henry Wellcome Building, which housed the University of York's Department of Psychology. Ellen had not seen Maggie James since their days at university. From Maggie's profile on the university website, Ellen had learned that the therapist split her time between her primary job with the Probation Service and a part-time lecturing post with the university.

Ellen paused at the door of the building. "You don't have to come with me, Sarika. You can stay in the car. As far as you know, I am consulting with Maggie James as a profiling expert, end of."

Sarika opened the door. "Who just happens to be Vicky Richards' Probation Service therapist. Let's just get on with it."

Ellen showed her badge to the porter at the reception desk and was given directions to the main lecture theatre. As she was early, she stopped to pick up a sandwich in the cafeteria. The lecture still had about five minutes to go, so they slipped into the nearest free seat at the edge of the auditorium. There were about fifty students in the room, many with laptops open, others busy scribbling notes. At the podium, Dr Maggie James stood in front of a whiteboard, black marker in hand.

She had seen the two detectives enter and nodded in recognition. Fifty heads turned Ellen and Sarika's way.

Maggie turned to the whiteboard and wrote two words on it in large letters. "So, to recap, we have these two important questions: 'Why?' and 'How?'"

"Why?" Maggie said, turning to face the auditorium. "That is the question every investigator must ask. It is the key to finding any perpetrator and the key word for this module. Why does one human being kill another? What is their motive?" She wrote the word 'motive' on the whiteboard, underlining it twice for emphasis. She turned back to the room and paused. Ellen looked around the auditorium. Maggie James had the full attention of every student in the room.

"The act of killing is a game changer. Killing someone is an act with enormous consequences, psychological and otherwise. A sane person will not take another person's life unless there is an extremely good motive. And by that I mean an extremely good motive from their frame of reference. That's the key. Getting into the head of your killer and seeing the scene from their perspective. Why did someone kill this person, in this way?"

Ellen opened her sandwich without caring about the noise the plastic wrapper was making. Several students turned to look at her and she stared them down.

In the front row, a woman who looked to Ellen to be in her fifties raised her arm.

"Yes?" Maggie said. "Gigi, you have another question?"

Ellen wondered if Maggie knew the names of all of her students.

"Surely it would be more scientific to start with forensic evidence? Less subjective than what you have just outlined," Gigi said in a condescending tone, "which is, in effect, guessing?" She spoke with a strong accent, probably Spanish, pronouncing the word 'subjective' with a 'y' — 'subyective'.

Ellen rolled her eyes. She remembered her own lectures made infinitely more excruciating by the interminable questions of the mature students. They couldn't seem to resist demonstrating their own extensive knowledge. Ellen saw several emotions flash over Maggie's face before she answered — irritation turning to resignation.

"Thank you for bringing me to my next point, Gigi. As you rightly point out, knowing the 'Why?' is not enough. But it is a good starting point, a way of directing our often scarce resources in the most useful direction. It is not enough to know who the murderer is likely to be. We must be able to prove who he or she is in court. And this brings us to the next important question. 'How?'"

Maggie drew a circle around the word on the whiteboard.

"The answer to the question 'Why?' is useless without the answer to the question 'How?', and vice versa, as any good detective will tell you."

Maggie paused and looked in Ellen's direction. "Actually, we have a senior detective here with us today. Detective Inspector Ellen McClure of the North Yorkshire Serious Crimes Team. This is an elite unit who focus solely on serious crime, primarily murder."

To Ellen's extreme discomfort, Maggie now gestured up towards her. The entire student body turned as one to stare at her, and she wished she had not just taken a huge bite of her sandwich, which was bulging out of her cheek. There was a ripple of laughter.

Ellen looked down at her feet, making it clear that she was not about to participate in some impromptu question-and-answer session. She couldn't possibly speak anyway, not with her mouth full.

"I'm sure DI McClure would agree that a detective very often has a hunch right at the outset as to who the murderer is. This is generally based on the 'Why?', on the question of motive, but that is never enough."

Maggie drew a circle around the word 'Why?' on the whiteboard.

"A detective's hunch is not admissible in court. A bloody screwdriver with the murderer's fingerprints on it is. How did the murderer kill his victim? With this screwdriver. This is something we can prove."

She underlined the word 'How?'

Maggie scanned the audience. The students were all paying attention. Ellen had to concede that Maggie's lecture was skilful and seamless. She remembered her own short-lived foray into lecturing, when she had been asked to speak to a group of new recruits. There were only seven of them, but she had lost their attention within minutes. One of them had even been texting while she was talking, for God's sake. Not one of these students was texting. Maggie knew what she was doing.

"But which comes first? Unless the murderer's fingerprints are already on the computer system, then the forensic evidence cannot help us. However, if the detective acting on the 'Why?' question looks to the most likely person and obtains their fingerprints or DNA, then the forensic evidence can come into play, either to eliminate or to convict."

A bell sounded in the corridor outside. The students started to pack away their things and Maggie turned to wipe down the whiteboard.

Ellen and Sarika walked down to the podium, Ellen dumping the remains of her sandwich in a bin marked 'paper recycling'.

"I was surprised to hear from you, Ellen," Maggie said, shuffling her papers into a leather satchel. "It's been a while."

"It's not a social visit, I'm afraid. It's about the woman found this morning at Heworth Green." Ellen pulled out the photo of Connie Taylor and Vicky Richards she had taken from the crime scene. Maggie looked at the photo and frowned.

"I saw it on the news."

"Have you got a few minutes to talk?"

"I have to get straight back over to Probation Services, but I can walk and talk if that's okay."

The three of them made their way through the double doors of the lecture theatre.

Ellen pointed at the photo. "The one on the left is Connie Taylor."

Maggie took the photo from Ellen and studied it closely.

"Why are you showing this to me?"

Maggie was too clever to be drawn so easily.

"The other woman is Vicky Richards. She's a friend of the victim. Do you know her?"

Maggie hesitated for several moments before she spoke.

"I do, as it happens," she said, pulling open a fire door and standing back to let Sarika and Ellen through. "I run a group therapy session for offenders out of HMP Askham Grange. I first met Vicky when she was in prison maybe six years ago. I've been working with her on a one-to-one basis since."

"Six years in therapy? You must know her pretty well," Sarika said.

"Yes, very well. Vicky is one of the success stories."

"Not too many of those, I'm guessing," Ellen said.

"Enough. I've seen Vicky straighten herself out completely. She has a child now, Kallie, five years old."

"Do you still see her?"

Again Maggie hesitated. Sarika caught Ellen's eye, she had seen the hesitation too.

They had reached the front door. Maggie fished her keys out of her satchel. She turned towards Ellen.

"You clearly know I am her therapist, Ellen. Why else would you be here?"

"I never said I didn't."

"I'll talk to you, but Vicky is my client. I can't tell you anything that would betray her patient confidentiality."

Maggie's phone rang and she indicated to Ellen that she had to take the call. After a few seconds she spoke quietly into the phone.

“Just keep her there, however you can. I have a police detective with me now who needs to speak to her urgently. Don’t let her leave. We’ll be there in five minutes.”

Maggie looked at Ellen.

“It’s Vicky. She’s at my office in the Probation Service. It’s five minutes from here — Lowther Street.”

CHAPTER FIFTEEN

National Probation Service, Lowther Street, York

The Probation Service was housed in a modern, red-brick building on Lowther Street in York. Ellen and Sarika pulled into the reserved parking area behind Maggie. When they got as far as reception, they found that Vicky was gone. The receptionist, a young Polish girl of about nineteen, looked sheepishly at Maggie.

"I told her you were on your way with a detective."

Ellen cursed. "For Christ's sake!"

The girl flushed. "I was the only one on the switch and the calls were coming in one after the other."

"It's okay, Aga. No one is blaming you," Maggie said.

Ellen threw her eyes up to heaven. "I am. What the hell were you thinking?"

The girl was visibly upset now, tears welling up in her eyes.

"I saw her go into the waiting room, but when I went to find her, she was gone."

The receptionist confirmed that Vicky had had a child with her. Ellen and Sarika ran outside and looked up and down the street but could see no sign of them.

"Damn it!" said Ellen as they walked back into the building.

"Should I put out an alert to any cars?" Sarika asked.

"No. You heard Monroe, if he catches wind, he'll know I'm out looking for her."

The waiting room had a permanently gloomy aspect, in part due to four fluorescent tube lights, one of which was flashing intermittently. Perhaps it was the pain and misery which had been absorbed by the paint and the furnishings; the echoes of abuse, addiction, and abandonment which had seeped out from those that waited here.

A television mounted in the far corner of the room was tuned permanently to Sky News. One Sky reporter was camped outside Lockton House, another outside Pear Tree Field.

Dog-eared magazines lay on a coffee table in the middle of the room. In the corner was a toy where children could run beads along wires, which wound up and around each other. The toy was chained to the adjacent radiator. The smell of gone-off milk, full nappies, and disinfectant mingled in the air.

The Sky reporter was now at the New Earswick scene. In the background, Ellen saw Lewis Samuels in the crowd of media surging around DI Matt Jackson. Jackson was appealing for anyone with any information on Connie's friends and working-girl associates to come forward.

Maggie gestured for Ellen and Sarika to follow her into her office, which was to the right of reception. As Ellen walked behind her, she was reminded of how stylish Maggie was. At college, she had had the knack of throwing things together that just worked. Today she wore a black turtleneck, teal-coloured fitted trousers, and high heeled boots.

Maggie wore her strawberry-blonde hair down now and it suited her. Ellen still wore her dark hair pulled into a functional pony tail, the way she had always worn it. The two had been as different in the way they dressed as in their personalities. Maggie prided herself in getting on with people, always able to put them at their ease. Ellen seemed to possess the opposite quality. She got people's backs up, often surprisingly quickly.

The two had met at the University of Bradford. They had been assigned a room together in halls in the first year. At first, Ellen had baulked at sharing with Maggie. No one who knew them would have put them together, but there was something in each of them, a deep and well-hidden wound, that the other recognised. It had drawn them together and, ultimately, it had ended their friendship.

Graduating first in her class, Ellen had eventually gone into the Fast Track Programme in the police service. Maggie had chosen to keep studying and gained her PhD in clinical psychology.

"I see you're still with Rob." Ellen pointed at a photograph on Maggie's desk. "No surprises there."

Maggie smiled. "Must seem very boring, but yes."

"How is he?"

"Fine, it's . . . he's fine." Maggie handed Ellen a framed photo of two smiling children, the girl auburn like her mother, the boy dark like Rob. "Amelia is eleven and Max is nine."

"Nice," Ellen said, barely glancing at the photo.

"How about you?" Ellen saw Maggie glance at her ringless left hand.

"I was married. That's over now."

Maggie's face was full of unwelcome concern. "Sorry to hear that."

"Don't be," said Ellen, rummaging in her bag and producing a notebook. "I've got a teenage daughter who wouldn't be here otherwise." A pregnant silence hung in the air for a few moments before Ellen brought the conversation back to business.

"So, Vicky Richards. What can you tell us?"

"I've been seeing Vicky every month for six years. She was due here for her usual appointment last Thursday" — Maggie indicated to Ellen and Sarika to sit down — "but she didn't show up. First time ever. She texted me a few days later. Told me specifically not to speak with the police, and I happen to know she has good reason for that."

Ellen raised an eyebrow.

"I'm hardly just the police, Maggie. For God's sake, you know me."

"Look, I'm not sure how much I can tell you. There's a confidentiality issue. I certainly won't be handing over my file."

Ellen and Maggie locked eyes.

"We both know that if I need that file I can get it through a judge."

"This is . . ." Maggie hesitated, glancing over at Sarika, ". . . sensitive. You may want to hear what I know alone."

Ellen straightened in her chair.

"You can talk freely in front of DC Kaur."

"Fine. But what I am about to say might rock a few boats for you."

Ellen threw Maggie an incredulous look, as if to say, "You really think I care about rocking boats?"

Maggie had seen first hand in college her propensity for getting into fights. She would end up falling out with everyone, even those she was so valiantly defending. Confrontation was as inevitable for her as breathing. She was protective of those she cared about, but even she recognised that she never seemed to know when to stop.

Ellen and Rob had been friendly enough to start with. When Rob had cheated on Maggie, Ellen had been furious with him. Even after Maggie had forgiven him and taken him back, Ellen had kept up the fight, refusing to speak to him. It had ruined their friendship. Maggie left halls and moved in with Rob in the second year. It was a tough time, Ellen had felt abandoned. She and Maggie hadn't really spoken since.

"You haven't changed then," Maggie said, smiling. "Still fighting other people's battles."

Ellen rooted in her bag for a pen, ignoring the jibe.

"Can we start with what you know about Connie Taylor?"

Maggie sat back in her chair.

"Connie and Vicky met in care at about twelve years of age, here in York. The care home is closed down now. It was called Lockton House."

Ellen's head shot up.

"That's where the head was found this morning, at Lockton House," she said. "Why didn't you ring this in immediately?"

Maggie looked uncomfortable.

"I only saw the news just before the lecture this morning. The bulletin only mentioned a house in Heworth Green. I didn't have time to make the connection."

Ellen was unimpressed.

Maggie continued. "I can assure you that I would never willingly hide evidence. There are protocols which I follow to protect the client."

Ellen sighed. "Fine. Just tell us what you know."

Maggie leaned forward on her desk

"They looked out for one another. Connie was the muscle, Vicky was the prettier one who got on better with people. The care home was sponsored by a well-known businessman and charity campaigner."

Ellen held her gaze. Could this be the unidentified businessman that Connie had told Samuels about?

"I'm not leaving here until you tell me his name."

Maggie shook her head. "I can't give you his name. The man is a monster, and he has a reputation for suing anyone who says a word against him."

Ellen thought hard. A well-known local businessman who must be in his late fifties or sixties by now with a reputation for suing. A few names sprung to mind. One, in particular, matched both the age profile and the propensity for suing. Harry Gascoyne. His name had come up in relation to the brothel in Leeds where Ana Petrescu had been kept.

"We both know you are talking about Harry Gascoyne, CEO of Gascoyne's supermarkets."

Maggie's face dropped. Her reaction confirmed to Ellen that she was right. Harry Gascoyne. The man was a household name because of the spectacular success of his supermarket chain. He was rumoured to have frequented the brothel in Leeds. His black Range Rover had been logged on CCTV images from the area. But nothing had ever been proven and he had escaped justice. Until now.

"A smile in every aisle," Sarika said, mimicking the television ads Gascoyne Supermarkets ran on several channels.

Maggie looked puzzled. "Sorry?"

Ellen nodded. "Gascoyne Supermarkets' tagline. 'A smile in every aisle.' Don't you watch daytime television? His ads come on mainly around *The Jeremy Kyle Show*, his target demographic."

Ellen knew she had to play this carefully. She needed Maggie to confirm it was Gascoyne who Vicky had named.

"Just tell me what you know, Maggie. You are only confirming information I already have. I was approached by a journalist, Lewis Samuels of the *York Press*. Did Vicky ever mention him?"

Maggie sat back in her seat. "No, but he did ring me. Several times. Trying to get me to talk to him about Vicky. Which I didn't, obviously."

"Connie approached him," Ellen told her. "She was priming him for a story on Harry Gascoyne, an exposé claiming Gascoyne was a sexual predator, and that he had friends in the police. Friends who possibly covered up for him."

Maggie crossed her arms.

"Look, I never mentioned Gascoyne," she said. "I have a duty to keep my client's confidentiality."

"You had a legal duty to report what that bastard did to Vicky, even if it was thirty years ago. A duty you failed to perform."

Maggie looked worried.

"Now hold on. That is just not true. Vicky was not a child when she spoke to me about the abuse, therefore I had no professional duty to report it. There are ways these things have to be dealt with, protocols, which I have followed to the letter."

Ellen felt her temper rising.

"Protocols my arse. How do you know Harry Gascoyne hasn't been abusing other girls over the years? He might still pose a risk to children to this day!"

Maggie's face reddened. "Don't you dare come in here suggesting I would shirk my duty to protect a child in danger. You know nothing about what I did or didn't do."

Ellen leaned forward.

"When you saw the news this morning, and you recognised Connie Taylor as Vicky's friend, why didn't you come forward then with whatever you knew?"

Maggie met Ellen's gaze.

"I'm talking to you *now*, aren't I?"

"Only because I came to you. Were you even going to call the police?"

"I took Vicky to Harrogate police station two months ago. I did that myself, in my own time. If it wasn't for me, she would never have reported Harry Gascoyne, and look where that got her."

Ellen had Maggie now. She had named Gascoyne.

"What happened after she reported?"

"Nothing. Just a shit load of intimidation, possibly from one of your fellow police officers, so don't you dare talk to me about my duty."

Ellen stood up.

"If whoever killed Connie Taylor is trying to get to Vicky Richards, then you need to stop hiding behind this professional bullshit and tell me exactly what you know, right now."

Maggie stood up and walked slowly over to the window. She was stuck between a rock and a hard place. If she told

Ellen everything she knew, then she would expose herself to a suit for professional negligence. If she didn't, then she might well be endangering the life of an innocent child and her mother.

Maggie turned around. "Okay, but you won't like it."

CHAPTER SIXTEEN

Maggie sat back down at her desk, facing Sarika and Ellen.

"Lockton House was one of a number of care homes sponsored by Gascoyne Supermarkets. Harry Gascoyne took a personal interest in this one, a kind of pet project."

Maggie took a deep breath.

"Gascoyne selected Connie and Vicky for special treatment shortly after they moved into Lockton House. He spent time grooming them, taking them on day trips, that kind of thing. After that, Connie and Vicky were given the privilege of waitressing at private functions arranged by Gascoyne at his mansion in Middlethorpe."

Ellen's eyebrows shot up in disbelief.

"Seriously?"

"We're talking thirty years ago, well before Jimmy Saville and other revelations. It was a different world. It was an honour to be offered work experience with a powerful businessman who might give you a job some day. Anyway, that's when the abuse proper started. All of it away behind the closed gates of Middlethorpe House, Gascoyne's mansion. Gascoyne arranged parties attended by wealthy paedophiles, men he wanted to influence, perhaps even blackmail. Vicky was by far the prettier of the two, and Gascoyne took her for his own exclusive use. Connie was forced to perform sexual acts with different men."

Ellen frowned. "How long did the abuse go on for?"

"Years. Both girls were eventually moved to a home in Leeds, out of Gascoyne's reach. If anyone in authority knew the truth they never spoke up."

Ellen willed herself not to lead Maggie with her next question. She wanted to confirm the information Lewis Samuels had given her. She stood up and walked over to the window. Outside, it had started to snow.

"And Vicky reported this exact information to a detective at Harrogate?"

"Yes. I went with her. I was in the room when she told the detective all of it. He basically accused her of making it up."

Ellen felt ashamed that one of her colleagues could have failed the woman so badly.

"The detective, do you remember his name?"

"Yes. He was on the news just now, at the press conference. I recognised him immediately. Jackson. Detective Inspector Matt Jackson. Do you know him?"

Ellen nodded. "Unfortunately."

"I remember he just looked at her. There were tears running down her face with the relief of having reported at last. His expression was so cold. He said, 'Didn't Mr Gascoyne just complete the sale of his chain to an American supermarket group for over a hundred million? And you thought you could just walk in here with that cock-and-bull story? Cash in on his good fortune?'"

Ellen flinched. That sounded like Jackson alright.

"Is that true? The hundred million bit?" Sarika asked.

Maggie shrugged. "I don't know. But it wasn't about the money. *I* was the one who persuaded Vicky to go to the police. I believed she would only get closure if she reported Gascoyne. I forced her in a way, and I really regret doing that now."

"And Connie?" Ellen asked.

"I didn't know she had gone to that journalist, but it doesn't surprise me. Once she realised someone was trying to shut them up, she twigged there was money to be made. Her motive was always money. Money and revenge."

Maggie suddenly looked exhausted.

"Anyway, the case died on Jackson's desk. Connie sent Gascoyne a letter threatening to expose him to the papers unless he compensated both her and Vicky. She was looking for a hundred thousand each."

"Maybe not the cleverest move," Ellen murmured.

"No. That's when the intimidation started. Threatening notes were left in the letterbox, phone calls in the middle of the night. Connie took it as a sign that they had rattled Gascoyne, that it was only a matter of time before he paid up, but Vicky was really frightened."

Ellen looked down, ashamed at being part of the system that had failed Vicky and Connie. An image of Jackson's smug face came into her mind. Monroe's clear order for her to leave this alone. She would follow this up no matter what the consequences, but first she had to find her witness.

"And you said Vicky didn't show up for her appointment last week?" Sarika said.

"That's right, her monthly appointment. I've been seeing her for years, she would never not show up without a text. I phoned and texted, but nothing."

"Do you know if she worked anywhere?" Ellen asked.

"She worked at a care home in Stockton, but they told me she hadn't come in for two weeks. I went to her flat. No answer. The lady next door, Mrs Nazeem, let me into the flat, but there was nothing to suggest where she was. She told me Vicky's dog had been found dead, that Vicky had left with Kallie in a hurry, dragging a suitcase."

"And she never got in touch?" Sarika asked.

"Only once, and there's been nothing since," Maggie said, picking up her mobile phone and scrolling through her text messages. "It was a few days after. Saturday, I think."

Maggie read the text aloud.

"Dr James. I'm sorry for not coming. I have to stay low for the moment. Please don't talk to the police if they ask you about me."

Maggie sighed and looked at Ellen.

"Now do you see why I didn't say anything straight away?"

* * *

Ellen stood outside the Probation Service building and took a call from the office manager at Fulford Road station, who was keeping her up to date with any developments. Nothing of major significance had turned up so far.

Next, she took a call from Professor Featherstone's secretary. The post-mortem would be performed at the mortuary at York Hospital at four o'clock. She ended the call and looked at the time — 2:38 p.m. If they got a move on, they could drop by Vicky's flat en route to the hospital. It would be disobeying a direct order from Monroe, stepping over a clearly defined line, but with this new information connecting Connie and Vicky to the care home, she would surely be able to justify her actions. If what Vicky had told Maggie was true, then she had been badly failed by the system. Ellen was not about to fail her again.

PART TWO

CHAPTER SEVENTEEN

Clifton, York

Sarika pulled up in front of the row of council-built flats on Evelyn Drive. Vicky's ground-floor flat, number six, was locked. Ellen peered in through the window and could see the room was in disarray. Sarika silently indicated with her head that the net curtains in the neighbouring window were twitching. Ellen strode over and knocked on the door. No reply. She could hear a child whining on the other side, and a woman shushing her.

She knocked again, louder this time, and flashed her ID in front of the spy hole.

"Mrs Nazeem? Police. Open up please, I can hear you."

There was a sound of a safety chain being put on, and the door was opened a fraction by an elderly Indian woman in a pink sari. She eyed Ellen warily. A young child of two or three clung to her neck. The smell of spices wafted out into the street.

"My husband is not here," the woman said in a strong Indian accent. "Come back another time."

"I'm enquiring about the lady who lives next door to you, Vicky Richards," Ellen said. "We are worried her disappearance may be connected to the woman who was found this morning. You might have seen it on the news?"

"I don't watch television, and I can't tell you anything," said the woman. "Vicky left a few weeks ago."

"We are very worried for her and her child's safety," said Sarika, stepping forward. "Perhaps she said where she was going?"

"I told you, I know nothing more," said the woman, and started to close the door.

Ellen jammed her foot in the gap to stop it.

"You can take the door off my foot and talk to me," said Ellen, "or we can have this conversation down at the station. Up to you."

The woman's face filled with alarm. Sarika leaned forward so that her face was in the gap. She spoke softly in what sounded to Ellen like an Indian language.

After a few words back and forth, the woman smiled at Sarika and reached for the chain. Ellen removed her foot and the door closed first before being re-opened.

"The old Punjabi coming in handy?" Ellen asked, while waiting for the door to open. "What did you say to her?"

"Hindi, actually," Sarika replied. "My family speak Punjabi, but I know a bit of Hindi too. She said she was afraid of getting Vicky into trouble."

The woman beckoned them into a tidy hall. Ellen and Sarika stepped in from the freezing cold into the warmth and were met with a strong tang of spices. The woman looked up and down the street before closing the door behind them.

"I don't know what I can tell you," she said, jiggling the child up and down on her hip.

"Like I said, we just want to know if Vicky said anything which might help us find her," Ellen said.

Mrs Nazeem looked agitated.

Sarika spoke several reassuring words in Hindi.

"All I can tell you is that my husband and I met Vicky outside about ten o'clock a few weeks ago. She was carrying a suitcase."

"Did she say anything?" Ellen asked.

"Anything at all?" Sarika added. "Anything you can remember might help us find her."

"She told me she was leaving, that someone had killed the little dog and she was frightened to stay."

"Did she say where she was going?" Ellen asked.

Mrs Nazeem put the child down, who now clung onto her leg.

"No. But she looked worried. I told the doctor lady all of this already and I told the other policeman who came."

The hairs on Ellen's neck stood up.

"A policeman came here?" she said.

"Yes, last Thursday night. I let the doctor into the flat and just after she left he came. He knocked very loudly on the door. Said he was a detective and asked me to let him into Vicky's flat, so I did. He made a terrible mess, left the door wide open. I had to pull it shut after he was gone."

"Did he give you his name?" Ellen asked.

"No. He was asking the same questions as you. About where Vicky said she was going. I have answered all of this before."

"There's no record of anything on the system," Sarika whispered into Ellen's ear.

Ellen's mind was racing. Whoever this man was, he was either posing as a policeman, or he was a policeman who didn't want his enquiries on record.

"This man," said Ellen. "Was he in uniform?"

"No." The woman shook her head. "He didn't have a uniform, but I remember he definitely said he was a detective."

"Can you give us a description of him?" she asked.

"I don't know. It was very late and it was dark. I only spoke to him for a short time, I was on my own here and . . . he was rude, a rude man."

"Please, try and remember something else. Was he tall, short?" Sarika asked.

"Taller than both of you, I think."

"His face, do you remember anything distinctive? Was he clean shaven, or did he have a beard?"

"I don't know, he was wearing a hoodie and he kept it up the whole time over his head."

"A hoodie? You're sure it was a hoodie?" Sarika said, scribbling notes.

"Yes," Mrs Nazeem said. "I said to my husband, everywhere standards are dropping. Police will be wearing tracksuits next."

Ellen handed Mrs Nazeem a card with her contact details.

"I doubt very much that this man actually was a policeman, so if he calls again, don't answer the door. Call me instead."

Mrs Nazeem reached down and gathered the little girl back up onto her hip.

"He had a badge, like yours. He told me he was a policeman." Her voice was trembling.

"You weren't to know. But I need you to trust us now and let us into the flat," Ellen said.

Mrs Nazeem opened a drawer in the hall table and retrieved a key. She walked ahead, still with the child on her hip, and unlocked the door to Vicky's flat.

"I didn't go in, it is not my business." She disappeared back into her own flat, instructing them to pull the door behind them.

"Thank you, Mrs Nazeem," Sarika called to the closed door.

Ellen surveyed the room. It was in disarray, the contents of shelves and drawers strewn across the floor.

"The place has been trashed!" Sarika said, pulling on a pair of blue latex gloves from her bag.

"Clearly the work of Mr Hoodie, whoever he is," Ellen said. "Wonder what he was looking for?"

"And did he find it?" Sarika said, walking over to the sofa.

A bookcase stood empty, its contents hurled onto the floor. Framed photos lay shattered in front of it. Ellen hunkered down and picked one up.

"Someone has stamped on these." She shook the glass from the photo. It showed a dark-haired child holding a small knitted yellow bear. The girl's head was thrown back in a belly laugh. Ellen held the photo up for Sarika to see.

"Who would stamp on a photo of a little angel like that?" she asked, shaking her head.

Removing the remaining shards of glass, Ellen retrieved the photo from the frame and put it in her bag. Her phone rang. It was Lewis Samuels. Monroe had given her a specific order not to speak with him. Disobeying him could be a disciplinary offence. She killed the call and put the phone back in her pocket.

"Look at this." Sarika was kneeling in front of the sofa, its arms worn through to the yellow foam stuffing. On the wood-effect flooring was a reddish-brown patch.

"Looks like dried blood here, with white dog hair embedded into it."

Ellen squatted down. "I'd say that was the dog, Rocky," she said, noticing flecks of dried blood on the sofa.

"So Vicky comes in from work, sees the dog lying here, butchered. She packs a case and scarpers. Good call on her part, by the looks of it," Sarika said.

Ellen walked into the small kitchen and opened the fridge, which stank of old food.

"The fridge is full." She flapped a hand in front of her nose.

She could see vegetables, cheese, an uncooked chicken, and, in the meat drawer, a pack of mince, dated a week before. She held the fridge open for Sarika to look.

"She must have been in some hurry to leave all this food," Ellen said. "Question is, who was she running from?"

The flat's only bedroom contained a double divan. Beside it, a travel bed was made up with a pink duvet and pillow. A child's drawings covered the walls, stuck on with drawing pins and blue tac. They showed a circular figure with stick arms and legs, holding hands with a much taller circular figure. Both figures had huge smiles on their faces. Vicky and her five-year-old daughter. Several drawings showed a blue house with yellow flowers on either side and a rainbow overhead. Sarika pointed at them.

"There's a blue house in all of these drawings. Do you think it's a real place?"

Ellen pulled a drawing off the wall, which she folded and put in her bag.

"Could be."

They went back into the sitting room and took a final look through the drawers and cabinets before locking up. They found the bins for the flats in an adjacent alleyway. There was a numbered lockup for each, all bar one were open and empty. The bins from these had been pulled out for collection which must have happened that morning. Only one lockup was closed. Number six. As she pulled open the door, Ellen noticed a nasty smell.

"It stinks!" she said as she lifted the lid and shone her torch inside. She recoiled as a dozen bluebottles flew up into her face, making her drop the lid.

Ellen lifted the lid again. At the bottom of the bin lay the maggot-infested remains of a small white dog.

CHAPTER EIGHTEEN

York Hospital Mortuary

The post-mortem on Connie Taylor was due to be conducted at York Hospital. On the short drive over, Ellen took the opportunity to google Harry Gascoyne. She found a recent article in the *York Press*, accompanied by a photo of Gascoyne and his wife, Jill, at a lavish function. He was in black tie, while she was wearing a full-length ballgown. The couple, both in their sixties, were standing in front of an enormous house, presumably the Gascoyne's mansion in Middlethorpe.

Sarika pulled up outside the mortuary building and the two detectives made their way inside. Ellen stopped to grab a coffee from a machine outside Post-Mortem Suite Number 2. It was a ritual she always performed before the ordeal ahead. There was something comforting about holding a hot cup of coffee in the icy atmosphere of the mortuary. The shrill sound of a drill came through the doors behind them.

"What's that, your fifth cup today?" Sarika asked, a note of concern in her voice. "You know, too much coffee is linked to early death."

"You know me, Sarika," Ellen replied, inserting two pound coins into the slot. "I like to live on the edge."

Ellen carefully positioned the paper cup. When the stream had stopped, she tore open a sachet of brown sugar and poured half of it into the liquid, stirring it with the wooden stick before snapping on a black lid. Her routine complete, she was ready for what lay on the other side of the heavy grey swing doors.

They were greeted by the strong smell of formaldehyde, that and something more familiar. Curry. Ellen could definitely smell curry. She sipped at her coffee. The room was awash with light from the fluorescent tubes which hung on chains from the ceiling. To one side was a bank of pristine stainless-steel sinks. They reminded Ellen of the kitchen at Lockton House.

On the far wall was a whiteboard marked into sections: lungs, heart, brain, stomach, liver, kidney, spleen. Underneath, various organs sat in clear plastic boxes. What looked like a liver was being weighed by a tall technician with dreadlocks. The smell of curry, Ellen assumed, was coming from the yellow-coloured contents of the stomach box.

The Home Office pathologist, Professor Giles Featherstone, was busy dictating into a machine. He spotted Ellen and gave her a small wave with a latex-gloved hand.

The head and body of Connie Taylor lay on a steel table in front of him. A female technician was stuffing what looked like white shredded paper into the skull cavity.

"Petechial haemorrhaging in the whites of both eyes consistent with strangulation. Ligature marks around the neck, under the site of the excision of the head . . ." Featherstone said into the Dictaphone.

He was dressed in bright pink scrubs, in sharp contrast to the muted blue of the two younger technicians. Over the years, Ellen and Giles had worked closely on a number of cases, and the two had become fast friends. At one time, there had been a mild flirtation between them. There was no doubt that Giles was physically attractive. But he was also a player, and he went through a ridiculous number of girlfriends.

"If it isn't my favourite detective? The lovely DI McClure," he said now, his eyes appraising Sarika's athletic body before settling back on Ellen.

"Apologies for starting without you, Ellen. I have a hit-and-run en route by ambulance, and a suicide waiting in the fridge, so I've had to stick to the schedule, I'm afraid."

He whipped off his latex gloves in one expert movement and deposited them in a yellow plastic bin marked 'medical waste'. He ran a tap and started washing his hands. "I'll be with you in a jiffy and you can do the introductions."

Ellen rolled her eyes. Featherstone was an outrageous flirt.

His assistant, who didn't look old enough to have left school, let alone university, had finished stuffing the head and was now fitting the top of the skull back into place.

"Makes you wonder," she said, "what motivates someone to do this to another human being?"

Ellen thought the same could be said of the young woman's career choice.

She smiled. "It really does."

More than once in the last few months it had occurred to Ellen that her job was doing her more harm than good. Jackie, Anthony, and even her daughter Zoe had questioned the wisdom of exposing herself to such horror on an ongoing basis.

"DC Sarika Kaur, meet Professor Giles Featherstone," Ellen said as the pathologist joined them, then, in a whisper so that the assistant couldn't hear, "serial womaniser."

Featherstone threw his head back with a roar of laughter. "Hell hath no fury like a woman scorned!"

"Screw you, Giles," Ellen replied, but she smiled at him.

Featherstone detailed his findings. Connie's organs had been weighed, stomach contents examined, blood checked for toxicity, and skin swabbed for DNA evidence.

"Female Caucasian. Muscle tone indicates her age to be between thirty-five and fifty. Based on body temperature, and the fact that rigor is pretty advanced, I'd put the time of death at somewhere between eleven o'clock last night and four o'clock this morning. Last meal was chicken curry and rice, which is undigested and had not yet passed into the small intestine, so she died within maybe one or two hours of eating."

Featherstone pointed at the head. The eyes had been taped open, the glassy eyeballs bulging from their sockets. "The head has been cut from the body post-mortem on a line one inch below the earlobes. There are eleven separate lacerations to the neck, so let's say the decapitation wasn't an expert job. Downward displacement of nasal cartilage. There are massive depressed skull fractures. The facial features are obscured by oedema and by extensive ecchymoses."

"Swelling and discolouration from bruising," Ellen translated for Sarika's benefit.

Featherstone nodded. "Gold star for DI McClure." He turned his attention to the torso. "Moving down the body, there are multiple lacerations on both breasts, also cigarette burns. Left breast almost severed. The burns, the knife wounds, and the blunt-force trauma to the face came ante-mortem."

Ellen inhaled. So she was right, Connie had been deliberately tortured before she'd been killed.

Featherstone pointed to some marks around the bottom of the neck.

"The cause of death was ligature strangulation, so she was already dead when she was decapitated."

"Thankfully," Sarika muttered in a low voice.

Ellen leaned forward to look at the ligature marks on the neck, just below the exposed flesh.

"There is evidence of two or three separate manual ligature marks, here, and again here, see?" Featherstone said. "Your victim was subjected to a prolonged ordeal involving repeated tightening and loosening of the ligature."

Ellen had seen this before. This method of tightening and loosening of the ligature meant that the killer could, in effect, strangle their victim several times, stopping short just enough each time to avoid finishing off their prey, forcing their victim to suffocate again and again.

"Any signs of sexual assault?"

"You would expect sexual assault with this kind of violence, but no, the victim was not raped. In fact, there is no evidence of interference with the genitals or anus, no semen. Nothing to suggest recent sexual activity."

Ellen stared at the tortured body in front of her. Maggie's words came to mind: "Find the 'Why?'" If sexual gratification had not been the motive, then what had? Featherstone left his assistant to finish up. The suicide had been prepared in the suite next door and he had to go.

As Ellen watched the assistant cover Connie Taylor with a green cotton sheet, she wondered if Lewis Samuels had been right. Had the killer tortured Connie Taylor to find out where Vicky was? Or was there another reason?

On her way out of the mortuary, Ellen arranged with Featherstone's assistant to send her a copy of the pathologist's report. Outside, she inhaled the cool winter air. It was a relief after the smell of curry and the stench of death.

CHAPTER NINETEEN

Fulford Road station, York

On the drive back to Fulford Road, Ellen tried to figure out what she had learned. Was it possible that Matt Jackson was somehow involved in Connie Taylor's death? Was he the man in the hoodie Mrs Nazeem had seen at Vicky's flat? Or had he passed on information to Harry Gascoyne? Gascoyne's car had been seen in the vicinity of the brothel in Leeds. If he was visiting the brothel, that would make him a piece of lowlife scum, but could he also be a cold-blooded killer?

As she and Sarika drove through the gates into Fulford Road station, Ellen was sure of one thing. If either Jackson or Gascoyne were involved in this, she would not hold back in exposing them, no matter what the consequences for herself.

Ellen headed straight for the Major Incident Room. Sarika was going to look at Connie's Facebook history, in particular any references to Vicky Richards. When she pushed open the door to the MIR she could hear a healthy background murmur of noise, which told her that the teams were still hard at work. She saw with relief that the twenty computer terminals she had ordered for the HOLMES 2 account were in place, and most were occupied.

She wanted to grab the red marker and write Harry Gascoyne's name in big letters on the central board, but that would see her taken off the case quicker than it would take Jackson to run to Monroe's office. He would claim that what Maggie James had revealed was just hearsay, the hearsay of a woman convicted for soliciting. She needed something concrete.

Instead, she picked up the red marker and tapped it on the board to draw everyone's attention. As the voices gradually died down, she wrote the words 'Lockton House' in the middle and underneath two names, 'Connie Taylor' and 'Vicky Richards'.

"Listen up. We now have a direct connection between Lockton House and Connie Taylor. Both she and her friend . . ." Ellen drew a circle around Vicky's name, ". . . were residents at a care home which used to operate from the house. We still need to find out exactly why Connie's head was placed there. Vicky Richards may be able to provide us with that information."

Ellen looked at the sea of faces. She couldn't see Jackson, although she could have sworn he had been present when she arrived. If he had run into Monroe, she would stand her corner. Vicky Richards had to be found.

Next Ellen asked the Incident Room manager, DS Diane Wharton, to bring her up to speed on the various teams' findings, what tasks had been completed, what remained to be done.

The fruits of their labours were displayed on four whiteboards that lined the walls. Jackson's team had been interviewing known sex workers in the area. Nothing useful had emerged, no surprise. Connie Taylor had not been active on the street scene for some years. A few numbers on her phone belonged to men who had used her services in the past, but all of them had so far been eliminated from their inquiries.

"The picture emerging from her neighbours was that Connie kept herself primarily to herself. While she may have been operating as a sex worker out of her house in the past, her neighbours reported that there was little activity of that kind lately. She had been in receipt of housing benefit for the previous decade. She had never married, had no children, and was single. The only consistent visitor to her house was a dark-haired woman and a child," said DS Wharton.

Ellen pinned the photo of Kallie she had taken from Vicky's flat next to that of her mother. DS Wharton continued.

"According to Connie's co-workers at Prufrock's café, she was not well liked. Opinionated and short-tempered — their words. In general, she avoided talking to customers, although she appeared to have struck up a friendship with one particular customer over the last few months. She took her break with him most days."

"Any luck tracking him down?"

"The officers waited to see if he would show up this morning, but there was no sign of him."

"We need to find him. Do we have a name, a description?"

"Only his first name. Tom. White, mid-thirties to early forties, medium height. Dressed casually — hoodie, trainers, sometimes a baseball cap."

Sounded like the man Mrs Nazeem had described.

"See if the CCTV team can pick him up on one of the cameras from yesterday. Should be easy enough if we find out what time he was in the café. We might get a car reg if he was parked locally."

"They've been on it for the last hour."

Thirty minutes later, Ellen was in the CCTV viewing room on the top floor. Suddenly aware of how hungry she was, she stopped at the vending machine by the lift and bought a Snickers bar, tearing at the wrapper with her teeth as she entered the room. There are an estimated five million CCTV cameras in the UK, one for every fourteen people. The city of York was well served. With any luck, hoodie man would show up.

DS Benton had been assigned to the CCTV team. Spending hours poring over grainy images from cameras was a job most officers avoided if at all possible, but Benton had volunteered for the job. Maybe it suited him to be sitting down, given his recent injury? He looked up as Ellen walked into the room and she caught a hostile look, quickly replaced with something more amenable. Too late. Benton could turn on all the charm in the world, but she knew he disliked her.

"Ma'am."

"Hope you've got something for me, Paul," Ellen said.

"We've got some images here that might be useful," he replied.

"Fire away."

She stood behind Benton, who was sitting in front of two screens. He gestured to the screen on the left. It was divided into smaller squares showing various different views.

"Here we have multiple live images from High Petergate, the street leading to Prufrock's café."

He pointed to the screen on the right.

"And on this one, a recording from a camera opposite Prufrock's from two days ago. You can see the time here." The digits in the corner of the screen read 11:27 a.m.

A man could be seen on this screen. He was exiting the café, facing the camera, which was mounted on a high position almost directly opposite.

"Can you zoom in?" Ellen said, leaning forwards.

Benton did so. The man was wearing a bulky jacket over tracksuit bottoms and white trainers. Under the jacket he had on a hoodie, the hood of which was pulled up over a baseball cap, obscuring his face. He was looking down, as if he were deliberately avoiding being caught on camera.

"He's been picked up on other cameras walking towards the Minster, but this was the only face-on angle, I'm afraid," Benton said.

"Is there anything you can do with the shot?" Ellen said, pulling up a chair.

"Nah, it's the camera. I've tried everything. That's the best I can get it."

Benton now played footage showing a group of Japanese tourists. At a certain point he froze the image and pointed at a figure standing towards the back of the crowd.

"Here he is, in the background. This is a minute after he's left the café, walking further down Petergate."

The man Benton pointed to was looking away from the camera, his face obscured by a baseball cap and hoodie. In the foreground, the Japanese tourists obscured his lower body.

"Do you think he knows where the cameras are?" Ellen asked.

"Looks like it." Benton clicked the mouse and another image appeared on the screen. "We have him here heading into Fenwick's department store. Same thing, head turned away, no image of his face."

"Can you get him inside or leaving?" Ellen asked.

Benton brought up another image with a few clicks. This time inside the department store.

"We got the footage from Fenwick's. Here he is entering the lobby."

The grainy picture showed the hooded figure, head down, entering the shop and then swinging right out of shot.

"We lose him here. There are multiple exits in Fenwick's, including a large underground car park. We've no way of knowing which of the hundred or so males milling in or out over the next half-hour are him. He could have taken off his cap, changed his jacket."

"How about earlier, arriving at the café?"

"I have him arriving," said Benton, "but it's the same camera, same poor image, this time from behind. Sorry, it's all I have."

The man was undoubtedly taking measures to avoid being identified, and that made him a suspect. However, his evasion had worked, at least as far as identifying him was concerned.

Ellen sat for some time with Benton playing and re-playing the videos. This guy was definitely acting suspiciously, which could mean they were looking at the killer. She looked at her watch. The café would probably be closing soon.

"Okay, get a police artist down to the café when it opens in the morning. We need to get a photofit drawn up. If several staff members can remember this guy, then we have a good chance of an accurate drawing."

Ellen left the CCTV room clutching a handful of printouts. It was impossible to see the suspect clearly with the jacket, baseball cap, and hoodie. Whoever he was, he knew where the CCTV cameras in the city centre were positioned. Could it be Harry Gascoyne or Matt Jackson? If the photofit resembled either man, then she wanted to be the first person with that information. Ducking back into the CCTV room she called out to Benton.

"Paul, good work. Oh, and that photofit — strictly for my eyes only in the first instance. Email it to me as soon as you have it."

She didn't trust Benton, and he had been put on notice to send the photofit to her first. If he didn't, she would have his guts for garters.

* * *

As Ellen passed the MIR, Sarika waved her over.

"We've managed to get access to Connie's Facebook account. I've found a page set up a few years ago called 'Survivors of Lockton House'. Lots of photos from the time. Women looking for friends they knew at the home. Bit of an online reunion thing going on."

Ellen pulled up a chair, placing the CCTV printouts on the desk in front of her.

"Good work. Maybe we can speak with some of them."

Sarika clicked on an old photo of five girls holding up ice creams for the camera. All were dressed in shorts and T-shirts. Several had big hair, reminiscent of Melanie Griffith in *Working Girl*.

In a comment under the photo, Connie had identified herself as the third girl from the right.

"Connie's the brassy one sticking her tongue out?" Ellen asked.

Sarika nodded. "That's her."

Ellen looked closely at the image. The young Connie Taylor bore no resemblance to the corpse lying on the slab at the mortuary. In the picture, Connie was plump, and although not exactly pretty, she had a youthful glow.

"Look here," Sarika said, scrolling down through the comments. "Connie identifies Vicky, to her right. Here."

The young Vicky was strikingly pretty, with plump lips and almond-shaped eyes.

"The girl standing to Vicky's right is also identified. Her name is Becky Tansey."

Becky Tansey was taller than the other girls by several inches, and had bleached-blonde shoulder-length hair.

"That photo was posted by Connie four years ago. Then, two months ago, there's a new post. The poster, who lives in Canada, identifies herself as Becky Tansey, says she has just seen the page. She and Connie have been messaging privately since, catching up on old times."

Sarika clicked into the private messages on Connie's Facebook page.

Ellen frowned. The woman appeared to be pumping Connie for information on Vicky. "What is she doing now?" "Where does she live?" Connie fills her in on both their lives, tells her she works in Prufrock's, that Vicky has a child now. That both she and Vicky live in York.

Sarika scrolls down the screen, clicking into various messages exchanged between the two women.

"Here, Becky talks about what she's been doing since Lockton House. How she went to British Columbia, got citizenship, joined the army, met her husband. How she never gets to come back home anymore, but she would love to get in touch with Vicky."

"Interesting. Can we get in touch with her?"

Sarika looked at Ellen.

"This is where it gets really interesting. I sent a message but got no reply, so I googled her. Becky Tansey, British Columbia. This came up."

Ellen squinted at the screen. It was a death notice on an online obituary site, CanadaObits, dated 12 March 2014.

> Roberts, Rebecca: August 2, 1975 — March 9, 2014
>
> Rebecca (Becky) Roberts (née Tansey), aged 38, passed away in Victoria BC, after a short illness.
>
> Rebecca was born and raised in York, England where she attended college in Nottingham. Upon graduation she left the UK to take a Master's degree at the University of British Columbia. She gained Canadian citizenship and subsequently joined the Canadian Army at the age of 23.
>
> Rebecca left the army in 2007 and moved to Victoria BC to start her family.
>
> She is survived by her spouse, David.

Ellen scratched her head. "So, if Becky Tansey died in 2014, then someone has been using her identity to contact Connie."

"Looks like it, and that person was *very* interested in Vicky. The conversations are all around her and what she is doing. Even asks for her address to send a postcard."

"Did Connie give it to her?"

"No. Connie told 'Becky' that Vicky moved around a lot, but that she could send it to Prufrock's and that Connie would make sure Vicky got it."

Ellen's mind was racing. Connie's killer poses online as Becky Tansey. Stalks her through this Facebook page. This could be just what she needed to bring to Monroe, to show him that finding Vicky Richards has to be a priority.

Ellen picked up the CCTV printouts from the desk.

"It's a bit of a long shot, but I'm wondering if our friend here with the hoodie could be the same person who was posing as Becky. Maybe even Mrs Nazeem's 'detective.'"

"Could be," Sarika said. "And before you ask, I've got the tech team tracking the IP address and they've promised to get it to me in the next hour or so."

CHAPTER TWENTY

Fulford Road station, York

Ellen shut the door to her office and sat down at her desk. It was six thirty already, and she still had to gather whatever information her team had gleaned that day, collate it, and present it in report form for Monroe to read first thing. The Facebook lead on Becky Tansey would go into that report. The visit to Vicky's flat in Clifton would not.

Ellen glanced at her phone and saw the missed call from Lewis Samuels from earlier on. If she had half an eye on her career, she would follow Monroe's order not to speak with him. She would block his number, forget she had ever spoken with him. However, Samuels had been right about everything he had told her so far and she could not afford to freeze him out. His information could prove invaluable to the case.

It was almost 8:15 p.m. by the time she had completed the report and emailed it to Monroe. Most of the team had started to pack up for the day. She groaned when she saw Matt Jackson waiting for the lift. They stood in silence and the ride down was filled with tension. He must have heard about the Facebook lead, and the icy atmosphere told her he wasn't happy. Ellen stepped out of the lift without looking at him. As she passed the duty sergeant on the front desk, she made sure he had her details and knew to phone her if anything new came in.

Sitting in her car, Ellen googled Lewis Samuels on her phone. The *York Press* had offices a hundred yards down the road from Jackie's flat. A number of his articles were available online. Most had appeared in the *Press* but several had been published in the *Guardian* and the *Telegraph*. Scrolling through, Ellen could see a theme. Political corruption, police corruption, miscarriages of justice. The tone was passionate. Samuels was undoubtedly what her father would have called a 'bleeding heart liberal'. The latest article attacked Gascoyne Supermarkets for selling out to an American company, with the inevitable loss of jobs that would entail.

Her mobile rang. Speak of the devil.

"If your mission is to screw up my career, Mr Samuels, it's working."

"I gather what I told you checked out?"

"Look, that's as maybe, but let's just say I am being kept on a very tight leash. You know my history?"

"Why do you think I approached you?"

"To wreck whatever chance of advancement I have?"

"Because you're not afraid to stand up for what's right."

Ellen reached over to the glove compartment and retrieved her emergency cigarette packet. She lit up and inhaled deeply, opening the window to blow out the smoke.

"Ellen, you saw what happened to Connie. If we don't find her, Vicky could be next, and I don't want that on my conscience."

An image of the framed photos crushed on the floor of Vicky's flat flashed through Ellen's mind. Something about it had troubled her and now she realised why. All of those photos had been of Kallie, Vicky's daughter. There had been maybe five or six of them. All crushed under an intruder's heel. Was the killer looking for the little girl?

Samuels broke the silence.

"Your hands are tied, I get that. But mine aren't. Help me to find her."

Ellen took another pull of the cigarette and exhaled slowly. She knew what she had to do.

"I shouldn't be telling you this, but I have new information."

"What kind of information?"

"I have a lead on the identity of her abuser."

"Give me his name, I can sniff around. I'll be discrete."

Ellen had always trusted her instinct. Samuels was not like any journalist she had come across. He might be a fanatic, but she believed he was not just interested in turning a story.

"I can't give you the name, but I can tell you we've found a Facebook page Connie was on, survivors of Lockton House. Someone on there was fishing for information on Vicky. Someone using a false identity."

"Did Connie tell them where Vicky is?"

"Look, I can't say anymore on the phone. I'll contact you when I get a moment. Maybe tomorrow."

"How about now?"

"Can't now, but soon."

With that Ellen hung up.

CHAPTER TWENTY-ONE

Fossgate

Ellen managed to open the door to the flat while juggling the three steaming bags of fish and chips she was carrying. As soon as this case was over, she would get back to cooking proper meals. Maybe even do a lemon chicken with rice at the weekend. Zoe's favourite. Sit at the kitchen table instead of in front of the TV, like Zoe said they did over at her dad and Linda's place. Jackie would have given Zoe something nice from the café downstairs for her dinner, but who could resist a bag of freshly cooked chips bathed in salt and malt vinegar?

According to Zoe, Linda cooked everything from scratch — vegetables, sauces, the lot. All organic this, additive-free that. Zoe did a great impression, which always made the two of them laugh. Ellen smiled. Anthony could rot in tofu hell. Poetic justice.

She reached the top of the stairs and opened the door to the flat. The television was blaring. She looked at her watch — 8:45 p.m. Her sister Jackie's laugh rang out. Zoe was laughing too. The two were curled up together on the sofa re-watching the closing moments of *Strictly Come Dancing* that Zoe had recorded from the weekend.

Ellen watched them from the door to the sitting room. In many ways Jackie reminded Ellen of a *Strictly* contestant. She wore a permanent fake tan, summer and winter, which glowed orange under the shop lights. She put a lot of effort into her hair, which changed in colour from deepest black to pink to blue, depending on her mood. She had a barter system going with the hair salon across the road. The manageress of Snips got her lunch in the café most days for free, and in return Jackie got a cut and colour once a month. This was a blue month. If Ellen had got her hair cut in the last two years she could not remember.

Aunt and niece laughed in sync, an ease between them which both lifted Ellen's heart and caused it to ache. Of all the angry words Anthony and Ellen threw at each other now, only one thing really hurt. The accusation that she was never home. Never there for their daughter. She tried, she really did, but it wasn't easy doing it all alone. Ellen had just slipped into the kitchen to put the fish and chips down when Jackie appeared.

"You're here! We saw you on the local news, skulking away from the cameras."

Ellen didn't like Zoe knowing too much about her job, but this case would be all over the television for the next few days. As if reading her mind, Zoe appeared behind Jackie.

"We saw you on the telly, Mum." She spotted the brown bags. "Chips! I thought I could smell them."

"And you're the SIO," Jackie said. "Well done you! But how come you weren't at the press conference?"

"Long story." Ellen didn't want to discuss work in front of Zoe.

Jackie snatched up her keys and mobile phone. "Got to fly."

"I've got chips for you too, Jackie. What's the rush?"

"*You* might have no social life, but I do. And you are just in time. I was seriously considering bringing Zoe with me to the wine bar."

"Another Tinder date?"

"Yes. And before you say it, I'll be careful."

"It's the normal-looking ones that'll turn you into a lamp shade," said Zoe, who was busy spilling fish and chips out onto the two IKEA plates with the leaf design. The same ones Ellen had seen in Connie Taylor's kitchen.

Ellen and Jackie looked at each other, dumbstruck.

"Jesus, Zoe, where did you hear that?" said Ellen to Zoe's back as she carried the plates through to the sitting room. Linda had two older boys, aged fifteen and seventeen, and Ellen knew that Zoe would be watching all sorts with them. She would have to have a word with Anthony.

"I'll keep that in mind," Jackie said, kissing Zoe goodbye. "I'll only stay if he doesn't look normal."

Since embracing online dating several months previously, Jackie had been out on lots of dates, only one of which had led to a short-term romance. The rest, without exception, had led to disappointment. Jackie was an eternal optimist. Ellen, on the other hand, was deeply suspicious of Tinder. As a cop, she disapproved of any app that used GPS to track its users, even if only to offer them suitable local dates. Jackie was too eager, and in spite of Ellen's warnings, she tended to meet these guys in person far too quickly. As far as Ellen was concerned, Tinder was to a potential serial killer what a playground was to a paedophile. After fifteen years in the job, she had a habit of putting herself into the shoes of a criminal. If she were a serial rapist or killer, the first place she would head for would be Tinder.

As Jackie was leaving, she indicated with a gesture of her head that she needed to talk to Ellen out of Zoe's earshot. Ellen followed her out to the landing, closing the door behind her.

"Zoe got into trouble today. Her form teacher was waiting when I went to collect her."

Ellen was shocked. "Her form teacher?"

"Yeah, a nice woman, Mrs Telford. Suggested you pop in for a chat tomorrow morning, when you drop Zoe off.

She commutes from Harrogate, gets in at seven thirty ahead of the traffic."

"I'm running a murder investigation, Jack. What kind of trouble are we talking about?"

"I got the impression she's worried about her. To be honest, I think you should go. Zoe's not a happy bunny right now. You know it as well as I do."

"Can you go and talk to her, find out what it's about?"

Jackie had made her way down the stairs now and turned back to face Ellen.

"No, Elle. I'm not her mother, you are. Can't you get Anthony to go?"

Ellen wasn't about to give Anthony any ammunition against her.

"Okay, okay, I'll do it."

* * *

Ellen changed into her pyjamas and she and Zoe ate their fish supper in front of the TV. When they had finished, Ellen cleared the two plates and, without telling Zoe, threw them both into the bin. After kissing her goodnight, she retrieved Zoe's dirty gym gear from the hall where she had left it last week and put on a wash.

She stood for a minute outside the bedroom, the long day catching up on her. She could hear Zoe through the open bedroom door, talking to Anthony on her phone. From the conversation, she remembered that he was flying to Zurich the following morning. He worked in a marketing capacity for a Swiss pharmaceutical company and once a month made the trip to their headquarters.

Her phone rang. It was Sarika, who was still at Fulford Road station. Ellen walked into the storage closet she used as a study and closed the door behind her. The room was not big enough for a bed and had no window, but she had been able to fit a small table, on top of which stood a cheap whiteboard. Any files she took home from work stayed in this room, away from curious young eyes.

"Sarika, what have you got?"

"We've hit the jackpot with the IP address."

"Go on then, put me out of my misery."

"It's an internet café, a few doors down from the Shepherd's Dog."

The Shepherd's Dog was a pub in an old Victorian building around the corner from the North Yorkshire Police headquarters in Harrogate. Due to its proximity to the station, it was a popular spot with the nick. There was a bank of shops in the same row, including a shop where Ellen picked up her paper in the mornings.

"Before you ask, there's no CCTV outside the café, only outside the pub. I doubt they'll still have anything, but I'll check before I call it a night."

"This is really good work, Sarika. I'll be on my phone if anything comes of it."

Ellen picked up a marker pen and wrote the following names on the whiteboard.

Harry Gascoyne
Matt Jackson
Vicky Richards
Connie Taylor
Tom?
Becky Tansey

She underlined the name Becky Tansey and sat back on the office chair. Whoever was pretending to be Becky Tansey had to be a police officer based in Harrogate Police HQ. The coincidence was too great. This person, whether it be Matt Jackson or someone else, was trying to get to Vicky Richards. That same person may have killed Connie Taylor.

Vicky Richards and Connie Taylor knew each other from Lockton House. Harry Gascoyne abused both girls while they were residents there. The customer at Prufrock's,

'Tom', couldn't be Gascoyne as the description Connie's co-workers gave was of a younger man. Could 'Tom' be Matt Jackson?

Ellen's phone pinged and the doorbell sounded at the same time. The text was from Samuels.

I need to see you now.

Who the hell was ringing her doorbell at this time of night?

CHAPTER TWENTY-TWO

Ellen looked through the peephole before opening the door. Lewis Samuels was standing in the street carrying a takeaway pizza and a bottle of red wine. She opened the door and Samuels' eyes flashed over her pyjamas. He smiled. She forced herself into professional mode. "How did you find out where I live?"

Samuels nodded at the hand-painted sign overhead.

"You mentioned Fossgate, and your surname is over the door."

Ellen glanced at the sign over Jackie's shop: 'McClure's Mellow Fig Café'.

Samuels grinned. "I'm an investigative journalist. It wasn't too hard. I did send you a text."

Ellen held up her phone.

"Yeah, thirty seconds ago."

Samuels shrugged, a sheepish expression on his face. She hadn't noticed how tall he was when she had met him at the Lazy Days Café. He towered over her now. Her guess was that he had to be at least six foot five. He had a confidence that, in spite of her better judgement, she had always found attractive. He paused, gazing at her with a look of amusement. He was enjoying himself. More worryingly, she realised, so was she.

"I was passing your door. My office is just down the road."

"And . . . ?"

"Look, Ellen," he said, holding up the pizza and the wine. "I have something you might want to hear, but it can wait until tomorrow. Or you can help me with these and I'll fill you in?"

Ellen thought for a moment. If Samuels had something, she definitely wanted to hear it.

"You can come up for five minutes. My daughter's in bed, so we'll need to be quiet."

* * *

Ellen climbed the stairs ahead of Samuels. When she reached the landing, she poked her head into the bedroom. Zoe's light was off. She had headphones on, and her eyes were closed. As she pulled the door shut, Ellen saw Samuels standing at the open door to her office, where she had left the light on. He was looking at the whiteboard.

"Harry Gascoyne . . . Jesus, really?"

Shit.

Ellen strode over and pulled her office door closed in what she realised was a futile gesture.

"You weren't meant to see that."

Ellen stomped ahead into the kitchen. She wondered how to play things. There were no flies on Lewis Samuels, he would have seen everything on the whiteboard. Was it better to reveal everything to him and have him working for her, or tell him nothing and risk having him working against her?

"Did the therapist give you the name? Remember, you got that tip from me."

Ellen wished she had time to weigh up her options.

"Maybe," she said in as non-committal a way as possible.

Samuels set down the pizza on the kitchen table and held the bottle of wine up.

"If you can provide a couple of glasses, I can tell you more about Harry Gascoyne. I know quite a lot about him, as it happens."

There was that smile again.

Ellen fetched two glasses and a corkscrew, which she handed to Samuels. She excused herself and slipped into the bathroom. For a moment she stood with her back to the door. If whoever impersonated Becky Tansey turned out to be from Harrogate nick, then she would have to be careful about what information she introduced there. Monroe had made it clear that she was on borrowed time. Lewis Samuels had no connections to Monroe that she knew of. He had information about Gascoyne and a reason to get to the bottom of what happened to Connie. He could be a good ally and a terrible enemy. But could she trust him?

While washing her hands she looked at herself in the mirror. *Jesus.* Had she even stopped to brush her hair that morning? Her only hairbrush was in her bag in the kitchen, so she pulled out her ponytail, ran her fingers through her hair then decided, no, that was definitely not going to work, before quickly tying it back up again. She sniffed under her arms, realising she badly needed a shower. Instead, she sprayed some deodorant and hoped for the best.

Ellen was slow to trust people. Trust was something earned in her book, and few people had earned it. She had few friends bar Linda, who had betrayed her, Dan, who was more like family, and Jackie, who actually was. At work she was suspicious of co-workers until they earned her trust. Sarika Kaur was one of the few colleagues she allowed herself to rely on. The same went for romantic relationships, although she had barely thought about dating, let alone going on a date, since the split with Anthony. The truth was there were few men she found attractive enough to bother with. Lewis Samuels was the first man in a long time to cause a reaction.

Back in the kitchen, she saw that Samuels had set the table with two plates, knives and forks.

"I love your place. The wood, the pitched ceiling, very cool."

He opened the bottle of wine and poured two glasses.

"My sister runs the café downstairs. I've always loved it up here, but it's really too small."

"It'll cost a few pennies to find a bigger place around here."

Ellen pulled out a chair and sat down.

"I'm actually doing up a houseboat, out at Bishopthorpe. Hoping to be moving on board in the next few weeks."

Samuels handed her a glass of wine.

"No shit? You bought a boat?"

"It was my dad's, he died last year. He always meant to finish *Gypsy*, but never did."

Samuels lifted his glass in a toast.

"I lost both my parents in the last year too, not easy. To our parents, wherever they might be."

Ellen clinked her glass against his. Samuels opened the pizza box and pulled a slice onto her plate. She was still full but decided to have one slice. She picked it up and bit into the warm, juicy filling.

Samuels pointed at a photo on the fridge of Ellen, Jackie and Dan taken on the deck of *Serendipity*. "I'm guessing that's your sister and your father?"

"My sister and my dad's friend," Ellen said with a full mouth. "That's his boat."

"You and your sister don't look in the least bit alike."

Ellen smiled. "So I'm told." She didn't feel the need to explain that both she and Jackie had been adopted and were not blood relatives.

The pizza was delicious but she really couldn't eat more than the one slice. Samuels worked his way through the rest.

"I'm amazed it's Harry Gascoyne," he said. "I've written a lot about him over the years."

Ellen filled their glasses with more wine.

"Maybe that was why Connie approached you."

"She never would tell me his name, but it would explain a lot. He's a big player in Yorkshire. That deal he signed with the American supermarket group a few months ago? The guy's worth millions."

"Powerful man," Ellen agreed.

"From what I hear, he has a lot of ex-police working for his organisation in security consultancy. That's what I've been looking into."

Ellen took a mouthful of wine. "Go on."

"Your colleague, Matt Jackson. Is he a friend of yours?"

"No. He is definitely *not* a friend of mine."

"Good. According to my source, he's been to the Hong Kong Sevens for the last four years running."

"The rugby tournament? Plenty of the lads go. It's hardly a crime."

"He stays at the Ritz Carlton, one of the most expensive hotels in Hong Kong."

"What are you suggesting?"

"Gascoyne attends the Hong Kong Sevens every year. Hosts a dinner, entertains clients. Always stays at the Ritz Carlton."

Ellen considered this information. It would make sense that Jackson was working for Gascoyne. Receiving payment in kind and no doubt straight cash as well.

"I'm sure lots of people stay at the Ritz Carlton."

He raised an eyebrow. "At maybe two grand a night during the tournament? Not bad on a DI's salary."

"You think Jackson was behind the notes? The intimidation?"

"Or worse."

Ellen poured the last of the wine into both glasses and downed hers. She had made the decision to let Lewis in on what she knew.

"Look, someone approached Connie on Facebook using the identity of a woman who has been dead for a few years. This woman was supposed to be in Canada, claimed she was at Lockton House."

"I'll assume that's Becky Tansey. The last name on your list."

Ellen raised an eyebrow.

"Jesus. Have you got a photographic memory or something?"

"Years of training," Samuels said, a smile on his lips. "Go on."

"We've checked the IP. It turns out to be an internet café in Harrogate, on Otley Road. Not far from Harrogate nick, where Jackson is based."

Lewis Samuels whistled.

"That's some hot potato you've managed to catch. You think it's Jackson, I presume. How did Monroe react?"

"I haven't had time to tell him. I'm guessing he won't be too pleased to find out one of his own officers could be a potential suspect in a murder inquiry."

"What makes you think Monroe doesn't already know?"

Ellen gaped at him. Shit, why hadn't she even considered that?

"You think Monroe is involved with Gascoyne?"

"Look, I don't know. I'm not saying he is, but it's a possibility."

Samuels looked around.

"Do you mind if I use your bathroom?"

"Sure, it's just there," Ellen pointed to the door to the right of the kitchen. The automatic fan whirred into life as Samuels closed the door.

The bedroom door opened and Zoe appeared.

"Just getting some water."

Zoe's timing was suspicious. Had she been listening at the door?

"There's a journalist here to discuss the case I'm working on," Ellen told her, gesturing towards the bathroom. "He'll be gone in a few minutes."

Ellen watched Zoe's eyes take in the wine and the pizza, her mother's flushed face.

Ellen suspected that her daughter had a fantasy that she and Anthony would get back together. This in spite of the fact that Anthony was now living with Linda. After her parents had split, her mother had had a stream of men in her life. Ellen had resented them all, and had resented her mother for bringing these men into their home.

There was no question of her ever patching things up with Anthony. She wouldn't have him back if he was the last man on earth, which was what she had told him when he had begged her to come back. It had been his second strike. She should have ended it on the first.

"It's fine, I'll just go back to bed."

Zoe sloped back to the bedroom and closed the door.

When Samuels emerged from the bathroom, Ellen had his coat in her hand.

"Sorry, you've got to go," she said. "My daughter's awake. We'll pick this up tomorrow."

CHAPTER TWENTY-THREE

Ellen hopped out of the shower at 6:30 a.m. and threw on her clothes. She had forty-five minutes to get dressed and leave for Zoe's parent-teacher meeting. Plenty of time. Sky News was playing the item about the murder every twenty minutes, and she repeatedly heard Monroe say the words 'sex worker Connie Taylor' at yesterday's press conference. Monroe knew how to spin a story for the media.

The next clip was footage from Lockton House that Jackie and Zoe had seen. Why hadn't Jackie insisted she get her hair cut? Or maybe she had.

She got Zoe out of bed and ten minutes later the two of them were out the door onto Fossgate. The ancient street packed with independent shops, bars, and restaurants was already busy with morning commuter traffic. Ellen's car was parked around the corner in Peel Street.

At twenty past seven, Ellen drove through the gates at St Mary's School. She had to make this a five-minute in-and-out affair. Instead of driving to the visitors' parking area, she parked in one of the teachers' spaces at the front of the building. Zoe groaned and got out of the car. Ellen took the opportunity to call Lewis Samuels.

"You're up early," he said.

"Parent–teacher meeting," Ellen explained. "Don't ask."

"Why don't you swing round here after, have a coffee, and continue last night's discussion?"

"I can't, I'm heading straight to a meeting. That's actually why I called. I need you to acknowledge that everything we discussed last night was off the record."

Ellen heard Samuels take a drink of something and swallow.

"Agreed. But keep me in the loop."

Ellen ended the call without confirming she would.

The school was housed in an old mansion, with sweeping parkland, tennis courts, and hockey pitches. It looked more like a grand hotel than a school. It was a far cry from the comprehensive Ellen had attended. Zoe was bright and had managed to snare a scholarship.

Inside the main hall, Ellen found the reception desk empty. Zoe reluctantly accompanied her to Mrs Telford's office then skittered off. Helen Telford, a woman in her fifties, gestured for Ellen to take a seat. She pulled out Zoe's file from the pile on her desk.

"Where do I start with Zoe?"

Mrs Telford launched into the reports from Zoe's teachers. Zoe was consistently late for class, consistently failed to hand in homework assignments, and consistently flouted the uniform code by wearing a non-uniform jacket to and from school. Ellen snatched a look at her watch, she needed to go.

Mrs Telford hadn't finished. Zoe had been caught smoking on several occasions and did not participate in any after-school activities.

"Look," Ellen said, "I get it, she's being a teenager, a general pain in the ass. I'm on it."

Helen Telford leaned forward. Her voice softened.

"There's more going on than that. Zoe is struggling here. She hasn't made any friends, she's isolated."

Ellen stood up and put her bag on her shoulder. She didn't want to hear this, didn't want to acknowledge it was true.

Zoe's form teacher continued. "I've been a school counsellor for twenty years, and I know a kid in trouble when I see one."

This was nonsense. Zoe was always first in her class since she started school at five. Maybe she was struggling a bit, but she would be fine.

Ellen turned for the door. "I have to go. I'll sort it."

"Zoe tells me she has been feeling down in the dumps, and that she has been having panic attacks."

Ellen halted in her tracks. Panic attacks? Zoe was thirteen, for God's sake. What has a thirteen-year-old got to be feeling down about?

Ellen opened the door.

"Look, I appreciate you trying to help, but I have to go."

Five minutes later Ellen emerged from the confines of the school into the open air with Zoe at her side, who she had tracked down in the cafeteria. Zoe refused to talk until they were in the safety of the car.

"What's all this about you having panic attacks?"

"Just take me home."

"I'm not leaving you at home on your own all day, Zoe. I have to go to work."

"Of course you do. You *always* have to go to work."

Zoe pushed open the car door. Things were clearly not fine. Ellen felt a stab of anxiety deep in her chest. If she was a good mother, she would drive Zoe home and spend the day with her, but that was just not going to happen. Not today. Not with a murder investigation to run.

"Look, it's a half-day. You're going to Dan's after school," Ellen said. "I'll pick you up later. How about I cook us a nice dinner and we can watch a movie together?"

Zoe sighed and stepped out of the car.

"Whatever."

* * *

Ellen drove the few miles to Fulford Road in a daze. *Zoe, having panic attacks?* The fallout from the court case, the marriage breakdown, her promotion and subsequent move to York had turned Zoe's life upside down. Zoe had been happy in Leeds. She'd liked her school and had had lots of friends.

She slammed her palm against the steering wheel. Of course it wasn't easy for Zoe to move home and school, to start over in a new place. But for Mrs Telford to imply that she was depressed — well, that was ridiculous. Wasn't it? She was a teenager, for God's sake.

Ellen didn't have time to linger on the thought. She had a team briefing at nine. She had to focus.

CHAPTER TWENTY-FOUR

I sit at my desk eating a breakfast roll I picked up in the canteen. It is surprisingly good. Juicy sausage, crispy bacon, topped off with an egg, the yoke of which is running out over my fingers. To think I've been paying over the top for what passes for breakfast at Prufrock's these past months. Smashed bloody avocado on everything and three times the price.

The new girl on the switch waves over at me conspiratorially and I wave back. She reminds me of Connie Taylor. The same bovine expression. Same desperation to be liked. From here I can see her desk. I can tell that she is slacking off, indulging herself in a spot of googling. There is no writing, no notes being taken, no activity emerging from the time spent on screen. Her job is to answer the phones, which she manages to do despite her low threshold for stress, which manifests itself when more than one call comes in at a time. She wears an agitated expression, as if she is constantly surprised by the demands of her menial job. Like it is a surprise that a person employed to answer the phone should have to do that over and over again.

The agitated expression only relaxes when she engages in these periods of non-work-related googling, during which time she shamelessly redirects her calls back to the switchboard. No doubt she is googling 'Is my weight gain caused by an overactive thyroid?' Intermittently, furtive eyes flicker left and right before pudgy fingers feed her mouth from a stash of pink marshmallows hidden in the folds of her skirt. Does she really think no one sees her stuffing herself?

My so-called mother used to stuff herself in a similar fashion. Morbidly obese, she couldn't keep her trotters out of a bag of jellies for long. They acted like a drug, numbing the guilt she might otherwise have felt. Her weakness disgusted me. Make-up covered her own bruises. She pretended not to see mine.

To lie, to deceive, to hurt others — these are human sins. Unfortunate but necessary sometimes. To lie to oneself, however, that is contemptible under any circumstances. In my quest for justice, I have lied and I have certainly deceived others. But I take full responsibility for my actions, at least to myself. I do these things because I need to. On occasion because I want to. You don't hear me bleating on about how the world has fucked me over. Like my mother, Connie played the victim card her whole life. She deserved what she got. If someone wrongs me, I don't take refuge in alcohol, or drugs, or food. I take revenge.

When I reached eighteen, adulthood, Dr Michael Daly was finally able to upgrade my diagnosis from conduct disorder to antisocial personality disorder. He cited my tendency towards violence. My propensity for deception and manipulation. While he stopped short of labelling me a psychopath, he did tell my parents that psychopaths are considered to have a severe form of antisocial personality disorder. My father cut me off. Refused to have anything more to do with me. I could see the fear in his eyes. He was terrified of me. That at least felt good.

Some time ago, I googled 'Am I a psychopath?' A riddle came up in one of my search results which intrigued me. It was developed by an American psychologist to test if a person has the mentality of a psychopath. The riddle goes like this:

> *While at the funeral of his own father, a man meets an attractive woman whom he does not know. He thinks this woman is amazing. In fact, he falls in love with her straight away. However, he never asks for her name or number, and afterwards cannot find anyone who knows who she is.*
>
> *A few days later the man kills his own mother.*
>
> *Question: Why did he kill his mother?*

Answer: He reasoned that if the woman appeared at his father's funeral, then she might appear at his mother's funeral.

I answered correctly. No surprise there. Maybe I am a psychopath. If I am, I wasn't born that way. I was made.

Forbes *magazine published a list of jobs most attractive to psychopaths. The list is interesting because it lists my own profession.*

1. *CEO*
2. *Lawyer*
3. *Media (television/radio)*
4. *Salesperson*
5. *Surgeon*
6. *Journalist*
7. *Police officer*

Like this creature on the switch, Connie also had a low threshold for stress. Having cigarettes put out on your breast is certainly stressful. Connie revealed to me with her dying breath that Vicky was moving from place to place, staying in Airbnb's. When she gave me the information, she probably fooled herself into thinking I would spare her. I didn't. I killed her anyway.

To access Vicky's Airbnb account, I needed her email address and her password. With the first splash of acid, Connie screamed her friend's email address. Hilarious how easy it was. She didn't know the password, and it has so far evaded me. From what I know of Vicky, it will have some reference to her daughter. People are so predictable in these matters. I have tried every combination that I can think of. Callie1, Callie2, Callie3, Callie123, Callie456, and a hundred more. I sit back and toss the final piece of roll into my mouth, washing it down with a slug of tea. I wonder where Vicky came up with the name and type 'meaning of name Callie' into Google.

The name Callie is a Greek baby name meaning 'most beautiful'. Alternative but rare spelling is Kallie.

Of course! My heart lurches with adrenalin. Trust the stupid bitch to give the child an 'individual' spelling. I bring up the Airbnb login and this time type in Kallie1. Nothing. I type Kallie123. I laugh out loud and shout "Bingo!" The girl on switch looks over and I wink at her. She goes pink in the face. I feel revolted.

I turn my attention back to my computer screen. I am in to Vicky's Airbnb account. I open up her 'trips' page and see that she is staying in an apartment here in York, on Margaret Street. I can't quite believe I have found her. There are still twenty-eight hours to go until the deadline, and I am ready as I'll ever be. I open my top drawer and take out my car keys. I open the bottom drawer and take out my knife.

CHAPTER TWENTY-FIVE

Margaret Street, York

Vicky was sitting by the window of the flat watching a man on the street corner below. At the table, Kallie was drawing with a new set of crayons. She looked at her phone. Another text message from Dr James.

Please, Vicky, I can help you. The detective is a friend of mine. She wants to help. You can't do this alone.

Since yesterday she had been running on adrenalin. She couldn't believe Dr James had gone to the police. Vicky looked back down onto the street where the man was still standing. She tapped into her missed calls. Four missed calls from Dr James. She found her therapist's number, her thumb hovering over the call button. She had no choice but to trust her. Before she could press it, Kallie drew her attention.

"Come and draw with me, Mummy."

Vicky's shopping bags lay on the floor beside her.

"In a minute, love," Vicky said, her eyes back on the man on the street below.

She had only gone to the Spar on the next street to get the essentials. Tea, milk, bread, and the box of crayons to keep Kallie happy. Was it him? The monster who killed

Connie? Had he spotted her on the street and followed her home? She inhaled deeply. She couldn't afford to let the terror take hold.

"I want you to draw with me, Mummy," Kallie said, her face crumpling in tears. Kallie always knew when Vicky was scared. Vicky couldn't hide it from her, much as she tried.

Before today, she had been so careful, taking long detours around the place she was staying, never entering the property until she was 100 per cent sure she hadn't been followed. Why had she dropped her guard today? Last night was her third in this Airbnb. She had paid in advance for another four, but she couldn't stay now. Not after what had happened to poor Connie.

Like most of the places she had stayed over the past few weeks, it was a dump, but it was affordable and functional. She always selected a place on a street with few shops or businesses on it. That way, anyone hanging around would be immediately obvious. That's how she had spotted the man outside.

Kallie had abandoned her crayons and was pulling at Vicky's arm.

"Not now, Kallie," Vicky snapped, with more anger in her voice than she had intended.

The man was wearing a hoodie which covered most of his face. He was on his mobile phone now. *There.* He definitely looked up at her. Vicky darted back behind the curtain. *Did he see me?*

Kallie was wailing now.

"Mummy, I want you to draw with me."

The man was moving now, striding towards her building. He was still on the phone, looking up at her window. *Who is he talking to?*

Her heart pounding, she lifted Kallie up and tried to comfort her. She needed her to be quiet. There was no time to phone Dr James now. She had to focus on the escape strategy she had worked out earlier on. Her car was parked around the corner. This apartment had two entrances, one at the front of the building and one at the back. It also had a small walled balcony which was separated from its neighbour's balcony by a two-foot gap. She had already placed a chair up against the wall on the inside of the balcony in readiness.

Leaning out from behind the curtain, she noticed that the neighbour's balcony door was open a fraction. She would have to jump. And with a wriggling child in her arms. Could she really do it?

She slipped back behind the curtain. Below on the street she heard high heels on the front step of her apartment building and a young woman emerged. She saw the man with the hoodie run like lightning to grab the door before it closed behind her. *Oh God! He's in the building.* Carrying Kallie, she ran to look through the peephole in the front door, where she had a view of the landing and stairs. Suddenly he was there, rounding the staircase. Her stomach lurched. *This can't be happening.* He was looking at her apartment door, his face still obscured by the hoodie he was wearing. She grabbed her handbag and darted to the balcony. *This is it. If I don't do this, he'll kill us both.* She kissed Kallie, who was wriggling in her arms. She stepped up onto the chair and then onto the balcony wall. She could hear the man pounding on the door. He was shouting her name. She had no choice. *You have to do this. Now!*

CHAPTER TWENTY-SIX

Fulford Road station, York

Ellen briefed the team then headed to the canteen for breakfast. Before she had taken a bite of her toast, Sarika appeared.

"Glad I caught you on your own, boss. Just saw this come in on the system. Do you think it could be Vicky and her daughter?"

Sarika handed Ellen a printout of a callout to Margaret Street, made half an hour ago. An elderly woman reported that the neighbouring flat had been broken into by an intruder, and that an unknown woman had entered her flat, carrying a female child. Ellen grabbed the toast from her plate.

"Let's go. Margaret Street's not far."

Ten minutes later Ellen and Sarika turned the corner into Margaret Street, which contained several blocks of near-identical red-brick apartment buildings.

Sarika pointed to a police car parked outside one of the buildings. Several residents had gathered at the front door and directed the detectives up to the first floor, where they found the door to one of the flats completely smashed in.

From inside the flat a young uniformed police officer appeared, presumably the first responder. Sarika and Ellen showed him their badges.

"The old dear next door called it in. Scared out of her wits when a woman appeared on her balcony."

They followed him into the sitting room and out onto a tiny concrete balcony. He indicated a chair, which was propped up against the low wall of the balcony.

"The woman was carrying a young child. She must have stepped up here onto that chair and jumped across."

Sarika looked over the balcony at the twenty-foot drop below.

"She must have been desperate to have jumped with a child."

"How is the old lady?" Ellen asked.

"In shock, I'd say. We've not been able to get a lot of sense out of her. I'll let her know you want to talk to her."

Ellen looked around the flat. From the front window, she could see the gothic-style arched windows of St George's Roman Catholic Church. After the potato famine in Ireland there had been a huge influx of Irish Catholic immigrants to the Walmgate area of York, and St George's had been built to accommodate them. For the first eight years of her life, Ellen had been part of that Catholic community. She knew the church well — she had made her First Holy Communion there. Jackie still had the photos. She remembered the dress her mother had paid a fortune for, much more than she let on to her father. She'd had a white mantilla and lace gloves, but her prized possession had been a white beaded handbag.

"Do you have an ID on the woman staying here?" Sarika asked the PC, interrupting Ellen's reverie.

"Name is Vicky Richards. We've been onto the owner. He rented it to her three nights ago, she was due to stay another four."

Sarika picked up a bag on the floor by the window. Inside was tea, milk, and bread. "So, she came in from shopping, was spooked by something, dropped the shopping here and climbed into next-door's flat."

The kitchen table was covered with crayons and paper. Ellen picked up one of the drawings. She recognised the artist. Kallie. Like the pictures at the flat in Clifton, this too showed a blue house. A woman and a child were holding hands beneath a rainbow. Around them were tall yellow flowers. Ellen folded the drawing and put it in her bag.

In the main bedroom the double bed had been slept in. Discarded pyjamas, underwear and a damp towel lay on the floor.

A second bedroom contained a single bed which had not been slept in. An open suitcase of clothes lay on top. The young PC appeared and indicated that the lady in the adjacent flat was ready to speak to them.

Mrs Allsop was being tended to by a female PC. The elderly woman sat in a faded armchair, a cup of tea in her trembling hands.

"Hello, Mrs Allsop. I'm DI McClure, this is DC Kaur. We need to ask you about the woman who came in from the balcony."

Mrs Allsop looked at the female PC then back at Ellen. She seemed incapable of telling anyone anything. Ellen tried to contain her impatience.

"Look, I know you've had a shock, but we really need you to answer our questions . . ."

Ellen felt a hand on her elbow. It was Sarika, who indicated with a nod of her head that she wanted to have a go. Sarika squatted down beside the lady, whose name the PC said was Vera.

"Hello, Vera, my name is Sarika." She pointed to the photographs on the table beside Vera's chair.

"Are they your grandchildren, Vera?"

Vera smiled for the first time.

Ellen sighed and backed away to the window. This was not a skill set she had, and she admired it in Sarika. She put people at ease. Her voice was soothing. Over the next few minutes Ellen paced back and forth, checking her phone while Vera told Sarika about her three grandchildren, their names, their ages, what they were all doing.

After being handed a second cup of tea, Vera eventually described what had happened.

"I heard banging on the door, next door. Loud it was. A man's voice shouting 'Open up,' something like that. Next door is rented out. All sorts coming and going. I didn't want to get involved."

"Had you seen the woman who was staying there at all?" Sarika asked.

"I passed her once or twice. Said hello, that was all. I assumed it was some kind of domestic. The man might be her husband, come to get her back. Anyway, I'm sitting right here and next thing I hear a clatter out there on the balcony and the door bursts open and she runs right past me and out the front door."

Vera's hands had started to tremble again, rattling the teaspoon in the saucer. Sarika took the teacup and placed it on the table beside her.

"I'm sorry to have to keep on, Vera, but we need to know. Did she say anything to you, the woman, anything at all?"

Vera shook her head. "That's all I remember. Then she was gone."

"Did you hear the man in the apartment next door come out. Did he see her?"

"I didn't see him but I think she went down the back stairs. The door is right next to mine out there. I closed the door, then I went and looked out the front, out the window. That's when I saw her running over towards the church."

Ellen knew that right behind the church was a car park, a large open-air lot. She sometimes parked there if she couldn't find a space on the street nearer Fossgate.

"Peel Street car park," she said to Sarika. "Vicky might have gone there."

A few minutes later Ellen and Sarika had reached Peel Street. The car park was bounded on one side by the east wall of St George's and on the other three sides by a mish-mash of council and private apartment buildings and commercial properties, including a working men's club called Tramways. The metal doors were propped open with kegs. A heavily tattooed man wearing stained overalls was painting over graffiti on the wall.

Ellen showed him her badge.

"Did you see a woman with a little girl come through here sometime in the last hour or so?"

"Yeah."

"We need to find her. Did you see if she got into a car?" said Sarika.

"She went down the back there. Looked scared out of her wits."

"Can you show us where her car was?"

The man hesitated.

"She's not in any trouble, but we do need to make sure she's safe," Sarika told him.

The man sighed and put down his paintbrush. He sauntered ahead of Ellen and Sarika, and took them right to the back of the car park.

"Here — she got into a car here. An old red Ford Fiesta. I was watching 'cos of the state she was in, kind of hysterical."

Ellen looked around. On the ground was the usual detritus of urban life. Empty beer cans, cigarette butts, plastic bottles. Something colourful caught her eye. She bent down and picked it up. It was a knitted yellow bear. She recognised it from the photo in Vicky's flat in Clifton. Kallie had been holding it.

"Did she speak to you?" Sarika asked.

"Nope. I asked her if she was okay. She looked like someone was chasing her. Kept looking over her shoulder."

"If you can remember anything else," Sarika said, "anything at all, it might really help her."

"She was mumbling something."

Ellen pounced on the comment. "What exactly?"

The man frowned in concentration. "Something about a blue house. Yeah, that was it. She kept telling the child, 'We're going to the blue house.'"

Ellen thought of the blue house in Kallie's drawings. That was where Vicky was running to. But where was this blue house? Perhaps Maggie might have some clue. Ellen dialled the therapist's number.

PART THREE

CHAPTER TWENTY-SEVEN

National Probation Service, Lowther Street, York

Maggie James was watching the news report on the waiting room television. It was the same segment on Sky News looping every half hour. The men's group she was due to facilitate were milling around reception and the waiting area ready for the 11:30 a.m. kick-off. Every Monday morning Maggie ran a rehabilitation programme for perpetrators of violent crime. Each week brought stories of rage, of hatred, of loss of control. In many ways, she had become somewhat immune to the cruelty human beings were capable of inflicting on one another.

She looked around the room. These hardened ex-cons were, in the main, a good-natured bunch. The weekly meeting was all that was keeping several of them from reoffending and finding themselves back in prison. It was heartening that they had all shown up, even with the freezing weather. Most of them were in tracksuits — only one or two were adequately dressed for the snowy weather.

The news segment showed the same clip from yesterday, and Maggie struggled to hear above the background din. Ellen McClure as she left the scene at Heworth Green, her distaste for the press evident as she pushed past without answering their questions. Maggie had driven past the crime scene two or three times a week for the last ten years, although she had never consciously connected the place with the care home Vicky had described. In fact, she and Rob had almost bought an ivy-clad Victorian around the corner from Lockton House before finding their dream home on South Parade.

Maggie had a gnawing sensation in the pit of her stomach. Ellen was due to arrive at any minute. She had demanded to see Vicky Richards' file. The detective had said very little on the phone, but her tone had screamed, "I mean business."

Ellen would go to the ends of the earth to protect those unable to defend themselves, a rare quality which Maggie had always admired in her. However, her impulsive nature meant she tended to charge into situations without weighing up the consequences for those she was actually trying to protect. Now she wondered if Ellen had changed, or if she was still just as reckless as she had been back then.

The scene on the TV changed now to the press conference from yesterday and the detective who looked like a boxer dog. DI Matt Jackson. She had recognised him immediately. He had taken Vicky's statement months before. She had worked for years to get Vicky to the point of reporting what happened to her to the police. It should have been a pivotal moment in her healing. An opportunity for her to be heard, to get justice for the violence which had been meted out to her. Instead, her story had been met by disbelief and, worse, derision. It was a horrible setback. A compounding of the years of abuse and marginalisation she had already suffered.

The intimidation had started just days after their visit to Harrogate station. The notes. The threats. Vicky had described feeling like she had poked a wasp's nest. Maggie now felt like she was standing at that wasp's nest with a spade, poised to open it right on top of Vicky and Kallie cowering below.

Vicky had been let down by the system throughout her unfortunate life. Born to a mother addicted to heroin, she had been taken into care by social workers who no doubt believed they were giving her the chance of a better life. Instead, she had been placed in the path of a monster. A monster who groomed her and then abused her, destroying any belief she may have had that people in authority could be trusted. Over the years, Maggie had fought to gain Vicky's trust. And eventually she had. She did so because Maggie never lied to her, never betrayed that trust. Could she betray Vicky now? Could she hand over the file to Ellen McClure after Vicky had specifically told her not to?

Maggie walked into her office and sat at her desk. Vicky Richards' file sat open in front of her. Her chest tightened with anxiety. She thought of the advice she regularly doled out to clients feeling similarly unpleasant sensations: "Just breathe through it." Absolute rubbish! It was impossible to breathe when you felt like you had a ten-ton weight bearing down on you. What she really felt like was a drink. A large gin martini. Ha! Some psychotherapist she was. Maybe that's what she should advise her clients from now on? Just go to the nearest pub and self-medicate with your favourite tipple.

Ellen might even have a warrant, given the information Maggie had already divulged. Maggie walked back out to reception. The men had exited in dribs and drabs onto the street and were braving the cold. Most of the men smoked. It would be two hours before they would have another chance and they were charging up with nicotine. Maggie looked up at the sky. It was heavy and yellow, with the promise of more snow. An unmarked car pulled in on the opposite side of the road. Ellen McClure was here.

* * *

Ellen and Sarika followed Maggie into her office, closing the door behind them. Ellen dropped her bag down onto

Maggie's desk and then took a chair facing her. Sarika sat down next to Ellen.

Ellen got straight to business. "Did Vicky ever mention a blue house to you?"

The therapist frowned. "A blue house? I don't think so. Why?"

"We've just come from a flat in Margaret Street where Vicky has been staying these last few days. This morning the door was smashed in by an unknown intruder. Vicky escaped by jumping from the balcony into the neighbouring flat. Took off in her car. She was heard telling Kallie they were going to the blue house."

Maggie gasped. "Oh my God! Is she okay?"

"We don't know. We don't know where she is, only that she took off from Peel Street car park."

Maggie took out her phone and dialled a number.

"I'll just try calling her again."

"She'll have ditched the sim card to avoid being tracked," Sarika said.

Maggie ended the call.

"Can you remember anything from your sessions? Any place Vicky mentioned that might match this blue house?" Ellen asked.

Maggie shook her head. "Vicky lived in care most of her life. I don't think she would want to revisit any of those places."

"Any friends or relatives?"

"Connie was her only real friend. She had no family, apart from Kallie."

"What about Kallie's father?"

"He died years ago — drug overdose."

"There has to be something in the file."

Maggie looked pensive.

"Look, I can go through it now and give you anything I think might be relevant, but I can't just hand over the file."

Ellen leaned across the desk.

"If you like, I'll show you the photos of Connie Taylor's face from the post-mortem. Her severed head sitting on the morgue table next to her tortured body. Vicky is only one small step ahead of this sick bastard. He will do this to her and then he will do it to her child. Now stop fucking around and give me that file!"

Maggie's face fell and she pushed the file forward.

"Take it."

"Thank you," Ellen said, drawing the file toward her. Then she reached into her bag and retrieved Kallie's drawing, placing it on the desk. She pointed to the blue house.

"This is a drawing Kallie did. I think it could be the same place."

Maggie picked up the picture. "Let me see."

"It's somewhere with a garden, and flowers," Sarika prompted.

Maggie suddenly pulled the file back towards her and started flicking through.

"What is it?" Ellen asked.

"Vicky was on a programme. She hasn't mentioned it in a while."

"What programme?"

"Here it is." Maggie pulled out a letter typed on headed paper. "It's a community-based programme teaching people how to grow their own vegetables."

The logo for the York Allotments Committee was printed on the top right-hand corner. It was a garden shed. A blue garden shed.

Maggie pointed at the logo. "Maybe Kallie's drawing isn't of a blue house — maybe it's a blue shed." She looked at Kallie's drawing. "And these yellow flowers, I think they might be cobs of corn. The other flowers could be vegetables."

Ellen glanced out the window. There was a light dusting of snow on the ground.

"Would you take a child to an allotment in this weather?" she asked.

Sarika nodded. "My dad's got a shed at his allotment in Bradford. Its cosy enough. You can make a cup of tea there, plug in a heater."

"Do you know where Vicky's allotment is?" Ellen asked Maggie.

Maggie picked up the phone. "It's not in Vicky's file, but I'll phone through to reception." She spoke down the line. "Aga, the York Allotments scheme. Vicky Richards was assigned a plot. Can you find out where?"

Three minutes later the phone rang. Maggie picked it up.

"Low Moor. Great. I'm going to have to cancel my eleven thirty. Tell the men's group I'll be in to explain in a minute."

Sarika was busy googling Low Moor Allotments.

"It's not far from the station on Fulford Road, just beyond the cemetery."

Ellen stood up. "We'll head there right away."

Maggie grabbed her coat off the back of the door.

"Give me five minutes and I'll come with you. I just have to hand over a few things."

Before Ellen could protest, Maggie was out the door.

Ellen would give Maggie five minutes. If Vicky was there, it may help to keep her calm having her therapist present.

CHAPTER TWENTY-EIGHT

Low Moor, York

Vicky parked her car off Kilburn Road, fifty yards from the allotments. She couldn't risk leaving the car any closer. After days of heavy skies, the forecasted snow had finally started to fall in earnest. It was freezing. They had left their winter coats behind at the flat on Margaret Street and only had what was in the car, a fleece for Vicky and a summer jacket for Kallie. Low Moor was quiet. The allotments were deserted at this time of year. Only the occasional regular would be here. People she knew to say hello to but who knew nothing about her. They would be safe for now.

Like all the allotment holders, Vicky had a key to the gate, but it was back in the flat at Clifton. It didn't matter. She knew there was a hole in the fence because Rocky had found it. She felt guilty that she hadn't had time to bury him. He deserved better. Looking up and down the path to make sure they hadn't been seen, Vicky pushed Kallie through the hole in the fence and squeezed through after her. She had stopped at a garage and bought milk, bread, and other supplies to last a few days. It would be cold, but at least they would be safe here.

She wondered how her attacker had tracked her to the flat in Margaret Street. She couldn't risk renting another place and have him track her down again. Nobody would think to look for her here.

They made their way past the familiar plots, each an extension of their owner's personality. Some had been cleared of the previous year's planting, compost dug in, all ready for the spring planting. Others were a tangled mass of weeds. The snow was settling on the ground now and Kallie amused herself stepping into Vicky's larger footprints.

The key to the shed was kept under the water barrel and she found it easily. The familiar musty odour wafted out as she opened the door.

The shed was crowded with chairs, tables, and tools. With relief she found the fan heater in the box she had kept here. She would have to pull all the furniture out to make some room, then get the heater on, warm the place up.

An axe lay just inside the door. She hoped she wouldn't have to use it. She remembered what Dr James always said to her: "Just think of a first small step, then take it. Then think of the next one, and take it. Keep going and only think of your next small step." She could not afford to give into panic. One mistake and they might be discovered.

She jumped when her mobile rang. They could find people by tracing their phones. Connie had told her that. She would have to get rid of it. She took the sim card out of the phone and brought the axe down on it, smashing it until she was sure there was nothing left to transmit a signal. Kallie squealed in delight.

Vicky lifted out two fold-up chairs and set them up. Then she stacked the remaining chairs at the back of the shed, along with a shovel, a watering can, and a rake. Finally, she shut the door to the bright white world outside. They were safer in the dark. She had taken one small step and she wasn't moving from here until she worked out what the next step was.

CHAPTER TWENTY-NINE

Ellen and Maggie drove in Maggie's car. Sarika followed behind. Low Moor Allotments were a fifteen-minute drive from Lowther Street at this time of the day. The traffic was slow with the weather. Maggie put the windscreen wipers on to clear the snow now falling steadily. Ellen looked at her watch. Thankfully Dan would have picked Zoe up already, so they wouldn't be caught out in it.

"I can only imagine the effect this will have on poor Kallie," Maggie said with a sigh. "She's a sensitive child as it is. Prone to anxiety."

Ellen instantly thought of Zoe. "Isn't anxiety an adult thing?"

The snow was getting heavier. Maggie put the wipers on full speed.

"I believe anxiety can set in at any age. But there's plenty we can do to help with it."

The traffic light leading to the Barbican Road ahead was only letting two or three cars through at a time. Ellen groaned. They were not going anywhere in a hurry.

She glanced at the Walmgate Bar to her right, the ancient gate in the city's stone walls, impossibly pretty now in the swirling snow. Her apartment on Fossgate was only a ten-minute walk, at the far end of Walmgate and over the bridge.

"I don't think I could do your job, Maggie. Listening to all that trauma, day in, day out."

Maggie inched the car forward then came to a stop. She turned to face Ellen.

"Are you for real? You don't think you deal with trauma? In your job?"

Ellen grinned. "Yeah, I see plenty of gruesome stuff. Some of that you could call traumatic. But what you do . . ."

What Maggie didn't understand was that finding the perpetrators of crimes and bringing them to justice was the easy bit. Sure, she had to break bad news to relatives on occasion, but she didn't have to sit hour after hour, week after week, with those same relatives. She wouldn't have the patience, for one thing. If she felt low, then she dealt with it by doing more, by working harder. How, then, was she meant to help Zoe?

They managed another five feet before Maggie cut the engine and pulled up the handbrake. The traffic was going nowhere.

"Tell me honestly, Maggie. Do you think counselling helps?" Ellen asked.

"Are you considering therapy?"

Ellen laughed.

"Me? No way. My parents are both Irish, remember? You know what Freud said about the Irish?"

"That they are the one nation in the world impervious to psychoanalysis. Only problem is, he never actually said it."

The light finally turned to green and Maggie shot across to the Barbican Road on the far side. The traffic was moving now at least. They drove alongside the city walls, which loomed high on the right side of the street.

Ellen shrugged. "It's my daughter, Zoe. Her teacher thinks she's . . . depressed."

There was silence for a moment.

"I'm guessing that's hard for you to hear?" Maggie said.

They swung left and passed Pings, the Chinese restaurant Zoe loved.

"I don't get it," said Ellen. "She's thirteen. *Apparently*, she's getting 'panic attacks'."

"Apparently?"

"That's what her form teacher told me. It's ridiculous, right?"

"And you're not so sure."

Ellen had forgotten how bloody psychoanalytical Maggie could be.

"I'm just asking."

"It sounds like you think she might be exaggerating, or lying."

"Of course not," Ellen said, then paused. "I dunno. Maybe she heard someone talking about panic attacks. You know what girls that age are like."

"How is she reacting to your scepticism?"

"She doesn't know."

"She knows." They continued driving in silence.

CHAPTER THIRTY

I had to scale the fence to get into Low Moor Allotments, ripping my knee open in the process. That group appearing outside the Probation Service was a stroke of luck. I was going to wait in the car outside for McClure, but then those men in their shabby tracksuits emerged for a fag. I hung around the reception area, keeping my face down. I saw Maggie James emerge and heard her tell the receptionist she was heading out to Low Moor with the police. They had to be looking for you, Vicky.

I only have a few minutes' head start before McClure gets here, but it might be enough. I know you're here. I passed your car round the corner. The same red Ford Fiesta I watched you drive away in at Peel Street not two hours ago. I cannot tell you how angry that made me.

There are maybe fifty sheds. You have to be in one of them. Maybe I'll find your footprints in the snow. You have to be here somewhere. The sheds all have locks on the outside. I have to find one without a lock.

This is useless, I am running out of time. Maybe I can frighten you out of your hiding place. I cup my hands and call out your name.

"Vicky!"

Silence.

"Vicky, I'm coming for you!"

No movement. Not a sound. My only hope is to ferret you out. Make you believe you are better off running. I cup my hands around my mouth again.

"I'm going to look in every shed until I find you. You and Kallie."

You deserve to suffer for what you've put me through. The fury burns like acid inside me. Speaking of acid, I tighten my grip on the bottle. Just a few moments alone with you is all I need. Just long enough to empty the contents onto your child's face and watch your world fall apart.

I lurch left, onto a parallel strip, looking for tracks on the ground.

"VICKY!" I roar. "If you come out now, I will let the girl live."

Rage surges up into my throat and I hear my father's words in my ears. "You're a Fuckwit! Even your own mother didn't want you!" I hear a car door slam and I spin round to see McClure in the distance. I duck down. Shit!

Then I see them. Footprints. Two sets — an adult's and a child's. Yes! I have you now. The prints lead to the left and around a large plot. They stop at the door of a blue shed.

CHAPTER THIRTY-ONE

Everything was silent, all sound muffled by the steadily falling snow. The trees were skeletal, any leaves long swept away by the bitter winds of the last few days.

Maggie was struggling to keep up, the soles on her boots had no grip in the snow. "Do you know I've passed this place so many times and didn't even know there were allotments here?"

"It's up there with pigeon-fancying and keeping whippets in my book," Ellen said.

"What is?" Sarika asked.

"Keeping an allotment. Something old men in braces do on a Saturday to escape their nagging wives."

Sarika grinned. "You're behind the times, boss. There's a whole new generation of apartment dwellers embracing the joys of allotment-keeping."

"I'll take my chances with Tesco, thanks all the same," Ellen said as they approached the entrance gate. It was locked.

A set of footprints led right up to the gate and ended abruptly. *Shit.*

"Someone's climbed over."

"Recently, by the looks of it," Maggie said, looking at the fast-disappearing prints.

Sarika placed her foot alongside one of the prints. It was a good three inches longer than her own.

"Someone male."

"Come on then," Ellen said, holding her hand out for Maggie to step up on. "If he's here then we can't hang about."

Sarika locked her fingers with Ellen's and between them they hoisted Maggie up and over the gate.

"Age before beauty," Ellen said, indicating for Sarika to assist her next. Sarika was in far better shape than she was and would not need any assistance.

Once inside, Ellen scanned the allotments for any movement. Nothing. A set of footprints went off to the right.

They ran past shed after shed, all of which were locked up.

Suddenly a woman's scream pierced the air.

Sarika pointed to the left. "Over there!"

Ellen took off at a sprint. She could see three sheds directly ahead. All had a two-inch layer of snow on the pitched roofs, bar one, indicating that heat was rising up from inside. A blue shed with footprints outside.

Sarika reached the shed five or six paces ahead of Ellen, her level of fitness showing itself. Without waiting for Ellen, she turned the handle and pushed the door open. Ellen was on her tail and pulled her back just as an axe came crashing down, lodging itself into the wood of the door step.

Vicky stood in the doorway, her hands still wrapped around the handle of the axe. Behind her, a little girl cowered in the gloom.

"He's here," Vicky whispered. "He said he's going to kill us."

"Did you see his face?" Ellen asked, stepping inside the shed and looking around. "What did he look like?"

Vicky shook her head. "No, I didn't see him. I only heard him."

Ellen turned to face Vicky.

"His voice — was it familiar?" She wanted to ask Vicky if she recognised the voice as belonging to either Matt

Jackson or Harry Gascoyne, but her training made her stop. If she asked Vicky straight out, it would be seen by a court as leading the witness, planting a positive identification where none had existed. She couldn't risk it. Instead she said, "Can you remember anything distinctive about the voice?"

Vicky started to shake.

"She's going into shock," said Maggie, prising the axe out of Vicky's fingers. She slipped off her coat and wrapped it around the woman's shoulders. "You need to leave her alone, just for a few minutes. Please."

In the distance Ellen heard a noise. She turned and caught sight of a figure scaling the entrance gate.

"Over there!" she shouted. "He's just gone over the gate!" She and Sarika took off, leaving Maggie to tend to Vicky. As they reached the gate, they heard a car driving off at speed up the road. Ellen put out her clasped hands for Sarika, who sprang up on them to look over the gate.

"A dark-coloured SUV. Made a right turn up the top." The DC looked down at Ellen. "Sorry, I didn't catch the reg."

Ellen helped Sarika down and kicked the gate. *Damn it! We almost had him.*

"Ring it in," she told Sarika. "If there's an SUV within ten miles of here, I want it stopped."

Ellen walked slowly back towards the shed, grateful for a moment alone to think. Monroe would hear about the SUV and would be in touch, probably within minutes. What Samuels had told her last night would give her some justification for following up on Vicky Richards. However, what she really needed was something concrete to pass on to him about Jackson's connection with Gascoyne. She took out her phone and dialled Samuels' number. He answered straight away.

"I've found Vicky hiding out at Low Moor."

"Low Moor?"

"She was hiding in an allotment shed. We got to her just in time. There was someone just ahead of us. He got away in an SUV, we didn't get the plate."

"Did she see the guy?"

"No. He ran off and we only saw him from a distance."

"And Vicky? How is she?"

"She's fine. Listen, I've had to put out an alert on the SUV. It's only a matter of time before DS Monroe hears, and he'll be looking for answers from me. Have you got anything concrete? Anything to tie Vicky with Jackson and Gascoyne?"

"Not yet, but I'm working on it. You do know Harry Gascoyne drives an SUV?"

Ellen remembered the details of Gascoyne's car from the Ana Petrescu investigation. A black Range Rover. She ran back to Sarika and mouthed, "Was it a Range Rover?"

Sarika nodded.

The hairs on the back of Ellen's neck stood up. It could be a coincidence. There were lots of dark-coloured Range Rovers in North Yorkshire. It certainly wasn't something she could bring to Alastair Monroe. But it could also be that Harry Gascoyne had just made his first mistake. Under pressure, Ellen knew that even the most careful villain often ended up getting sloppy, taking unnecessary risks which inevitably led to their arrest.

If Harry Gascoyne had Jackson in his pocket, there was no way Ellen was bringing Vicky and Kallie into police custody. She would have to find somewhere safe to hide mother and daughter, and quickly.

"I have to go, Lewis. Let me know the minute you get anything I can bring to Monroe."

CHAPTER THIRTY-TWO

Maggie got blankets from the boot of the car and wrapped them around mother and daughter, who huddled together in the back seat.

"They can stay at mine until we decide what to do," Maggie said. "I've cleared the next few days off work."

Ellen frowned. "I don't know if that's a good idea. You've got your own family to think of."

"Look, I'm ex-directory. My address isn't listed anywhere."

Ellen wasn't going to argue. It made sense. The last place she wanted Vicky right now was in a police station.

"Rob works from home so there'll be someone with us at all times."

Ellen nodded her agreement. Vicky had been through so much lately. If anyone could provide a haven of safety, it was Maggie.

Sarika and Ellen followed Maggie back to her house at Micklegate. Sarika constantly checked the rear-view mirror to a make sure they were not being followed. There had been no sightings of the SUV. It had gone to ground, but they couldn't take any chances.

South Parade was an elegant terrace of Georgian townhouses, just a hundred yards south of the city walls. Ellen whistled. Maggie had done well for herself. The street was cobbled, and the original street lamps and ornamental ironwork gates were still in use. Maggie led the way down to the garden-level door, which opened into an enormous open-plan kitchen/living room. At the far end, double doors looked out onto a courtyard garden.

Rob was standing at the hob, apron on. He was cooking dinner, spaghetti bolognese by the looks of it. He hadn't changed much with the years, Ellen thought to herself. A few grey hairs, but otherwise he had aged well. Two children were doing their homework at the table, a girl and a boy. Ellen thought of Zoe over at Dan's boat, waiting for her to come home.

Rob was all charm, but Ellen saw right through him. Once a cheating bastard, always a cheating bastard, no matter how smooth the patter. Back in college she had caught him red-handed. Walked into a pub to find him wrapped around some girl. He had been seeing Maggie for at least six months at that stage. He had even met her parents. Rob was the first boyfriend Maggie had ever brought home, the first boyfriend she had really cared about. He had given her some rubbish about the girl just being a friend, that Ellen had made a mistake. Ellen knew what she had seen, and Rob knew she knew.

Maggie's kids took Kallie off to their playroom to watch cartoons. Kallie was reluctant to go at first, but went with the bribe of sweets. Rob took himself off to his office. Maggie made a pot of tea.

Ellen needed to hear Vicky's story first hand.

"I know this is hard, Vicky, but I need to know about your connection with Harry Gascoyne," she said, pulling out a chair and sitting down beside Vicky at the table.

Vicky threw Maggie a pleading look.

The therapist's voice was soft. "Go ahead, Vicky, you can trust Ellen."

Vicky looked down at the table before speaking.

"I was nine when I was taken into care. Twelve when I was moved to Lockton House."

Maggie poured four mugs of tea and passed them around the table. Vicky smiled at Maggie, then her expression hardened.

"I didn't know anyone there, most of the girls were older than me. Harry Gascoyne came a lot. He was on the board, I think. He acted like he felt sorry for me. Picked me out for special treatment."

Vicky paused and took a sip of her tea. Ellen's phone vibrated with a text. It was from Monroe. *Shit.*

"What kind of treatment?" Ellen asked. "Can you tell me what happened exactly?"

Maggie shot Ellen a warning look, which she ignored.

"The abuse started . . ." Vicky covered her face with her hands. "I can't! I can't! It's too much."

Ellen was losing patience. "Vicky, we don't have time for this. Just tell us—"

Maggie stood up and indicated with a jerk of her head that Ellen was to follow her into the hall. Sarika sat down beside Vicky and Ellen saw her gently place the mug of tea into her hand.

Shutting the hall door, Maggie got straight to the point. She spoke in a low voice.

"Have you any idea how hard this is for her?"

"Of course I do," said Ellen, holding up her phone by way of explanation. "But I have my boss breathing down my neck looking for answers. I can't keep him waiting much longer."

"Fine, you have a job to do. But so do I." Maggie pointed at the kitchen door. "If you push her, she will freeze up and she won't be able to tell you anything. So go easy."

Ellen followed Maggie into the kitchen and sat back down.

"Look, Vicky, I'm sorry if I was rushing you. Just tell me what you can in your own time."

Vicky nodded.

"The abuse started almost immediately. He took me out for car trips, to get ice cream, to the park. At the beginning, there were other girls." She looked up. "That's when I met Connie."

Maggie put a gentle hand on her shoulder and whispered, "It's okay."

"After a few weeks it was just me and Connie he took out. He stopped taking us for ice cream. We just went straight to his house. There was a basement with a bed and video equipment. That's where he always took us. He told us if we told anyone he would show our families the videos. They would never want us back."

Ellen swore under her breath. She would get this bastard behind bars even if it meant the end of her career.

"Did he ever wear a mask?" She was thinking of Ana Petrescu and the masked man Ellen had code-named Satan.

Vicky nodded. "When he was filming. A black rubber mask. I told the policeman at Harrogate. He didn't believe me."

Vicky had started trembling. Maggie took Vicky's hands and rubbed them between her own.

"Look at me, Vicky. It's okay. All of that was in the past. DI McClure, Ellen, she believes you. It's over now. You are safe. You and Kallie are both safe."

"I do believe you, Vicky," Ellen said. "And I promise you, he won't get away with what he did to you."

Maggie looked at Ellen. "Vicky's mother, Karen, was living on the street when Vicky was taken into care. She was a vulnerable person. Gascoyne told Vicky that he had friends in the police. Friends who would make Karen's life hell. That he only had to ask."

Ellen leaned forward. "Did he say those very words, Vicky? That he had friends in the police?"

"Yes," Vicky answered in a quiet voice. "He told me that if I went to the police, they wouldn't believe me. That they would tell him, and he would kill my mother. I should have listened. He killed Connie and now he's coming after me."

CHAPTER THIRTY-THREE

Ellen decided not to phone Monroe back. Instead she had texted him, saying she would be at the station in half an hour or so and would explain all then. An intense anger was brewing inside her. It was clear that Vicky's story was true. That she had been a vulnerable innocent whose childhood had been ripped apart. Bastards like Gascoyne got away with their crimes because people in authority turned a blind eye. People like Matt Jackson. No one had fought for Vicky or Connie when they were children. No one had stood up for Ana Petrescu.

They drove down Scarcroft Road, and when they reached the junction with Bishopthorpe Road, Ellen gestured to the right.

"Right here."

Sarika glanced over at her.

"It's left for the station."

"I said turn right."

Sarika made the right turn. They drove in silence, passing terrace after terrace of Victorian houses. After a mile or two they were out in the open country.

"Are we going where I think we're going?" Sarika asked.

Ellen looked out over the rolling fields, now blanketed in white. What she was about to do might have huge consequences for her career, and not positive ones. She couldn't think about that now.

"Turn left here."

Sarika pulled off Bishopthorpe Road into Middlethorpe, a hamlet of old red-brick buildings, a model of good conservation and taste. Most of the houses, a mixture of grand and modest properties, were hundreds of years old. The Gascoyne's mansion was accessed via a long lane surrounded by acres of open fields stretching as far as the eye could see. The fields glowed white, despite the falling dusk. Ellen pressed the buzzer on the gate and announced herself. She noticed that the security camera at the gate was not in operation, its camera pointing at the ground. A female voice came onto the intercom. "Mr Gascoyne will see you."

Passing through the gates, they drove up the tree-lined drive towards a renovated farmhouse, complete with a pair of brand-new two-storey extensions, built to look like barns on either side of the main building. In the middle of a cobbled courtyard, alongside a raised fishpond, stood a giant reproduction David, the statue spouting water from its mouth. Clearly Harry Gascoyne had more money than taste. Another camera was mounted near the fountain — it too was out of operation.

A cream-coloured Bentley sat on the drive. Ellen noted the personalised number plate. GAS 100. Beside it was a Range Rover, also with personalised plates. GAS 200. The Bentley was covered in a layer of snow, while the Range Rover was clear.

Sarika parked alongside the Range Rover.

"It's been driven recently," Ellen said, indicating the SUV.

She got out and walked over to look in the pond, surprised to see several Koi under the netting. There was steam rising from the water.

"Even the bloody fish have a heated swimming pool!"

Sarika stood by the car, arms folded. "With all due respect, boss, are you sure this is a good idea?"

"I'm not going to ruffle any feathers . . . not just yet, anyway."

Sarika looked unconvinced. "You know, there are more than a few detectives in North Yorkshire who are counting on Gascoyne for their retirement jobs."

Ellen glared at Sarika for a moment then relented. She knew there was a lot at stake for Sarika in cementing her promotion to DS. She had completed her exams and had worked bloody hard to take that next step up the career ladder. Whatever risk Ellen took with her own career, she couldn't risk Sarika's.

"I'll take full responsibility. Just let me do the talking."

Harry Gascoyne answered the door himself. Ellen recognised him immediately from the photos she had seen online. He was dressed in an expensive-looking pinstripe suit with a crisp white shirt and a blue silk tie. It was hard to believe he was sixty-six, he looked early fifties at most. His black hair had a vaguely purple hue. His teeth were out of a toothpaste ad.

"Sorry to disturb you, Mr Gascoyne. I wonder if I might ask you a few questions?"

"Of course. Come in, glad to see you so soon." Ellen and Sarika exchanged a bemused look as Gascoyne stood back to allow them inside.

The entrance hall was a two-storey affair complete with a grand fireplace. A full-length portrait of Gascoyne himself hung in pride of place over the mantelpiece.

Gascoyne was talking. "It must have happened last night. Two of the security cameras were smashed. Bloody inconvenient. They were expensive pieces of kit."

Now Ellen understood why she had been let onto the property. Gascoyne clearly thought they were here about his cameras.

A blonde woman appeared at the top of the grand staircase wearing an elegant wool suit. Ellen recognised Jill

Gascoyne from the press photos too. A coat was folded over her arm. In contrast to her husband, she looked her age. Her face had a pinched look, as if some overpaid Harley Street surgeon had tucked a little too tightly.

"I thought I heard voices." Jill had reached the bottom of the staircase. "We only got those cameras installed a few weeks ago, cost a fortune."

"We're not here about the cameras, Mrs Gascoyne," Ellen said.

"Oh, for God's sake. Then who is dealing with the cameras?" Jill Gascoyne asked.

Ellen ignored the question. "It's actually you we need to speak with, Mr Gascoyne. Perhaps we could have a word in private?"

She had wanted to catch him unawares. She had hoped that without lawyers, without time to prepare his answers, the man might betray something of himself. However, right now, he was giving nothing away.

He put an arm around his wife's shoulder. "Anything you have to say can be said in front of my wife, Inspector."

A clock on the hall table chimed the half hour. *It's now or never.*

"We are investigating the murder of a woman found in York yesterday. You might have seen it on the news?"

Jill looked scornful. "The sex worker found in Heworth Green?"

"Yes," Ellen replied, looking at Gascoyne. "Did you know her?"

Jill made a scoffing noise. "How on earth would my husband know that . . . that unfortunate woman?"

Gascoyne scratched his eyebrow. Behind him, Ellen could see a stairway leading down to a basement.

"The victim's name is Connie Taylor. Does that name mean anything to you, Mr Gascoyne?"

"This is absolutely ridiculous!" Jill Gascoyne fumed.

"Can you answer the question please, Mr Gascoyne?"

Gascoyne ran his fingers through his hair.

"Connie Taylor? As you can imagine, DI McClure, I meet a lot of people in my line of work. Some names I remember, many I don't. Connie Taylor, you say? I really don't think so, but as I say . . ."

Gascoyne was stalling.

Jill Gascoyne wriggled out from under her husband's arm.

"What are you suggesting? Why would my husband have any connection with that woman?"

Ellen ignored her.

"How about the name Vicky Richards?"

"I really don't know where you are going with these questions, Inspector," Gascoyne said. His voice was cold now.

"Just answer the question, please."

Gascoyne cleared his throat. "Vicky Richards, did you say?"

"Yes. She's a friend of the murder victim."

"Again, not a name that rings any bells. If you can tell me how you think I might know these people, then I might be able to be of some help."

"That's strange," Ellen said, "because I've just had a long chat with Vicky Richards, and she remembers you very well. From Lockton House. Ring any bells?"

Jill Gascoyne stepped towards the front door.

"We need to go now, Harry. We'll be late for our appointment."

"I'll be right there, love," Gascoyne said with a smile. Jill stomped off across the snow-covered gravel. He waited until she had reached the Range Rover then turned back to Ellen. His voice was low.

"How dare you come onto my property like this, and on the word of a lying slag like Vicky Richards?"

Ellen bristled. "So you do remember her?"

"Does Alastair Monroe know you're here?"

Sarika rattled the car keys. It was time to leave.

"I see your Range Rover has recently been driven, Mr Gascoyne. Can you tell me where you were in the last hour and a half?"

"My wife and I went to the cemetery to place flowers on her mother's grave. You can ask her if you like. She'll confirm it."

It was conceivable that Gascoyne could have parked near the allotments to visit the cemetery, which would explain why his car was seen.

"I'm sure she will. You should know that Vicky Richards is in a safe place. A place where you can't get to her."

A contemptuous smile appeared on Gascoyne's lips.

"I recognise you. You were on the news. The whistle-blower losing her shit on the steps of Leeds courthouse."

Gascoyne leaned in until his face was opposite hers. "I hope you and your daughter are settling well into York."

* * *

They drove in silence for most of the way back to Fulford Road station. Ellen played Gascoyne's words over in her mind. He had mentioned her daughter. It was a threat, there was no doubt. She phoned Dan. He would hold onto Zoe at *Serendipity* and bring her back to the flat at about 7 p.m. From now on, Zoe was not going as far as the corner shop alone.

"You do know there will be a whole heap of trouble coming our way from this?" Sarika said.

"I'll take full responsibility. You were just following orders."

Ellen wondered how long it would take for the news of her visit to Middlethorpe House to filter through to Monroe.

CHAPTER THIRTY-FOUR

Fulford Road station, York

It was nearly 6 p.m. and dark when Sarika pulled into the parking space at Fulford Road. The desk sergeant told Ellen that Monroe was on the warpath, that she was to report to his office as soon as she arrived.

She went into her office and shut the door. She could see the first stirrings of a migraine floater just to the bottom left plane of her vision. She needed to take two pink Migraleve and calm herself down. Rooting round her bag, she found a single paracetamol but no bloody Migraleve. She searched the side pockets in desperation and was relieved to find a couple of pink tablets sitting loose in the bag dust.

In the lift up to Monroe's office, Ellen rehearsed what she was going to say. She would show him the CCTV stills from Prufrock's café. They had a clear suspect there. She would also show him the printout from Connie's Facebook page and the entry on Becky Tansey's death from CanadaObits. She would inform Monroe of what Maggie James had revealed to her about Harry Gascoyne. The sexual abuse of both Vicky and Connie at Gascoyne's hands. The intimidation experienced by both women since reporting the abuse to police. That Vicky's flat had been ransacked. She breathed out slowly. The body of evidence presented clear reason for including Harry Gascoyne as a person of interest in Connie Taylor's murder.

As she entered Monroe's office, the detective superintendent stood up and came around from behind his desk, shutting the door behind her.

"DI McClure. About time," Monroe said, gesturing to the chair in front of his desk. "I think you know why you are here."

Ellen noticed a carafe of water on the desk. She needed to swallow the Migraleve tablets, which she still clutched in the palm of her hand. The aura was starting to expand now, narrowing the field of her vision.

"If I can explain, sir—"

He cut her off. "Sit down."

Ellen took a seat opposite him.

Monroe lifted his phone and spoke.

"She's here."

A minute later there was a knock at the door. It was Matt Jackson.

Monroe addressed Ellen. "I gave you a specific order to drop the Vicky Richards line of enquiry. You apparently took it upon yourself to disobey my order."

Ellen reached for her file. "There have been a number of developments on the case, sir. If I can go through them with you now, I'm sure you will understand."

"Off on a wild goose chase," Jackson spat. "Following up on a pile of shit you were told was going nowhere."

He was trying to bait her, make her lose her temper. Well, it wasn't going to work. The migraine was starting in earnest now, a deep throbbing at the base of her skull. She needed to slow this confrontation right down.

"Do you mind, sir?" Ellen said, pouring a glass of water from the carafe on Monroe's desk. "I have to take some medication." She took a gulp of water and swallowed both tablets down.

"Did you honestly think we wouldn't find out you'd been to Harry Gascoyne's home?" Jackson's tone was triumphant.

"Well?" Monroe glared at her.

Ellen took a breath. "I was speaking with Dr Maggie James, Vicky Richards' therapist, and she confirmed that Harry Gascoyne is the man Vicky identified as her abuser. You might remember her, DI Jackson? Dr James came in with Vicky to make her statement. The statement that never went anywhere."

Jackson scowled at her. "The witness was deemed unreliable. I wouldn't believe Vicky Richards if she'd told the shrink that Jimmy Saville himself had abused her."

"I've managed to find her. She's telling the truth."

"Enough!" Monroe thumped the desk with his fist. "You took it upon yourself to appear at Harry Gascoyne's property without any concrete evidence bar the word of a discredited witness, *and* after being explicitly told not to pursue it."

"I had several sources—"

"Several sources who had spoken to the same discredited witness, sir," said Jackson to Monroe.

"There is more evidence emerging. If you could just let me explain—"

"No excuses," said Monroe. "My letting you take the lead on this case was a mistake. From what I hear, you've hardly been here. DI Jackson has been directing the team in your absence."

Ellen's voice rose as she struggled to defend her actions. "Sir, Vicky Richards' flat was ransacked this morning. She was targeted by a man in the Airbnb she had rented in Margaret Street. She escaped, but only just."

"Probably her pimp," Jackson muttered.

"She hasn't been on the game in six years!" Ellen shouted at him.

Monroe pursed his lips. "I want you to listen to me now, and listen—"

"We have evidence that Connie was targeted through Facebook," Ellen interrupted him. "By someone looking for

Vicky. That person may have been posing as a customer in Prufrock's. We have CCTV of this person clearly evading the cameras."

Monroe paused.

Ellen continued. "I found Vicky and her daughter. I interviewed her. In my opinion, she's a highly credible witness. She named Harry Gascoyne as having abused her and Connie Taylor when they were residents at Lockton House. Connie Taylor's head was placed by her killer at Lockton House for a reason. I believe that reason was to serve as a warning to Vicky Richards."

Jackson snorted. "The whole thing is a try-on. Two whores making up a pack of lies to squeeze money out of a public figure."

Ellen glared at him. "Not according to her therapist. Someone has been trying to intimidate Vicky ever since she gave her statement."

"Did she report it?" asked Monroe.

"No. She doesn't trust the police, which is not surprising given the intimidation started the night she spoke to DI Jackson."

"Are you seriously accusing me of intimidating a witness?" Jackson exploded.

"If the cap fits."

Monroe was on his feet.

"Stop right there, McClure, before you get yourself and everyone else embroiled into a shitload of trouble."

"Ask DI Jackson about his financial connections with Harry Gascoyne, sir."

An icy silence fell over the room. Ellen knew she had gone too far. She had no evidence whatsoever to demonstrate Jackson's financial involvement with Gascoyne. She had crossed a line and there was no going back. She knew it, and so did Jackson. More importantly, so did Monroe.

Monroe sat back down.

"How dare you," he said, all trace of the patient mentor gone. "How dare you come into my office and throw unfounded allegations around. I gave you a chance after what happened in Leeds because I heard you were an excellent detective, and I believe everyone deserves a second chance."

Ellen didn't speak. There was no point, and she didn't trust herself not to make things worse.

Monroe heaved a sigh.

"I knew your father, you know. He would never have dreamt of pulling this kind of stunt. He was all about loyalty."

"She doesn't know the meaning of the word," Jackson growled under his breath.

"You've given me no choice," Monroe continued. "You can pack up your desk. Consider yourself on leave pending a disciplinary hearing."

Ellen was frozen to the spot.

"I feel sorry for you, Ellen. You're not a team player. You think of no one but yourself and your own glory. Not your team, not your superiors, certainly not your family. Sarika Kaur is a talented detective who hasn't put a foot wrong, until now. Have you thought for one moment about what effect your behaviour today will have on her?"

Monroe's words cut her like a knife. He rose to his feet and opened the door, making it clear the meeting was over. Matt Jackson looked like the cat who had just got the cream. Her father would have despised him, but he would never have let his temper get anyone else in trouble. Ellen stopped in the doorway.

"Sarika did everything she could to stop me going to Harry Gascoyne's property, sir. She had nothing whatsoever to do with this."

"Well, do her a favour and clear your desk. Hand over your badge when you leave."

Monroe closed the door behind her.

She stood in the empty corridor.

She suddenly felt exhausted and desperately needed to be with her daughter. She was going home.

CHAPTER THIRTY-FIVE

Ferry Lane, Bishopthorpe

Zoe was sitting in the galley on *Serendipity*. Dan never called it the kitchen, it was the galley. Just like the bedroom was the saloon, the toilet was the head. Boat people had their own words, that was just how it was. Zoe loved it here. It was the only place in her life that hadn't changed. Dan had been here as long as she could remember, living in the next boat along to her grandad's. When she was small, she had spent holidays and weekends running between the two boats.

Dan lit the wood-burning stove first thing in the morning and kept it going all day. A supply of wood was piled up on the roof under a huge tarpaulin. Everything had a place and only one place. Dan didn't have a lot of things, but he was very particular about where each thing went. He had four mugs for tea which sat on a shelf to the right of the stove beside the kettle and the tea bags. The grater for the cheese was kept on a hook hanging off a rail behind the two-ring cooker, along with two knives. The one with the broken handle was for cutting vegetables and meat, the other was for cutting bread. There used to be four plates, but now there were only three. They were kept on the shelf to the left of the stove, along with the five glasses and the wicker tray for the cutlery. Dan had three tea towels. The clean one hung off the handle on the oven door. The dirty ones got soaked in the laundry bucket and were then hung out on the deck to dry.

Even Dan always looked the same. He had several fleece jumpers, all black, several pairs of jeans, all grey or denim. He smelled of cigarettes and diesel, reminding Zoe of her grandad.

Dan had made her a toasted cheese sandwich when they arrived back at the boat and now Zoe was finishing off her homework, seated at the galley table, which was covered with an oil cloth with pictures of onions. As a young girl she had loved tracing the onions with greaseproof paper.

Dan didn't talk much. He never asked her annoying questions like "How is school?" or "Have you made any new friends?" He knew when she was having a no-talking day. He just made her sandwiches and tea and after she had done her homework he would plonk a steaming cup of hot chocolate down on the table, sometimes with marshmallows on the top. Today was definitely a no-talking day.

"I'm to drop you back home when you've finished that."

"Thanks, Dan."

Dan picked up the wood bucket and squeezed past her up the steps to the deck. It was dark outside, had been for hours. The darkness here was not like in the city. It was black, so black you could barely see your feet ahead of you on the towpath.

Zoe finished her homework and put it away. She turned on the TV and sat down on one of the two old armchairs Dan had. Each one was covered with a scratchy blanket. The chairs were directly in front of the stove, so this was the cosiest spot on the boat. Dan's chair was the one on the right, his ashtray and glasses sitting on the cupboard beside it. Zoe opened the door of the wood burner and threw in a log. Black smoke and sparks drifted into the room. She loved the woody smell. From under the armchair she pulled out a pair of slippers she kept there and put them on, then curled up in her chair.

Dan had been gone ages. When Dan took ages, it meant he was smoking. He liked to sit outside even when it was freezing cold like tonight, looking at the river. He must have smoked two or three cigarettes by now. Zoe flicked through the channels. There was nothing to watch except cartoons. Suddenly she heard a crash on the deck above, like Dan had dropped something heavy. Dan was always rearranging his stuff up there and quite often when he was doing this, something would fall. Then there would come loud cursing. She waited for the familiar swear words, the really bad ones that only Dan was allowed to say. Nothing. Something was wrong. She got up and walked over to the sink, peering out of the window into the dark.

Suddenly she heard heavy steps walking across the deck towards the galley door. They were heavier than Dan's and definitely not her mother's. She clicked into her phone and brought up her mum's number. The door to the deck swung open, letting in a flurry of snowflakes. In the gloom at the top of the steps she could see a figure. Where was Dan? Why was that man just standing there? Her mouth had gone dry.

"Hello?" she said. The man did not reply.

Zoe took several steps back before bumping into the table. Her hands were shaking. The man moved into the galley and finally the light caught his face. Her eyes met his and she knew for certain that he wanted to hurt her. She darted down the boat towards the head, her slippers making it hard to run. The man was right behind her. She managed to fall into the head and shut the door but when she tried to close the latch the man kicked the door open.

The man lunged at her. His face was so angry. She tried to scream, but the sound that came out was weak. *Where is Dan?* A huge hand lifted her at the waist, the other covered her mouth. He was much too strong for her. She felt her body going limp.

The man dragged her back into the galley and forced her onto the rug, face down. The rough surface chaffed against her cheek. He pulled her hands tight behind her back and bound them. The skin pinched like it was being cut open. Suddenly the man wrenched her head backwards by the hair and put tape over her mouth. He dropped her head and her nose banged on the floor, sending a shooting pain up through her forehead.

Everything went black as she was rolled up in the rug. Next, she felt herself again being lifted, this time inside the rug. Her breath was forced out as the man threw her over his shoulder. She could hear the lapping of the water, and she knew they must be outside. *Where is he taking me? How will mum find me?* Panic rose up from her belly. Her breaths were coming too fast and she couldn't get any air through her nose.

He was walking along the towpath, he must be taking her to a car. Moments later she felt the man kick at something and she heard a door open. Was he taking her onto another boat? Steps down. The man kicked things out of his way. Next, she was falling through the air until she landed hard on her side. A searing pain in her left shoulder knocked all the air out of her. She lay perfectly still, not daring to move.

She was aware of things landing on top of the carpet she was rolled in. He was piling whatever was in the room over her, burying her deep. It went on for ages, until she felt she must be at the bottom of a small hill.

She heard a door closing and then the sound of feet walking on the pontoon. And then there was silence. The pain in her shoulder was so intense she thought she couldn't bear any more. She thought of her mother. She would come and find her. But how would she know where to find her?

PART FOUR

CHAPTER THIRTY-SIX

Walmgate, York

Ellen parked the car in Peel Street and stomped down Margaret Street to the Mini Market on the corner of Walmgate. She was fuming. On the short drive from Fulford Road she had played Monroe's words over and over in her head. *You think of no one but yourself and your own glory. Not your team, not your superiors, certainly not your family.*

If she had had a team she could trust, she could have been a team player. But Matt Jackson was a snake who was clearly on Harry Gascoyne's payroll. Monroe was wrong about her. Her actions had never been for her own glory. If he knew her at all, he would realise that. Her only regret was that she had neglected Zoe for the sake of that pack of wolves. And for what? Her career was in tatters. Monroe had made that clear. She fumed when she thought of the last few weeks, all the overtime, the time spent away from Zoe when she should have been spending that time with her.

Monroe didn't know what she knew. He didn't know that Harry Gascoyne's name had turned up in the Ana Petrescu case. He hadn't given her the chance to tell him. Surely that information would come out in any investigation of her actions. Monroe would be put wise, he would see she had been right. Wouldn't he?

The migraine medication had thankfully started to work, but she knew from past experience that it would help if she ate a proper meal. She took a basket and threw in four chicken breasts and a bag of rice, trying to remember the recipe for sticky lemon chicken, the only recipe she had tried from the only cookbook she owned, Gordon Ramsay's *Fast Food*, which Jackie had bought her for Christmas. All the recipes took fifteen minutes or under to prepare. She frowned in concentration. What was in it? Chicken, honey, lemons, and fresh herbs. That was it.

She felt calmer. This was what normal people did. Normal people with normal jobs. Life had been crazy of late. Too crazy. Monroe had unwittingly done her a favour. Tonight, she would talk over everything that had happened with Dan and afterwards she would watch a film with Zoe. Tonight, she would make sure to sit for the entire movie. No jumping up to put on a wash or to fold clothes. Tonight, she would turn off her phone. Tomorrow, she would think of her next move.

Reaching the flat, Ellen fumbled for her keys, trying not to drop the two bags of shopping. The steps were treacherous, the snow already turning to ice. The lights in the flat were off and she felt relieved that she had got home before Zoe. She would have a chance to get started on dinner. She carried the shopping up the stairs and into the kitchen, setting it on the counter.

The breakfast bowls were still in the sink, filled with milky water where she had left them in her hurry to get to Zoe's school that morning. So much had happened since then, it felt like a week had gone by instead of a single day. The clock on the wall said 7:10. Strange for Dan to be late. Not that ten minutes was really late, but Dan Dixon was always on time.

Ellen put the chicken on to simmer. She picked up her phone and rang Dan. It went to voicemail, but Dan never checked his voice messages. There was only marginally more chance of him looking at a text message. Instead Ellen rang Zoe, hoping that she had her phone charged for once. Again, the phone rang out and went to voicemail. This time she left a message.

"Zoe. You will probably be home before you hear this, but please answer your phone in future."

By the time the chicken was cooked and the rice drained it was 7:40 p.m. By now Ellen was pacing back and forth in front of the sitting room window with its view of the street. Why wouldn't they answer their phones? Maybe something had happened on the road. An accident? She looked out of the window, up and down Fossgate. No sign. She rang the station — no accidents had been reported.

By eight o'clock Ellen couldn't sit still any longer. She would have to go out to Ferry Lane and see what had happened for herself. She scribbled a note and left it on the kitchen table, just in case Zoe arrived back. Running down to get her car from Peel Street, she rang Jackie. Her sister answered on the fifth ring. She was clearly in a bar, judging by the noise in the background. No, she had not seen Dan or Zoe.

Ellen set off for Ferry Lane. As she drove, she kept alternatively phoning Dan and Zoe, with no success. A sense of alarm was building with each unanswered call. Although only a twelve-minute drive from Fossgate, Bishopthorpe had a rural feel. At the pitch-black cricket pitch she made the left turn onto Ferry Lane, a long and winding country road with high hedges and no street lamps. She drove on full beam, down as far as the river, passing no one on the way. Her stomach clenched with fear. Something was wrong. When she swung right onto the riverfront, she saw lights on inside *Serendipity*. Dan's car was parked in its usual spot, in front of the caravans. *Thank God, they're here!* But her relief quickly turned to panic as she made her way down the icy towpath. From twenty feet away she could see that the door to the galley on *Serendipity* was open. Dan was a stickler for keeping in the heat. If Zoe left the door open for a second, he would bark at her to close it. Ignoring the ice, she ran until she could see a dark shape slumped on the starboard side deck. As she leaped up onto the deck, she could make out Dan's distinctive grey hair. He was lying face down. Ellen's heart was racing. *Where was Zoe?*

She crouched over Dan and felt for his pulse. It was weak, but at least it was there. The back of his head was covered with blood. *Please God, where was Zoe?* Her training kicked in and she managed to stay calm enough to dial 999 and ask for an ambulance and police. She called out for Zoe, but there was no reply. Panic surging through her body, she left Dan and scrambled down into the galley. Zoe wasn't there. Ellen ran through to the cabin behind. Empty. Back in the galley she saw the fire in the wood burner had died down to a few embers. Zoe's school bag and coat lay on one of the chairs. Her school shoes were underneath, as if she had just slipped them off.

Her phone pinged. A text from an unknown number. She could only see the first line on her screen.

I have your daughter.

Darkness closed in around her. *No, please.* She leaned on Dan's chair. *My baby.* She dared not open the text. *Please, please, this can't be true.* Opening the text would make whatever was happening here real. Harry Gascoyne's words played themselves over in her head. *I hope you and your daughter are settling well into York.*

With trembling fingers she tapped into the text.

I have your daughter.

In 24 hours I will kill her if you have not given me what I want.

Await instructions.

If you want to see her alive again, do not call the police.

Ellen stared at the message. She had already called the police. *Think! Think!* But she couldn't think, she could barely breathe. She slid down onto the chair behind her, her legs too weak to stand. She was no longer a detective, but a mother.

She considered instigating an amber alert, the child abduction alert system. Every police officer in the country, private citizens, concerned parents, would all be out looking for Zoe within minutes. But if this was the same person that had killed Connie Taylor, then she could not risk him taking his spite out on Zoe.

She scrambled back up on deck and screamed Zoe's name. Nothing. The lights were all off on *Gypsy* and the door to the galley was locked. She ran over to the caravan park and zigzagged through the mobile homes. The place was deserted. Back on *Serendipity*, she put her fingers to Dan's carotid artery again. His pulse was getting fainter. She pulled off her parka and placed it over him.

Tears ran down her face. "Don't leave me, Danny Boy. Please don't leave me now."

If only Dan could talk to her, he might be able to tell her what had happened, who had attacked him. Where was the ambulance?

All the statistics showed that the first few minutes and hours in an abduction case were critical. *Abduction.* The word sucked the last bit of energy from her. She thought of the abduction cases she had worked on. How many children were never found.

She was becoming paralysed with shock and she needed to snap herself back into action. She managed to dial Sarika's mobile, but while it was ringing a terrible realisation dawned on her. If she told Sarika about the text, then the DC would have to alert Monroe. He would tell Jackson. She had already put in a call to the police, but she didn't have to tell them that Zoe had been kidnapped. She didn't have to tell them about the text, at least not straightaway. The kidnapper had shown no mercy to Connie Taylor. He had tortured her before slaughtering her. How might he take his revenge out on Zoe? She killed the call.

She called Anthony, but his phone went straight to voicemail and she remembered he was in Switzerland. He would be out drinking now with the sales team in Zurich. She left a text message. He would quite possibly not see it until the morning, and, in fact, she hoped that he wouldn't. If he phoned her, she would have to tell him about the kidnapper's text. He would want the police involved. Everything would be taken out of her hands.

She heard the ambulance in the distance, its siren echoing across the empty fields for what seemed like an age before she finally saw the blue lights. Two paramedics finally came onto the deck and squatted over Dan. She wanted to tell them that Zoe was missing, she wanted to scream it to the world, to get help to find her baby, but she dared not. Whatever she did next could mean life or death for Zoe.

Dan was lifted onto a gurney and loaded into the back of the ambulance. As the flashing lights rounded the lane and moved out of sight, Ellen was thrown once again into darkness. She had never felt so alone.

She ran to her car and started the engine with shaking hands. As she drove up Ferry Lane she dialled Sarika's number again. The police artist had been to Prufrock's that afternoon, so where the hell was the photofit? She had asked DS Benton to send it to her as soon as it came in. Sarika answered her phone on the third ring.

"I'm out at Ferry Lane, Dan's been attacked. He's on his way to hospital."

Ellen heard Sarika gasp. "What about Zoe? Is she okay?"

"I can't talk now, Sarika. Just get out here and make sure the scene is processed. I need you to talk to the uniforms. I'll fill you in as soon as I can."

"I'm on my way, but what about Zoe—"

"Before you leave, track down that photofit, the one from Prufrock's. Send it to me."

Before Sarika could get the truth from her, Ellen rang off. She knew where she had to go. She rang Lewis Samuels' number and relief flooded through her when he answered on the first ring. She filled him in on what had happened to Dan and Zoe. There was only one thing she could do and she needed him for backup. He agreed to meet her at Middlethorpe in ten minutes.

CHAPTER THIRTY-SEVEN

The rug smelled old and dirty. Diesel, mould, and mildew. The smells of a boat. It was freezing, and her shoulder felt like it was broken. When she moved, it felt like needles were being stabbed into her, sending shocks down her arm.

She hadn't heard a sound for ages. When the man had left, she had heard his feet clomping up the floating pontoon. A car had started up, driven away, leaving silence. She had only heard one man, but there could have been more. Even if one had driven away, another one could be in the room for all she knew, watching her, waiting for her to do something wrong. She knew she was in a cabin in a boat, not far from *Serendipity*. She could hear water lapping against the hull.

After he had left, her body had started shaking, like people she had seen on TV after a car accident. Her teeth had chattered, every muscle had trembled. The weight of the things the man had piled up over her felt heavier. The tape on her mouth was pinching and she could only breathe through her nose. She desperately needed water. Her throat was bone dry.

Her thoughts raced. What had happened to Dan? The man must have hurt him. Her mum would have missed her by now, she must be looking for her. How would she know to find her in this boat? What if the man came back?

A wave of panic seized her. She had to focus on the pain and not on her thoughts. Her shoulder throbbed and her wrists were chafing badly, so there was plenty to focus on. Whenever the thoughts came of what the man might do to her, she would move her hands against their binding and the searing pain would block them out. Suddenly she heard something. A scratching sound, skittering feet. She was not alone after all. She had seen enough rats to know that she didn't want them getting anywhere near her feet. She pulled them further into the rug and started to sob.

CHAPTER THIRTY-EIGHT

Middlethorpe, York

Ellen drove the half-mile to Middlethorpe, staying on the fresh snow where possible to avoid any ice. She felt like she was running on autopilot, pure adrenalin forcing her on. As she pulled off the road past Middlethorpe House, Samuels' car came into view behind her and she almost cried with relief.

The gates to the property were open. She killed the headlights and drove slowly down the drive. Samuels followed her lead, driving behind her in darkness.

The Bentley and the Range Rover were parked outside the house. Ellen and Samuels parked up and she showed the journalist the text she had received.

Samuels took her by the shoulders so that he could look into her face.

"Look, Ellen, for what it's worth, I think you did the right thing, not ringing it in. We both know Jackson is all over this. I suspect Monroe is too. But breaking into Gascoyne's property? If we get caught, what happens then? You'll have to tell them, about Zoe."

Ellen stared at Samuels. Damn him if he was chickening out. She shrugged his hands off roughly.

"If you won't come in with me, then I'm going in myself."

Samuels sighed.

"Look, I'm here, aren't I? I'm just saying we need to be careful, for Zoe's sake. I wouldn't let you go in there alone, okay?"

Ellen took a deep breath. She had to hold it together. Samuels meant well and he was right to be cautious, but she couldn't sit by if Zoe was inside. They had to go in, now, before it was too late.

"He said not to involve the police and you're not the police," Ellen said. "I have to take this chance. If she's in there, then I'll find her. If she's not, then I might find something to tell me where she is."

Ellen looked out over the pristine snow covering the drive in front the house. There had been no fresh snowfall, so any car that had driven down the drive in the last few hours would have left a track. The only tracks were hers and Samuels.

"Do you think it's weird that there are no lights on in the house and yet both cars are here?" Ellen whispered. "I don't get it."

Samuels shrugged. "Maybe they're in bed. I'm more surprised we've got this far — there's bound to be a good security system."

Ellen pointed at the camera by the fountain, still pointing towards the ground.

"Cameras are all down," she said.

Ellen made her way via the shrubbery towards a side entrance, Samuels sticking close behind her. The door had a glass panel. She peered in, using her hands to block out the light from the moon behind her.

"Utility room," she whispered. She could just about make out a fridge freezer and a sink. She turned the doorknob and looked back at Samuels in surprise.

"It's open."

Samuels swore under his breath as she pushed the door open. There was no going back now.

Warm air wafted out as she stepped inside. Samuels closed the door silently behind them.

"Heating's on," he whispered.

Ellen clicked on her force-issue torch and swept the light around the enclosed space, listening for any sound from within the house. Samuels clicked the torch on his phone. All was quiet. They emerged from the utility room into the kitchen, Ellen's torch illuminating a bank of cupboards and a granite-covered island. The kitchen would not have been out of place in a Manhattan penthouse, a room designed to impress rather than a place for a family to gather.

An Aga was the source of the heat. Through an arch to the right was a seating area with several enormous armchairs. These were turned towards the biggest flat-screen TV she had ever seen.

A black cat stared up at her from the floor by the Aga. Ellen froze. The cat shot out of the room towards the hall. They followed it. Off the hall was a study and a formal dining room, both empty. The cat walked up the grand staircase as they approached.

Ellen indicated with a finger that she wanted to follow the creature up the stairs. Samuels nodded and she was grateful to him. She was well able to handle herself, but finding Zoe hurt, or worse, was something she didn't want to face alone. Halfway up the staircase she turned to him.

"You get that smell?"

"Yeah, like an abattoir."

They moved on, steadily, purposefully. The carpet pile was thick, which helped them move silently. A door was open to the right of the huge landing. Ellen inched closer. She hesitated, not wanting to face what was on the other side.

Her phone vibrated with a text from Sarika.

Where are you? The uniforms are here. Is Zoe okay?

Ignoring it, she stepped into the bedroom. Samuels found the light switch and flicked it.

The room burst into view and what she saw sucked her breath away. A man's head sat on an oak chest of drawers in a pool of sticky blood, which ran down over the wood and pooled on the cream carpet below. A moan escaped from Ellen's lips. The features of the face had been burned away, presumably by acid. The tongue hung out past what little remained of his thin lips. Only the man's hair was untouched.

"It's Gascoyne. I recognise the hair," Ellen said, her eyes taking in the black-purple locks.

"Jesus Christ!" Samuels covered his mouth with the sleeve of his jacket. "The smell."

Harry Gascoyne's naked corpse lay on the floor in front of the window, his hands tied behind his back. A dark pool of blood spread over the carpet beneath the neck, where the head had been. As she approached, Ellen started to make out shapes in the blood in front of the stomach.

"What's with all the rope?" Samuels asked.

Ellen grimaced. "That's not rope. That's his intestines. He's been disembowelled."

This was why the smell was so intense. She had seen Harry Gascoyne alive and well not five hours ago, not long enough for decomposition under normal circumstances. However, putrefaction had already started due to the fact that the intestines had been ruptured.

This was where Gascoyne had been killed, and by the spray pattern of blood on the wall behind, Ellen guessed he may have been alive when he was decapitated.

A thought suddenly struck her. If Gascoyne was dead, then who had Zoe?

"Zoe," she said in a half whisper.

Samuels pulled her towards him before she fell.

"We will find her," he said, holding her close. An air of unreality had descended on Ellen, like she was watching the scene on television. Only his intense eyes, full of concern, were real.

"It's not Zoe in there," Samuels said, guiding her out to the landing. There was a blue upholstered chair and Samuels led her towards it. "We will find her. You've got to keep telling yourself that."

Ellen went to sit down, but already the detective in her was coming back online and she stopped herself just in time. There might be forensic evidence on the chair.

"I have to ring this in," she said, turning on the landing light. Only now, in the brightness, did she see there was blood spattered on the landing carpet. There was more on the staircase. Samuels followed behind her. The blood led back to the TV room.

Ellen flicked on the light. The ceiling above the armchairs was spattered in arterial spray. Approaching, she found Jill Gascoyne's corpse sitting upright in one of the enormous chairs. Her perfectly coiffed head was sitting in her lap.

CHAPTER THIRTY-NINE

Within half an hour the house was swarming with uniformed police. Samuels had reluctantly left before they arrived. He told her he would meet her at the flat later on when she got home, which was surprisingly comforting. Sarika arrived first as she had come directly from the river. Ellen told her only that Zoe was missing, but nothing about the text message. The forensic teams were on their way. Monroe and Jackson were en route.

Ellen felt numb. It was hard to keep her attention on what Sarika was saying to her. A female police officer tried to put a blanket around her shoulders and she shrugged it off. If Gascoyne had not taken Zoe, then who had? Jackson? Had Jackson killed Connie Taylor and the Gascoynes? Was it him she'd seen scaling the gate at Low Moor Allotments?

Whatever happened, she knew she couldn't tell anyone about the contact from the kidnapper. Not even Sarika, whose career would depend on passing that information up the chain. She heard Monroe's voice in the hall. A minute later, he came into the sitting room. Ellen's heart sank. Where was Jackson? She needed to look Jackson in the eye — if he had Zoe, she would know.

Monroe's demeanour was markedly different from the last time she had seen him.

"Where's Jackson?" she asked, realising as she spoke that her question sounded odd.

"He'll be here soon," Monroe replied. "You can rest assured that Matt and I, and the whole team, will do everything humanly possible to find Zoe. I want you to know that."

Ellen was grateful for his compassion, but she had to be careful what she said.

"I told you Gascoyne was involved in this somehow."

The superintendent nodded.

"You did, and I'm sorry. I should have listened to you."

Tears fell down her cheeks and she wiped them away.

"I told you . . . I told you . . ."

Sarika put her arm around Ellen and guided her to the sofa. Monroe sat down beside her.

"I'm listening to you now, Ellen. I will personally move heaven and earth to find her, I promise you that."

Ellen stood up and began to pace the room.

"We need to go through this place, find out everything we can about Gascoyne. If he had any enemies, we need to know who they were."

Monroe was nodding, an expression of forbearance on his face.

Ellen wanted desperately to reveal all to Monroe, to tell him that she suspected Jackson was somehow involved. That, in fact, she suspected he was the killer and that he had taken Zoe. But her daughter's life depended on how she played her hand, and Jackson and Monroe were tight. She hesitated for just a moment before speaking.

"If Gascoyne had ears inside the police, we need to know that too."

Ellen saw the DS stiffen. It was like a shutter had been pulled down and she was now on the outside.

"I am personally taking charge of this murder investigation, Ellen. If there is any connection to Zoe's disappearance, I will find it."

Ellen could see she had lost him already, but she couldn't stop herself from pushing him further.

"Sir, Gascoyne was rumoured to have certain detectives in his pocket and we need to follow that up. Find out who was feeding him information, who was doing his dirty work."

Monroe reached out and took her hand. The gesture came as a shock, bringing her firmly back to reality. She didn't know if Monroe could be trusted.

"Ellen, stop this! I understand this is a nightmare for you, but you are not on the investigating team here. You can't be, you're too close."

"But I'm here now, and there might be something here, something to help us find Zoe."

Monroe stood up.

"You're not thinking straight. That's my point. You need to go home, Ellen, and wait there."

"We have to let forensics in first anyway," Sarika said gently. "There's nothing you can do here right now."

She was being shut out. Left on the outside.

"The monster who killed these people has my child," Ellen said forcibly. "We need to rip this place apart now, find something, anything."

"You don't know that for sure," Sarika said. "It's just as likely Zoe ran off after Dan was assaulted. That she'll turn up. It's only been two hours."

"No, that's not what happened!" Ellen shouted.

There was a battle going on inside her head. Should she admit that she had been contacted, so they at least knew someone had taken Zoe? Or should she say nothing and wait for instructions from the kidnapper? There was only one person who could help her make that decision. The person her father had regarded at one time as the best detective in the whole of the north of England. Dan Dixon. According to Sarika, Dan had regained consciousness. She desperately needed his advice now.

* * *

Ellen drove straight to York Hospital. She found Dan in A & E having a nasty-looking wound to his head sewn up. The skin on his right cheek was discoloured from where he had fallen.

"I'm so sorry, Elly, I didn't see a thing. The bastard came at me from behind. They told me that Zoe is missing. Please tell me you've found her."

Ellen shook her head. She took Dan's hand in hers, careful to avoid the IV cannula which had been fitted. He flinched as the nurse put the final stitch into the back of his head.

"Did you hear anything, before he hit you? A car, a boat, anything?" she asked.

Dan's face had turned white and she grabbed a plastic bowl and held it in front of his mouth while he vomited. She then poured water into a plastic cup and he rinsed out his mouth.

"All I remember is sitting looking upriver. I'd just lit up a smoke. I remember thinking how quiet it was, with the snow. Next thing I know I'm here."

"How about earlier? Did you notice anyone around the moorings?"

Dan thought for a moment.

"There was a guy at the caravans when I was driving in with Zoe after collecting her from school. I only saw the back of him. Medium build, dark jacket."

Ellen jotted this down in her notebook.

"Anything else?"

"He had a hoodie pulled up over his head. I couldn't see his face."

Ellen stopped writing.

Dan looked at her. "Are you going to tell me what's going on?"

The nurse left, pulling the curtain around them behind her. It would be fifteen minutes or so before a porter would be free to bring Dan up to one of the wards. He would need to stay in overnight for observation.

Ellen explained everything that had happened, the text she had received, and the discovery of Harry Gascoyne and his wife.

"I don't know if I should tell them about the text. I'm terrified if I do, it might make things worse for Zoe."

The wave of sorrow that had been building inside her finally crashed, and Ellen let herself be pulled under. The sobbing lasted for several minutes, during which time she and Dan clung to each other. She realised he was sobbing too.

Eventually she looked up.

"What's on your mind, Dan? Whatever it is, just say it."

"Nineteen seventy-eight. Carly Matthews."

Ellen wiped her face with her sleeve.

"I remember that case, Dad told me about it. That was when you were in Leeds."

Dan sighed. "Yeah. Carly was ten years old. A beautiful little girl. Her father was an industrialist. These were wealthy people. When I say wealthy, I mean seriously rich, money no object. Carly was lifted from a friend's house. Parents got a ransom demand the same night. They trusted in the system, trusted the police knew what to do. I followed the correct protocol. Tried to enter into communication with the kidnappers, but something spooked them."

"Go on." Ellen wasn't sure she wanted to hear the rest.

Dan sighed again. "Carly's body was found on waste ground near the airport six weeks later."

Ellen froze.

"You think I shouldn't tell them about the text?"

Dan reached out and took one of her hands.

"The police have two priorities. Get Zoe home, and make sure any future kidnappers know that ransoms are not paid. *You* only have one priority."

Ellen kissed Dan on the forehead and left. She couldn't involve Sarika in what was to come. Not because she didn't trust her. Rather, she didn't want to expose the young detective to what could be a dismissible offence — withholding information.

Instead, she called Jackie and told her Zoe was missing. Despite the late hour, she asked her to go to the flat and to let Lewis Samuels in if he reached it before her. They had a long night ahead.

CHAPTER FORTY

Fossgate, York

Zoe's gym bag was in the hall. She must have forgotten it that morning. It was as if Ellen was being punished for failing her, for not being a good enough mother. She sat in the kitchen, exhausted but unable to rest. Half the North Yorkshire police force were out looking for Zoe. There had been no sightings, no leads. The trail was most definitely cold. There was nothing for it but to wait for another text from the kidnapper.

Jackie tried to persuade her to take one of her Valium, but she couldn't switch off and Ellen instead begged Jackie to get a few hours' sleep herself. She was afraid that if she did drop off, she might not hear her phone. She briefly phoned Maggie and filled her in, making sure she would keep Vicky in the house, and that she hadn't told anyone about her visitors.

Samuels arrived and forced her to lie down on the sofa. She felt paralysed with fear, too exhausted to cry. She hadn't realised when she got the call to go to Lockton House that she would be drawing her daughter into the path of a psychopath. Maybe Anthony had been right all along.

Her job was incompatible with being a mother. She hadn't wanted to admit it, not even to herself, but she could see it now. If she ever got Zoe back, that would be it. She would happily say goodbye to her career if she could only have the chance to see Zoe's beautiful face again.

Ellen woke some hours later with a start. She must have dropped off. Samuels had covered her with a blanket, lifted her head and placed a pillow under it. Half conscious, she felt his hand stroking her forehead. He didn't speak, there were no words. His tenderness was welcome and unbearable at the same time, reminding her of the way Zoe loved to have her head stroked. She would give anything to do that again.

Several times she opened her eyes to see Samuels sitting in the armchair beside her, watching. She was woken by the ping of her phone. It was 5:35 a.m. Samuels had heard it too. Their eyes met. He handed over her mobile. Her mind screamed at her not to look. Zoe could have been found, mutilated like Harry Gascoyne, like Jill, like Connie Taylor. On the other hand, perhaps she had somehow escaped from her captor, been found alive?

She clicked into the text and read it aloud.

You have hidden what I want.

I have hidden what you want.

Let's swap.

One daughter for another.

Yours for Vicky's.

Time is running out. You have seven and a half hours left.

Ellen stared at the text. Did this monster really expect her to take Kallie from her mother's arms and hand her over to him? It was unthinkable. And yet she could not imagine that, given a choice, she would leave Zoe to her fate, knowing for certain that she would never hold her daughter in her arms again.

Samuels spoke softly. "You don't have any choice, Ellen . . ."

Ellen stood up. "I want proof Zoe is alive, video proof. Then I'll make the swap."

CHAPTER FORTY-ONE

Ellen caught her reflection in the rear-view mirror. Her face was pale, the skin around her eyes dark and heavy. It was 8 a.m. and Anthony had finally phoned from Zurich. He was trying to get on the next flight. Once he arrived, the texts would be public knowledge and any communication with the kidnapper would be taken out of her control. She had to get to Middlethorpe House. Perhaps she could find something that might help her find out who had taken Zoe.

As she drove down the drive, she could see the property was teeming with police. Sarika had phoned half an hour before to give her an update on the search for Zoe. There was nothing. No sightings, no leads. Sarika had been back at the scene after only four hours' sleep. She let slip that Monroe and Jackson had been there first thing, but that they had gone back to the station an hour ago. She was under strict orders not to allow Ellen near the crime scene.

Ellen was directed by a young uniformed constable to park on the drive. She retrieved her protective clothing from the boot and pulled a plastic mask over her nose and mouth. No one would recognise her among the other white-suited SOCOs. An ambulance was parked up with the rear door open, presumably waiting for the pathologist to give the all-clear to remove the bodies. She spotted Giles Featherstone's BMW parked up alongside the ambulance. She walked up to the police tape which cordoned off the mansion.

Sarika appeared from the front of the house, clipboard in hand.

The two detectives made eye contact and Sarika walked over.

"You shouldn't be here, boss. If I'm even seen talking to you . . ."

"I'll be in and gone in fifteen minutes."

"You can't sign in, they'll know."

Ellen grabbed the clipboard and pretended to sign in.

"No one will know. No one will recognise me. Please, Sarika, for Zoe."

Sarika looked to see if anyone was watching, then lifted the police tape for Ellen to duck under. Ellen owed her, big time.

"Professor Featherstone is here. Just make sure he doesn't see you," Sarika said.

"Giles and I go way back, Sarika. He'll be fine."

"Well, Monroe is on his way to hear his findings, so you'd better be quick."

As they entered the house, Ellen was hit by the stench, which had intensified overnight. Sarika held out a tub of Vicks VapoRub, but Ellen shook her head, preferring to hold out for now.

In the hall, Harry Gascoyne's portrait looked down over the activity, lending a macabre air to an already unreal atmosphere. Sarika led her to the kitchen and they squeezed by a female technician who was busy lifting prints in the doorway.

The Aga was still belting out heat, speeding the rate of decay of the corpse in the adjacent TV room. The smell was overwhelming, in spite of the Vicks, which Ellen was now daubing liberally underneath both nostrils.

Jill Gascoyne remained where Ellen had found her the night before. Giles Featherstone was bent over her. Ellen approached the pathologist and quickly pulled down her face mask. He stopped what he was doing, a bemused look on his face.

"Ellen, what are you doing here? I thought you'd been axed . . . fired . . . banished from grace!"

Giles's tone was jovial. He had clearly been told she had been taken off the case, but hadn't heard about Zoe. It was just as well. She hadn't time to explain what had happened to him now.

Ellen replaced the mask.

"I have been, Giles. I just need to hear your report then I'm out of here. You never saw me. Clear?"

Featherstone looked puzzled. "Clear as mud, but mum's the word."

The woman's head still lay on her lap. The elegant wool suit was spattered with gore and clumps of hair. There was blood on the floor, up the walls, and crusted onto the ceiling, samples of which were being carefully scraped off and bagged by a technician.

"Blunt trauma to the face and skull, probably from a hammer or some heavy instrument. Frenzied, prolonged attack. The attacker would have been covered in blood." Featherstone pointed to a single arc of blood spatter on the ceiling above the armchair.

"See this spray of blood? This was caused by a blow from behind to the top of the head. It would have knocked her out, perhaps even killed her. I won't know for sure until I complete the PM."

He raised his right hand to mimic the blow to the head.

"My guess is that the perpetrator then walked round to the front of the body and hit her" — he made a jabbing motion — "repeatedly in the face with the weapon."

"So the attacker might have been hiding in the kitchen, came at her from behind," Ellen said.

"He came at her from behind, that's for sure."

"He? We're sure about that?"

"Almost certainly a man, due to the strength of the blows. As you can see, he completely obliterated her face."

Ellen grimaced. "Venting some sort of rage on her?"

"She would almost certainly have been dead after the first blow — if not, then definitely after the second. Which begs the question, why did he keep going?"

"And the decapitation?" Ellen asked.

"Decapitation came after death."

Ellen's gaze moved from the body to the yellow evidence markers pinpointing where drops of blood had been deposited, leading to the hall and up the staircase.

"Looks like he killed the wife first, then went upstairs looking for Gascoyne, trailing blood with him."

Featherstone nodded. "That's certainly what it looks like."

Sarika appeared from the kitchen, holding her phone. She looked worried.

"You have to go, boss. Monroe will be here in five minutes. Jackson's coming with him. He wants to go through the filing cabinets in person."

"What filing cabinets?" Ellen asked.

"In the basement. But you need to get out of here. Now!"

* * *

Ellen ducked into the hall. Instead of heading for the front door, she made her way to the staircase she had seen the previous day, which led down to a basement level. She slipped down the stairs.

A long, dark corridor led to an office. The room was filled with a mahogany desk and three mahogany bookshelves. Two filing cabinets stood in the corner. Ellen pulled open the second drawer from the bottom on the right-hand cabinet, marked 'O to U'. There was nothing under 'R' for Richards or 'T' for Taylor. Shutting the drawer, Ellen searched under 'C' for Connie and 'V' for Vicky. Again nothing.

There was a small window at ceiling height which gave a glimpse of the drive outside. Ellen froze. She had seen that window before. *Shit.* It was the same window in the video she had watched so many times. This was where Ana Petrescu had been taken. Where the videos were shot. There was no doubt in her mind now. Gascoyne was Satan.

Ellen heard a car pull up on the gravel out front. She turned her attention back to the room. If Jackson wanted to search Gascoyne's files himself, then perhaps he was looking for something personally incriminating. She had to find whatever that was before he did.

Her eyes fell on the large desk. Underneath was a matching set of drawers. She pulled open the first drawer. Stapler, rubber bands, pens. Wrenching open the second she found receipts, bills, and business cards. The third drawer contained printouts of what looked like annual accounts, but she noticed the drawer was stiffer, like it was sticking on something.

She could hear Monroe's booming voice. Sarika was insisting he sign in. She was running out of time.

Ellen got down on her hands and knees and pulled the bottom drawer completely out. In the space beneath the drawer was a cardboard file. She pulled it out and then replaced the drawer. On the file were written the names she wanted to see.

Connie Taylor.

Vicky Richards.

She hadn't time to look at the contents, so she opened her plastic suit wide enough to pull her jacket open and slipped the file inside. Her only hope was to brazen it out. Pulling the mask back over her face, she opened the door. Monroe and Jackson were coming down the stairs. Her heart thumping, Ellen put down her head and walked straight past them, up the stairs, and out the front door. Sarika was standing outside, her eyes wide. Ellen whispered "Thank you" as she passed her and didn't stop walking until she reached her car. Her heart was still racing as she drove through the gates. It was only then that she remembered to breathe.

CHAPTER FORTY-TWO

Ellen pulled in at the first opportunity. She retrieved the file and opened it on her lap. Inside were maybe twenty or thirty sheets of paper. On top of these were surveillance photographs of Vicky and Connie taken outside each of their houses. There was one of Vicky arriving at Stockton Nursing Home, her place of work. The first sheet of paper was a letter written by hand on a lined refill pad. The handwriting was just about legible.

Mr Gascoyne,

My name is Connie Taylor and I am writing to you for me and my friend Vicky Richards. You know what you did to us all those years ago at Lockton House. You sick bastard. We were 12 and 13 years old, Vicky was only 14 when she gave birth to your baby.

Congratulations on the sale of your supermarket. We saw how much you made out of it. It was all over the news. We think it is time you paid us for what you did, for the suffering you put us through. We want £100,000 each. Do not contact us, just put the money in the bank account, details below.

If you pay up we will not take our story to the papers. We have nothing to lose, but you do.

Connie Taylor

Ellen was stunned. Why had Vicky not mentioned a baby? That was a significant piece of information. Had Maggie known all along? Of course she bloody had. Was there any other important information Maggie hadn't told her?

She slammed the steering wheel with her open palm then placed the letter back in the file. She would look through the rest of it at home. She texted Samuels to tell him what she had found and to make sure he stayed put until she got home. She pulled out of the lane and turned right on Bishopthorpe Road, heading back towards town.

When she arrived home, Jackie had brought up some food from the café downstairs. Samuels was still there, waiting for news.

Ellen waved away the food away while explaining what had happened at Middlethorpe, the file she had found. She showed Samuels the letter from Connie to Gascoyne.

"Did Connie say anything about Vicky having a baby to you?" she asked him.

Samuels looked surprised. "No."

"Neither did Maggie James. I wonder what else they didn't mention."

Ellen spread the contents of the file out on the desk in her office.

"There must be something here, something that will help us find Zoe."

There was an envelope with a Post-it note on the front which she thought might be Jackson's handwriting. She had only seen a few examples, but she remembered the childlike scrawl.

She read out loud.

"'This is what Benton owes. Keep it somewhere safe.'"

She looked at Samuels. "It's Jackson's writing, I'm sure of it. No wonder he wanted to go through the filing cabinets himself."

Inside the envelope was a sheet of paper with five names and five amounts of money beside each. Each amount had the word 'paid' and a date beside it. Ellen handed the sheet to Samuels.

"These names mean anything to you?"

He looked at the names.

"They're backstreet bookies, all of them."

"You think Benton owed money to these people and Gascoyne paid them off?"

"The way these thugs operate, you owe five thousand, it becomes ten thousand, becomes twenty thousand, becomes violence, becomes other things . . ."

"There's over thirty thousand here."

"Looks to me like Benton was borrowing from Peter to pay Paul. Who is he, anyway?" Samuels asked, handing the sheet back to Ellen.

"DS Paul Benton? He works under Matt Jackson. So, he gets himself into a spot of bother gambling. Maybe he confides to Jackson or Jackson finds out. Jackson gets Gascoyne to pay the debt for Benton, and hey presto, Gascoyne not only has a DI but he now has a DS working for him as well. Could be they used him to do the dirty work, intimidating witnesses like Vicky Richards. Maybe it escalated to murder and kidnapping."

"Do you think one or both of them turned on Gascoyne?" Samuels asked.

"Could be."

Whatever the case, Ellen wanted to find out what else Vicky Richards hadn't told her.

"I'm going to meet Sarika, see if she knows anything about Benton," Ellen lied. "I'll be back in an hour or so."

Samuels stood up. "I'll come with you."

Ellen found his concern touching, but this was one interview she had to do alone.

“No, I need you here finding out everything you can about Jackson and Benton. We need to find out where Zoe is being held. Could be one of them has a caravan or a lockup, whatever. Just find out what you can.”

“Look, Ellen, let me come. I’ll stay in the car, just to make sure you aren’t followed.”

She smiled at him. “I appreciate your trying to help, but I’m a trained police officer. I can handle myself.”

With that Ellen was out the door.

CHAPTER FORTY-THREE

Micklegate, York

Ellen arrived at South Parade. It had taken her five minutes longer than usual due to the winding route she had taken. But she had definitely not been followed. She knocked hard on the door. Rob answered.

"Maggie told me about Zoe, I'm so sorry."

"Thanks."

"Maggie and Vicky are in the garden, building a snowman with Kallie and the kids. I'll call them."

"I'll wait upstairs."

Ellen took the stairs two at a time. She found the bedroom Vicky was staying in. Her few belongings were on the side table. Ellen rifled through them. She didn't know what she was looking for. There was a small wardrobe, which was empty, and a bedside table with no drawers. If she were trying to hide something in this room, it would have to be on top of the wardrobe or else under the mattress.

Standing on the bed, Ellen was able to see the top of the wardrobe. There was a white envelope. She stretched forward and retrieved it. Vicky's name and address in Clifton were on the front.

Bingo.

Ellen spilled the contents out onto the bed. There were two birth certificates, one for Vicky, one for Kallie, plus a passport, a letter, and two hospital wristbands. They were tiny — newborn size. There was a printed label on each. The first read 'Baby girl, Vicky Richards, 16 September 2013'. This was Kallie's wristband.

She picked up the second wristband.

'Baby boy, Vicky Richards, 26 January 1988'.

Vicky had given birth to a child when she was in Lockton House. Today was the 26th of January. The boy had been born thirty years to the day.

Ellen slipped both wristbands into the pocket of her jacket.

She unfolded the letter. It was written on headed notepaper from an adoption society, dated five months before.

Dear Ms Richards,

My name is Susan Whithorpe and I am a social worker working with Henley Trust, the adoption agency with which you placed your son, Kevin Richards, in 1988. Kevin, no longer his name, has been in touch and has expressed his desire to meet you. We have explained that you have registered a wish not to be contacted, but we are alerting you of his wish in case you may have changed your mind.

Please contact me at the number above as soon as possible.

Yours sincerely,
Susan Whithorpe
Social worker

Ellen could hear voices downstairs. A few seconds later Kallie came running up the stairs and burst into the bedroom, followed by Vicky. Vicky stopped at the door, her eyes taking in the envelope on the bed and the letter in Ellen's hand. She walked slowly into the room, picked up a packet of crayons from the bedside table and handed them to Kallie, who ran off back down the stairs.

"I heard about your daughter," Vicky said. "I'm sorry."

Ellen took a deep breath, she had no time for Vicky's sympathy now.

"The man who took Zoe wants me to exchange Kallie for her."

Vicky looked like she had been slapped. She stepped backwards towards the door.

"What? Why? I don't understand."

"He is demanding I hand over Kallie. In return, he will give me back Zoe."

Vicky stared at her. "But you're not going to do that, are you? We're leaving today, me and Kallie. We're going to get as far away from here as we can, start a new life."

"A man befriended Connie before she was killed. It may be the same man who broke into your flat in Clifton, the same man who tried to get to you on Margaret Street. He was caught on CCTV. He looks young, maybe thirties, too young to be Harry Gascoyne."

"I've told you everything I know."

Ellen stood up and waved the letter from the adoption agency at Vicky.

"When were you going to tell me about your son and his attempts to contact you?"

Vicky looked bewildered. "I don't understand. What's he got to do with all of this?"

"Tell me what you know about him."

"Nothing, I . . . I don't know anything. I don't even know his real name."

Ellen grabbed Vicky by the shoulders and pushed her up against the wall. When she spoke her voice was low, hard.

"Someone is trying to get your little girl and you know something, something you are not telling me."

Maggie appeared at the doorway. She rushed forward and pushed Ellen away.

"That's enough, Ellen! What the hell do you think you're doing?"

Tears were running down Vicky's cheeks, smudging her mascara. She walked over to the bed and flopped down. Maggie sat down beside her and put an arm around her shoulder. Vicky took a deep breath and looked up at Ellen. "I'll tell you whatever you want to know."

Ellen nodded. "Talk."

Vicky paused for a moment before speaking.

"Two months ago, I got that letter from the adoption agency where I placed my son."

"Harry Gascoyne's child?"

She nodded, looking down at her hands.

"I had him when I was fourteen. I had no one to turn to."

"And the letter?"

"He was only with me for a few weeks in the home. I couldn't even feed him or change him."

"Vicky was suffering from post-natal depression," Maggie explained.

A stream of tears ran down Vicky's cheeks. "I loved him, but I couldn't bear to look at him."

"The letter?" Ellen said. "Did you respond to it?"

"No. The social worker rang me a few weeks later. She said Kevin was desperate to meet me. That's not his name now, they didn't tell me his name."

"Come on Vicky. What else did she tell you about him?"

Vicky looked up.

"His adoptive parents both died in the last year. That's when he started looking for me. . ."

"Did you have any contact with him?"

"No. I told her to tell him I couldn't see him, that I had a new life now. That I wished him well . . ."

Ellen's phone pinged with a text and rang at the same time. She took the call. It was Sarika, who had arrived back at Fulford Road.

"What have you got, Sarika?"

"I asked Benton if the photofit from Prufrock's had arrived. He told me it had and that Jackson has it."

Ellen had specifically instructed Benton to give the photofit to her, but as she was off the case she could hardly argue.

"Have you seen it?" Ellen asked.

"No, he hasn't put it up on HOLMES yet."

There was no reason why a critical piece of evidence such as this should not have been put on the system straight away.

"Something's not right there."

"That's what I thought, boss."

Ellen was thinking. Gascoyne had paid off Benton's debts. Had he got Benton to befriend Connie, to get information out of her? Was it Benton on the CCTV footage emerging from Prufrock's café? He was the right age, the same build. He even wore a hoodie. Was that why he had been so obliging in manning the CCTV? Had he known he was on it and managed to blur the footage?

"Okay, see if you can find it and send it to me as soon as you can."

"I knew you'd ask, boss, so I took a look round Benton's desk, and round Jackson's, but they must have it with them."

"Fine, get someone to access his computer. I want to see that photofit ASAP."

CHAPTER FORTY-FOUR

Zoe didn't know how long she had been asleep. When she'd woken there was a searing pain across the back of her shoulder and down her arm. If only she could release her hands. It was so cold and she desperately needed to go to the toilet. She had held on since last night, but now it was starting to spasm, pain spreading out across her pelvis. To take her mind off it, she had started counting back from a hundred. 100, 99, 98, 97 . . .

She heard a boat passing by on the river, the water lapping against the hull behind her head. A man's voice was laughing. It took her a moment to realise that if she could hear him, then maybe he could hear her. *Shout!*

She tried to scream but the tape over her mouth muffled the sound into something she knew only she could hear. She listened. Nothing. She needed to breathe in before she could attempt to shout again. After taking a tortured breath in through her nose she tried again, but the sound that came out was even weaker than her first attempt. She listened for any sound, but the boat had gone past now.

Thoughts of her mum flooded her mind. She wished desperately that she was lying on the sofa, her mum stroking her forehead. She choked back her tears and wiped her nose on the filthy rug before once again drawing in a thin breath through her nostrils.

The man who took her might be the same man who killed that woman, the one from the news. The reporter said the woman's head had been chopped off. Zoe fought for breath. *Is that what he is going to do to me?*

She had to focus on anything other than her thoughts. The pain in her bladder was a sharp, insistent pain. Count. What number was she on? 96, 95, 94, 93 . . . She couldn't hold it any longer, the pain was too strong. Urine flooded her school skirt and the rug underneath her, a wave of blessed heat spreading down her legs. The mess didn't matter, it meant nothing compared to the very real possibility that she might never get out of this place alive. In the distance she heard the sound of a car door slamming, then footsteps getting closer. It could be her mother, or it could be him. Her heart was beating so loud she could hear the blood pulsing in her ears. She heard a door open, footsteps coming through the galley. Her stomach lurched. *It's him. I'm going to die.*

She felt the heavy things being lifted off the rug and then she was rolling, red hot pain shooting through her shoulder and arm, then a blast of freezing air. She was out of the carpet, looking up at her abductor. He was wearing a balaclava. A gloved hand reached towards her and ripped the tape from her mouth. She gasped full breaths of cool air. The man was holding up a phone and a newspaper. He was filming her. "Say hello to Mummy, Zoe."

CHAPTER FORTY-FIVE

I must have been about thirteen the summer I found the file. It was in my father's study. It was the annual sports day at my brothers' school. Achievement at sport, that was something my father valued, and my three younger brothers gave him plenty to be proud of. My achievements in the realms of creativity, my intellectual intelligence, these were not considered worthy attributes. I was 'an embarrassment'.

That day, my father had been uncharacteristically careless. He had left the keys to his study in the door. Perhaps he had been disturbed while locking up? His study was his private domain. I knew never to go in there. We all did. The room was always locked when he was not using it. That's why I was so thrilled to see his keys just hanging there in the lock.

For several months an older boy on our street had been taunting me with what I was certain was a bare-faced lie. He said his mother told him I had been adopted. I lashed out at him, but he kept coming back to humiliate me. His friends started joining in. I suffered in silence for weeks. I dared not reveal the insult to my parents, they did not look kindly on tattle-telling.

Instead I waited. I waited until the opportunity arose to look for the evidence I needed to prove that the boy and his mother were liars. That day, when I saw those keys in the lock of my father's study, I took my chance. When everyone was getting in the car to go to sports day, I announced that I was feeling sick. I had developed the ability to vomit on demand, a handy trick I reserved for special occasions. We were late. My father agreed to leave me behind.

When the car was gone, I slipped into the study. There was speculation among my brothers that my father had a hidden camera, which would be triggered when anyone entered his study. I smiled. It was just a lie he told them to keep us out.

In the corner, to the left of the desk, was the filing cabinet. The top two drawers contained various household documents — insurance policies and letters from the bank. My name didn't feature so I ignored these.

In the bottom drawer I found what I had been looking for. For each of us four children there was a file. Inside my hanging file were the usual school reports, vaccination records. There were also psychiatric reports from Dr Daly. However, I could not find my birth certificate. My brother's files all contained theirs, confirming, of course, that they had not been adopted. So, where was my birth certificate? My eyes fell on a sealed envelope with my name on it, which I placed on my father's desk.

I sat in the black swivel chair. The desk was old, it had belonged to my grandfather. My father had received thrashings while bent over that desk. The beatings had made a man of him, my father said, just as the beatings he gave me would make a man out of me.

My birth certificate had to be in that envelope. I decided to take the risk of opening the seal. As I painstakingly peeled back the sticky flap, I imagined myself waving the certificate for all to see. I would make the boys who had taunted me take back what they said. Inside the envelope there was a pile of documents which I carefully slid out. I flicked through them several times, but could not find my birth certificate. They were just letters, most with the same letterhead. I picked one up. "Henley Trust Adoption Agency." It took several moments for the words to register. Adoption Agency. *I dropped the letter without reading it. Instead, I started swirling around and around on the swivel chair. The world disappeared into a welcome blur as the room swirled by.*

I sat there for some time. My father would be back after the boys' races. He never stayed to socialise, preferring to leave that chore to my mother. I didn't want him to find me here. I didn't want him to know that I knew what I was pretending not to know.

As I straightened the letters, two words caught my eye on the top sheet. "Birth mother." Those words were like a slap in the face. Once

I had seen them, I knew I could never un-see them. Two words that would change my life forever. Birth mother. *Tears of anger fell onto the desk. I read a few lines. It was true. I had been adopted at six weeks old. With a scream that came from deep inside me, I tossed the letter along with all the papers onto the floor. I had been duped. The people I had assumed were my parents had been lying to me all my life. I hurled a glass paperweight at the wall. I felt violated, assaulted. My so-called mother and father had made a fool out of me.*

I understood at that moment why my father treated me differently to my brothers. I had thought it was because I was the eldest, but now I knew the truth. He was ashamed of me. My father never failed at anything, but he had failed, at least for three or four years, to father a child. My mother had never loved me in the same way she had loved my brothers, her true children. From the moment they had conceived their own child, I was surplus to requirements.

A question suddenly sprung to mind. Where are my real parents? On my hands and knees on the floor, I rifled through the papers until I found what I was looking for. The letter gave details of my real mother, but not her name. She was fourteen years of age when I was born. Fourteen? How could that be? I was almost fourteen and had never as much as come close enough to kissing a girl. The letter said she had lived in a care home for several years due to "family circumstances." The identity of my father was stated as "unknown."

I folded the paper and placed it into the front pocket of my jeans. I put the papers back in the envelope and back in the hanging file. I pushed the filing cabinet several inches to the left to cover the hole in the wall caused by the paperweight, which itself was undamaged. I locked the office door behind me and left my father's keys hanging where he had left them.

I told no one. Neither my parents nor my brothers. I learned to ignore the boys on our street. But for years I slept with that letter under my pillow. It connected me to my real mother, which is how I thought of her. I imagined her at fourteen, waking up to find I had been taken, stolen from her during the night. In my mind, she was crazy with grief. I replayed the scene in my head many times every night. It was a comfort to know that someone in the world wanted me so desperately. I imagined her each year checking with the adoption agency to see if I, her son, had made contact.

The years passed by. I imagined her looking forward to my eighteenth birthday, hoping against hope that I would initiate our reconciliation. I imagined her disappointment when my eighteenth birthday came and went and I had not made contact. That bastard Dr Daly had diagnosed me with antisocial personality disorder, at which point my father cut all ties with me. I never lived at home again. The need to find my birth mother took a back seat to university, but I never doubted she was waiting for me, eagerly anticipating my appearance in her life.

Several years later, with a degree under my belt, I finally wrote to the adoption agency to start the process of finding her. My letter was returned. The agency had closed down many years before. All of the records had been transferred, and it took several more years of searching to finally ascertain who was holding them. When I finally tracked down the agency which had them, I believed I was at last about to get back what had been stolen from me. The right to a mother's love.

The long-anticipated envelope arrived and I tore it open. I couldn't take in the words at first. "Your birth mother has registered a 'do not contact' request." How could this be? Why would my mother not want me to contact her? She loved me. Didn't she?

I pushed the social worker to write to her, to give her the chance to change her mind. The obvious reason was that she was trying to protect me, that she didn't want to hurt me by revealing the circumstances of my birth. She would come round, once the social worker explained that I needed her. Three agonising weeks later another letter came. My mother, Vicky Richards, was washing her hands of me forever.

The rage I felt for this woman was incredible. To be rejected once was bad enough, but for her to reject me twice was unforgivable. I determined then that I would not allow her to turn her back on me again. I would find her and I would make her pay for the suffering she had put me through.

I applied for and got my long-form birth certificate, which disclosed my place of birth, Lockton House. A search for Lockton House on Facebook led me to the Survivors' page. I found a photograph of Vicky there. She was standing with a group of friends, most of whom had posted to the group. One person had not posted at all. Becky Tansey hadn't posted because she was dead. It was easy to assume her identity.

I befriended Connie Taylor online, pretending to be Becky. Connie may have been dim-witted, but in fairness to her, she would never reveal my mother's whereabouts. I had to assume another identify and strike up a friendship with her in person to get that information.

Imagine my fury when I discovered what a doting parent my mother has been to my half-sister. To find out that not only did she wash her filthy hands of me, her first-born child, but that she transferred the love which was rightfully mine to her second.

That bitch! Soon she will find out what it feels like to lose someone she loves. I have barely enough acid left, but I won't need so much this time. Kallie has such a small face.

CHAPTER FORTY-SIX

Fossgate, York

It was almost 12:15 p.m. when Ellen arrived back at the flat. As she climbed the stairs her phone rang. It was Samuels. He'd left the flat to chase a lead.

"Paul Benton's family have a caravan on a site at Acaster Malbis. Poplar Farm, it's called."

Acaster Malbis was a village about six miles south of Bishopthorpe. Ellen used to go there for lunch with Anthony when Zoe was tiny. There was an old pub with great food, the Ship Inn.

"I know the site, it's on the river."

"Everything points to Benton. If Gascoyne paid off his debts, he would have been caught between a rock and a hard place. His debt was written off when Gascoyne was killed."

Ellen frowned. "I just didn't get that feeling off the guy. Jackson, sure, but Benton? I don't know."

"I'm heading out to Acaster Malbis now to have a look. Rumour has it, Benton's wife threw him out over his gambling and he's been living out in the caravan for the last few weeks."

Ellen remembered Benton's tracksuit bottoms and hoodie. He looked like a man with limited access to a washing machine.

"He has the photofit, from Prufrock's," Ellen said.

"What photofit?"

"I got a police artist into the café yesterday. The staff all saw the guy. It arrived this morning, but I haven't got to see it yet."

A text pinged on her phone.

"I have to go, I've got a text. Oh, and Lewis . . ."

"Yes?"

"Thanks. I really appreciate this."

Ellen cut the call. The text was from an unknown number with a video attachment. Her stomach lurched. It had to be Zoe's kidnapper. As she opened the door to the flat, she saw Jackie waiting nervously inside.

"It's him, the guy who's got Zoe. I can't look."

Jackie led her to the sofa and then sat down beside her.

Ellen took a deep breath and opened the attachment. The video showed a small, dark room which could have been the bedroom of a caravan. Zoe's face appeared. She looked startled. Beside her face was a newspaper with today's date. The skin around Zoe's mouth looked red, and she was holding her shoulder awkwardly. Ellen groaned. On the video, she heard Zoe's voice, barely audible.

"Hello, Mum." There was silence as she struggled to make any further sound. As Zoe tried to speak, Ellen heard the faint sound of bells ringing in the background. The video swung up, just for a second, before cutting off, exposing a glimpse of the room behind. Wooden walls and a round shape, a window or a mirror. The screen went black.

Another text pinged in.

St Andrew's church, Bishopthorpe, one o'clock. Bring the girl and her mother. Come alone and you will get Zoe back, alive. Any police and I will send her back to you, head first.

The phone slid out of Ellen's hand and Jackie caught it and read the text. Ellen's heart was pounding. She looked at the clock on the sitting room wall. It was half past twelve. How would she get to Micklegate in time to pick up Vicky and Kallie and drive them back out to St Andrew's for one o'clock?

Jackie was on her feet. "We have to move, Elly. We have to go now!"

"Wait," Ellen said.

She clicked back into the video and played it again.

Something was nudging at the edge of Ellen's memory. She replayed the video clip, listening carefully. There! It was a combination of sounds she knew well. A boat engine chugging past and a peal of bells. Jackie's eyes locked onto hers. She recognised the bells of St Andrew's too.

"She's somewhere on the river near the church," Ellen said.

Ellen had a flashback of being on her father's boat. It was one of those hot summer days. A Sunday. She and Jackie had been on one of their 'breaks' from home. Back then they didn't have a name for their mother's alcoholism. Their father had packed a case and had bundled the two girls into the old Ford. She and Jackie had always loved being on the boat, listening to the sound of those bells. Those days had been their happiest.

Ellen replayed the video again, this time looking for the round shape she had seen. There it was. She knew it. It was the lower half of a porthole, shuttered from the inside. Zoe was on a houseboat moored on the river, somewhere near St Andrew's. There was only one possibility along that stretch of the Ouse — the moorings at Ferry Lane.

It was only a ten-minute drive to Ferry Lane, but she would have to drive in the opposite direction if she were to collect Vicky and Kallie first. *Shit!* She wouldn't make it in time. *Think!* Samuels! He had said he was going out to Acaster Malbis — that was only five minutes from Ferry Lane. He could go to the boats and check if Zoe was there while she drove to Micklegate. She dialled his number.

CHAPTER FORTY-SEVEN

Samuels answered after one ring.

"I've only got a minute to talk, so just listen," Ellen said in a rush.

"What's happened?"

"Just listen. I've been sent a video. It's Zoe, she's alive. The text says I have to be at St Andrew's church at Bishopthorpe at one o'clock and I have to bring Vicky and Kallie for a swap."

"Shit. Where are you?"

"I'm picking up Vicky and Kallie from Maggie James's house at Micklegate. Any sign of Benton?"

"I'm looking in the window of his caravan. There's dishes in the sink, but he's not here now and neither is Zoe."

"You're sure she's not there?"

"I can see every inch of the place from the window and there's no way she could be in there. Sorry, Ellen. Look, I can be at St Andrew's church in ten minutes. Let me come with you."

"No!" Ellen said, her tone firm. "He says if he sees anyone but me, he'll send Zoe back to me in pieces. No one can come with me."

"For God's sake, Ellen, you can't meet him alone, it's too dangerous."

"Shut up and listen," Ellen snapped, pulling across the traffic on Blossom Street, narrowly missing a white van whose driver blared his horn at her. "I think I know where she is. Maybe we can get to her before he moves her to the church. I need you to get out to the riverside at the end of Ferry Lane in Bishopthorpe. I'm only arriving at Maggie's now, so I won't be there for at least fifteen minutes."

"I know where it is. Boats along the river, with a caravan park behind. What makes you think she's there?"

"I just know, okay? Look for an old houseboat with a porthole shuttered from the inside. There are only a few old boats there. It's not the first boat, *Gypsy*, or the one next to it, *Serendipity*. But look in the rest. I think she's in one of them."

Ellen heard the bleep of a car being unlocked.

"I'm already at my car, and before you say it, I'll stay out of sight."

* * *

Ellen double parked outside Maggie's house and ran to the door.

Rob came to the door on the second ring.

"Where's Vicky?" Ellen said, looking past him and down to the kitchen behind.

"She's upstairs with Kallie. What's going on?"

Ellen brushed past him, but realised she had better put him at his ease. The last thing she needed now was Rob getting all heroic.

"There's no panic, but I'm going to have to move them. There's a small chance there was a leak at the station. Better safe than sorry, as they say."

Ellen started up the stairs. Rob shouted up after her.

"Well, just hold on until Maggie gets back. She's on her way from the office. I'll put the kettle on."

Ellen pasted on a smile.

"Sure, Rob, that would be nice."

Ellen found Vicky still in her pyjamas, plaiting Kallie's hair in the bathroom.

"We need to go."

"Why, what's happened?" Vicky said, fear in her voice.

"Nothing to worry about, but I think it's best if we move you from here. My friend has a boat on the river at Bishopthorpe." Ellen looked away. "You'll be safe there."

Ellen glanced at her watch, painfully aware that precious time was being lost.

"It's freezing outside. I think we're better off here for the moment," Vicky said, continuing to plait Kallie's hair.

Ellen reached across and snatched the hairbrush out of Vicky's hand.

"Vicky, you need to trust me. It's my friend Dan's houseboat, he's an ex-copper. He'll be there to keep you safe, but we need to go, now."

Vicky reluctantly left the bathroom and took Kallie into the bedroom to get dressed. Ellen stood outside the door, watching the seconds ticking by on her watch. A few minutes later Vicky and Kallie emerged. Ellen went downstairs ahead of them and opened the front door.

"I just need to go thank Rob," Vicky said, turning towards the kitchen.

Ellen looked down the corridor to the closed kitchen door. She could hear the clinking of mugs.

"He said to just go. Come on, hurry."

Vicky looked unsure but walked out past Ellen, holding Kallie by the hand. Ellen closed the door silently behind her. Vicky got into the back seat beside Kallie.

Ellen started the car and screeched onto Blossom Street, running the red light at the junction with Nunnery Lane. It was 12:35 p.m. It would be a quarter to one by the time she reached the riverside.

Ellen put her foot down and picked up speed. Swerving right at the Swan pub, Ellen turned on the radio, hoping that it might deter Vicky from asking any questions. It didn't.

"Why did you need to move us?" Vicky asked as Ellen sped past York Racecourse. She was driving faster now that green fields had appeared on either side of the road.

In the rear-view mirror Ellen saw Vicky pull Kallie towards her and kiss the top of her head. What was the expression, a mother's love knows no bounds? It was true of Vicky, but it was also true of her. Kallie was looking up at Vicky now, innocent, trusting. *Damn it!* How could she even consider taking that child anywhere near that monster? Did that make her as bad as him?

She couldn't bear to meet Vicky's gaze in the mirror any longer. Instead she glanced at her phone. No texts. No missed calls. Where the hell was Lewis? Surely he would be at the river by now. Why hadn't he texted her? She considered calling him but thought better of it, not wanting to risk his phone being heard.

Five minutes later she pulled up behind some disused caravans. It was almost a quarter to one. There were berths on this stretch of the river for around twenty boats, but aside from *Gypsy* and *Serendipity*, there were only a couple of old houseboats. Behind the riverfront was a small caravan park with ten or eleven caravans, all empty. She turned in her seat to speak to Vicky.

"Stay here, out of sight. I just have to take a look around first, make sure it's all safe."

As Ellen got out and shut the door, she could hear Vicky protesting but ignored her. There was no time to waste. She glanced around. No cars apart from hers. No sign of Lewis Samuels, but maybe he had been clever enough to park his car somewhere out of sight. The sky was gun-metal grey, threatening yet more snow. It cast an eerie atmosphere over the entire place. Then she realised what was so strange. There were no geese or swans. The river was deathly quiet.

She opened the boot and lifted out a crowbar, the only weapon she had to hand. She moved from one caravan to the next, keeping her eye on the boats beyond. There was no sign of life by the dock, no evidence that any of the boats moored were occupied. She knew neither *Gypsy* nor *Serendipity* had a porthole with a wooden shutter. It was the two old houseboats she had her eye on. Looking all around, she darted down to the riverbank, alongside the first boat. Her breath formed clouds in the air in front of her. It had no portholes of the kind she was looking for. She hurried along to the second boat. It was an old narrowboat with peeling paintwork. Stained curtains were drawn over rectangular windows. Then she saw the porthole, shuttered just like the one in the video.

There were double doors at the stern, outside of which was a small deck which was level with the dock. The doors must have been forced at some stage — they were closed, but no longer locked. Ellen eased the doors open and listened. Silence.

She descended the steps into the galley. It was cluttered with ancient cans of paint, bottles of turpentine, dust sheets, and brushes covered in cobwebs. She stepped gingerly into the small living area, aware that if anyone were on the boat, they must surely be aware of her presence. Beyond was a partition open on the port side. Squeezing past into the saloon, she called Zoe's name. Nothing. At that moment her ankle caught on something sharp. She jerked back and stumbled, her ankle turning under her. She gasped in pain. *Shit!*

Pulling herself up to a standing position and leaning on her good leg, she looked around the room. In front of her she saw the porthole that she had seen on the video, but there was no one in the room, only a jumble of furniture and boxes stacked up on the port side. Then she heard it. A muffled sound coming from the pile of furniture. Looking closer, she saw two feet poking out from what looked like a rolled-up carpet at the bottom of the pile. Her heart leapt. *Zoe!* She recognised Zoe's school socks.

Ellen hopped over to Zoe and frantically started pulling the furniture off her, all the while keeping an eye on the galley. Where was Zoe's abductor? And where was Lewis?

She managed to unroll Zoe from the filthy rug and pulled the tape off her mouth. *Thank God!* Tears flowed down her face as she held her daughter tight. Zoe was alive. She was here. She was safe.

"My arms," Zoe said in a hoarse voice. Her wrists were bound with cable ties, which Ellen could not budge.

"Hang on. I'll be right back."

After easing Zoe back onto the floor, Ellen hobbled back into the galley and rooted round until she found a pair of scissors. She managed to hop back with them and cut the cable ties binding Zoe's hands. Zoe cried out with pain as her arms were released. There was something terribly wrong with her left shoulder.

"It's going to be okay, Zoe," said Ellen, although she knew that they might still be in terrible danger.

She needed to get Zoe to hospital, but her daughter could barely move, and her own ankle was throbbing painfully. Ellen took off her jacket and wrapped it around Zoe. Her phone pinged — it was a text from Sarika.

Here's the photofit.

She hadn't time for that now. Instead she dialled Sarika's number. The DC answered immediately.

"Sarika, I need you to listen very carefully. I've just found Zoe, tied up on a boat, six berths upriver from *Gypsy*. I think the man who took her killed Connie and the Gascoyne's. And I think he might be back here any second."

Sarika inhaled sharply. "Okay, boss. Hold tight and I'll be there in ten. See if you can lock yourself in somehow."

"Sarika, I think it might be Paul Benton."

"I've sent you the photofit. Just hang on, I'm on my way."

Half lifting, half pulling, Ellen managed to drag Zoe out of the saloon and into the galley. Taking the crowbar she had taken from the car boot, she managed to jam it through both handles on the door to the deck. It would not stop anyone determined to get in, but at least it would slow them down.

She cradled Zoe, who was shivering in spite of the jacket.

"I want to go home now, Mum," she said. Ellen looked at her watch. It was five to one.

"I promise we will be home soon, love, very soon."

Ellen was still clutching the scissors she had used to cut the cable ties from Zoe's hands. She hoped she would not need to use them. Remembering the photofit, she clicked into Sarika's text. *What the fuck?*

* * *

An icy shiver ran right through her. It was Lewis Samuels. The same pale eyes, the turn of the mouth. There was no doubt. Suddenly the door above them rattled — someone was trying to get in. Two seconds later the double doors crashed open and the crowbar clattered to the floor. Ellen looked up to see Samuels standing above them.

Instinctively, she slipped the scissors into her pocket, and then pulled Zoe towards her.

"It's him," Zoe whispered, confirming what Ellen knew for certain now.

Samuels' expression was cold. There was no trace of the amiable journalist Ellen thought she had known. In his hand he held a bottle of liquid. In one swift movement he had showered the contents over both Ellen and Zoe.

CHAPTER FORTY-EIGHT

Ellen gasped as the liquid splashed over them. The powerful fumes stung her eyes as the realisation hit her. Turpentine! Ellen scrambled to wipe the pungent liquid from her daughter's face using the cuff of her sleeve.

The air was so heavy with fumes that she and Zoe both started coughing. She looked up and saw Samuels' hand dart into his shirt pocket and produce an old-fashioned brass lighter. He flicked the cap, his thumb resting on the wheel. Ellen flinched. If he flicked the wheel on that lighter, the entire boat would go up in a fireball.

"I want the two of you up here, where I can see you."

Barely able to see with her streaming eyes, Ellen dragged herself and Zoe towards the steps. Sarika would be here in a matter of minutes. How would Samuels react if he heard a police siren? The steps were slick with the turpentine, and it was hard to keep her footing.

"Lewis, please . . ."

Samuels' eyes were as cold as ice. How could she have got him so wrong? There was no trace of the man who had tenderly ministered to Ellen during the night, stroking her head in comfort. Instead, she saw only a deranged killer. A psychopath.

As Ellen pulled herself up the steps, Zoe clutching on behind her, Samuels doused himself in the turps.

"Try anything and I'll turn this boat into an inferno."

Ellen clambered up the final step onto the deck. The surface of the deck was slippery, soaked in the flammable liquid. As she pulled Zoe into the open air, Samuels leaned forward and grabbed the girl by the hair. She cried out with pain, but Ellen dared not move to help her. Her eyes were trained on the lighter. One move and the entire boat would go up. None of them would escape.

Samuels forced Zoe into a squatting position, holding her at arm's length by the hair. Ellen's eyes flicked over towards the car, where Vicky and Kallie were waiting unawares. Samuels' gaze followed hers. He smiled.

"Get Vicky and her child here in the next minute or I'll happily burn in hell alongside the two of you. Tell her anything, but get her here."

"Okay, Lewis, please, don't . . ."

Ellen pulled out her phone and called Vicky's number. Her hands were shaking. She had a memory of being in a petrol station and reading a notice that it was dangerous to use a mobile phone around petrol fumes. Was turpentine oil as flammable as petrol? Vicky answered her phone.

"You can come down to the boat, Vicky. Bring Kallie. It's all clear."

She was aware of the strain in her voice but she had to persuade Vicky to come on board. It was the only chance she had of getting Zoe out of this nightmare alive.

"I don't know, Ellen. It's so isolated," Vicky said. "I don't think I want to stay here."

Ellen swallowed painfully.

"It's actually lovely, Vicky. Really nice and cosy. Tell you what, why don't you just come and have a look and if you don't like it, fine, I'll take you to my place."

There was a pause before Vicky spoke again.

"Okay. But I already know I won't like it."

No, you won't like it, Ellen thought.

"Great. It's the last boat along on the right."

She felt a stab of shame for how easily the words had rolled off her tongue. She knew she could be leading Vicky and Kallie to their deaths, but what choice did she have? She needed to play for time.

There was the sound of a car door closing. Samuels crouched behind the open door to the galley, pulling Zoe and himself out of sight. After a long twenty seconds or so Ellen caught sight of Vicky making her way towards the boat. She was carrying Kallie in her arms. The child looked to be asleep. Samuels was holding the lighter to Zoe's face.

"Wave at her," he instructed.

Ellen lifted her shaking hand in a wave. She fought to control the shaking in her limbs. She couldn't let panic overwhelm her, not now.

"I'm so sorry, Vicky. I had no choice," Ellen said as she helped Vicky up onto the deck.

Vicky's eyes widened in horror as Samuels stood up and she immediately stepped back.

"Do what he says. The deck is covered in turpentine. One move and we will all go up in flames."

Samuels was grinning. He looked manic, his eyes flashing with menace. He pulled Zoe roughly into a standing position. Her hands flew up reflexively, but she didn't make a sound. He lit the lighter and held the flame up to Zoe's face.

Ellen's breath caught in her throat.

"Please, Lewis, I beg you. She's just a child."

Samuels wasn't listening. His focus was on Vicky.

Vicky looked behind her, as if still considering making a run for it, but with a child in her arms, escape was impossible.

"I don't understand," she said, looking from Samuels to Ellen.

Samuels sneered. "Don't you remember me?"

"No, I don't. There must be some mistake." She looked away, avoiding Samuels' piercing stare.

"Look . . . at . . . me!" The venom was real and it shocked Vicky. "Look at me and tell me that you don't recognise me."

At that moment, realisation dawned on Vicky's face.

"Kevin?" she whispered. "Is it you?"

Samuels stared at Vicky for several moments before speaking.

"Yes, mother, I'm afraid, for you, it is."

He turned to Ellen. The fleeting sadness in his eyes had been replaced with a look of rage.

"We have you, Ellen, to thank for making this reunion possible. Without you, I might never have tracked Vicky down."

Ellen frowned. "*You're* Vicky's son?"

"Yes. Vicky is my birth mother. Also the woman who gave me away, and who subsequently refused all my attempts to contact her."

"Kevin," Vicky said in a gentle voice. "I'm so sorry, but you don't understand."

Samuels face flushed red. Still holding the lighter, he turned to Vicky and elbowed her violently in the face, sending her crashing back against the side of the boat, the child still in her arms. He stood over mother and daughter, hysterical with rage.

"Don't you dare speak, you fucking heartless bitch. You don't know the meaning of sorry . . . but you soon will."

Ellen's mind raced. It was clear that Samuels had set her up from the start to find Vicky. It was her fault that she and Kallie were here. Now she had to save them.

Samuels waved the lighter in the direction of a half-full bottle of turps, sitting beside the tiller. He turned to Ellen.

"Empty it over the two of them," he growled.

Ellen froze in shock.

"Do it now!"

Ellen leaned forward and retrieved the bottle, and started sprinkling the liquid over Vicky.

"And the child," Samuels roared, waving the flame once again.

Ellen poured the rest of the liquid onto Kallie's pink and yellow tracksuit bottoms. Vicky tried to shuffle away with

Kallie. Samuels took several steps forward, dragging Zoe by the hair with him.

"I could forgive you for giving me up for adoption. You weren't to know that my adoptive father was a brute who beat me. That my adoptive mother would laugh when he did so. I thought of you, every day, through all of it. I took comfort knowing that some day I would look for you and you would be there for me, that you would be waiting for me to get in touch."

"Kevin . . . I'm so sorry . . ."

"Shut up!" he blasted, spittle spraying from his lips. "Contact refused. Can you imagine how I felt when I read those words?" Samuels was standing over Vicky now and he let go of Zoe, who stumbled backwards. Ellen reached forward and pulled her daughter into her arms.

Vicky was speaking. "I should have written to you, Kevin, to explain why I couldn't ever meet you."

"You don't even know my fucking name," he shouted. "It's Lewis. My name is Lewis Samuels."

Tears streamed down Vicky's face.

"I couldn't bear for you to know the truth about your father."

"But I found out. Connie told me everything. Everything except what I most needed to know, where you were hiding. Her loyalty cost her her head."

Samuels was blocking any escape onto the pontoon dock, but Ellen realised that if she moved quickly, she could pull Zoe over the port side and into the water.

Lewis looked at his watch.

"Almost time, Mother. You do remember that's it's my birthday?"

Vicky's voice was barely audible.

"Of course I do. The twenty-sixth of January."

"Twenty-sixth of January, nineteen eighty-eight. Twelve minutes past one, to be precise. It's almost that time now. This is what sorry looks like, Mother. It's the look on your face when your precious child goes up in flames."

Vicky opened her mouth as if to scream, but nothing came out. Samuels looked at his watch again. He was counting down the seconds. "Ten, nine, eight, seven . . ."

Ellen had to stop him. Her only chance was to run at Samuels, and she needed to make some distance to give herself room to build up momentum. She took two small steps backwards, which was as far as she could go on the tiny deck.

"I always loved you," Vicky said, looking up at Samuels. "You have to know that."

Samuels hesitated. Ellen knew it was now or never.

She lunged forward, pushing off on her good ankle, her head down. The impact of her body slamming into Lewis Samuels' stomach launched them both off the boat and onto the floating pontoon dock. The flame from the lighter caught the fumes on their clothing as they fell with a crash. A whoosh of flame enveloped the two of them in a fireball, and Ellen felt a searing pain across her left shoulder and up the back of her head. She heard Samuels' desperate screams, but she couldn't see anything against the flames and smoke before her. In training she had been taught a protocol — she had to get to ground, roll out the flames. She blindly pitched herself forwards, hands flailing in front of her. She could smell her hair burning. Her hands went instinctively to her face as she fell forwards, her head knocked against something hard and metal. A second later she plunged backwards into the freezing river, the shock causing her to gasp and take in mouthfuls of water.

As she came back up to the surface, coughing water and gasping for air, she saw a moving fireball on the pontoon. It was Samuels, his arms flailing. Perhaps he thought he was headed in the direction of the river. He wasn't. He stumbled and fell on the grassy ground behind the pontoon, curling into a foetal position, the flames consuming him so that she could no longer make out his shape.

Vicky shouted to Ellen and reached out to pull her out of the water and onto the stern deck. The smell of charred skin hung in the air. Zoe was staring blankly at the burning mass. Ellen crawled to her and threw her wet arms around her daughter's rigid body, then held her face with both hands, forcing Zoe to look at her and away from Samuels.

"He's gone, Zoe. You're safe now."

Zoe looked through her but Ellen felt her daughter's hand squeeze hers back. She would survive, they both would.

CHAPTER FORTY-NINE

Ferry Lane, Bishopthorpe

Zoe slept with her arms wrapped around her mother, as she had every night for the last three weeks. She made a moaning sound in her sleep. Who knew what nightmares were playing themselves out inside her head. But Ellen did not wake her. The therapist had said it was better to let her sleep.

The pain from the burns still kept her awake at night, in spite of the strong painkillers she was taking. But she was lucky — new skin was starting to appear, and she had avoided any infection.

She looked at the alarm clock — 7:20 a.m. It was still dark outside. The bedside light had been on all night. Zoe couldn't sleep without it. In truth, Ellen was happy to leave it on too. The first boat of the day was already passing by and the wash gently rocked the boat. She had been awake for hours. She couldn't stop thinking about what had happened, that first approach by Lewis Samuels at Connie Taylor's house. What if she had refused to talk to him, had never met with him at the Lazy Days Café? Could the nightmare that unfolded have been avoided? Would Harry and Jill Gascoyne still be alive today?

More than anything, Ellen agonised over the night she allowed Lewis Samuels to inveigle his way into her flat, into her daughter's home. In so doing, she had brought Zoe to the attention of a monster who might otherwise never have noticed her. Zoe had survived, but only just. It was this thought that tortured her during the night. She could never allow Zoe's life to be endangered like that again. And if that meant giving up the career she loved, then so be it.

Very gently, Ellen prised herself out of Zoe's grip and out of the bed. She tiptoed to the galley, which smelled of fresh paint. She didn't need to turn on the light as the large windows on all four galley walls let in the breaking dawn. She could see Dan sitting on the deck of *Serendipity*, having his first cigarette of the day. Ellen filled the kettle.

The work on the boat was nowhere near finished, but she had accomplished a lot in the last few weeks on leave. Dan had been discharged from hospital after a few days' observation and had thrown himself into working on *Gypsy*. The galley was more or less complete. Dan had built the kitchen units himself using old cabinets salvaged from a skip outside a second-hand bookshop at Fishergate which had recently closed down. She opened the cupboard over the sink and took out two mugs. The wood was dark mahogany and had been painted with multiple layers over the years. The paint had worn through here and there so that the different coloured layers were visible. The top coat was a rich red, but worn patches of cobalt blue and sea green could be seen underneath. Dan's Belfast sink, which had been sitting under the tarpaulin on his boat for the last ten years, now had pride of place in the new kitchen, a solid oak worktop installed around it.

The kettle came to the boil and Ellen wet the tea. She pulled on her parka over her pyjamas and walked out onto the deck with the steaming mugs, whistling to Dan, who would come once his cigarette was finished. This was her favourite time of the day on the water, listening to the first stirrings of the birds. Paddy had taught her to distinguish one species from another — blackbirds, thrushes, kingfishers, water rail, reed and sedge warblers, and grey wagtails. She knew them all.

The work to get *Gypsy* habitable had brought Ellen, Dan, Zoe, and Jackie closer together. The renovations had given them all a common focus. It had been healing, but like the scars on her body, Ellen feared the scars in Zoe's mind might never fully go away.

Dan arrived and pulled out one of the newly painted chairs to sit on.

"Would you look at the amount of paint that daft lass has got everywhere," he said, pointing to where Jackie had dripped green paint on the deck.

Ellen pushed one of the mugs towards him. If Dan did anything, he liked to do a proper job.

"It will come off eventually. Don't you go saying anything to upset her. She's very pleased with herself, believe it or not."

"I'd well believe she is," Dan grumbled.

The two sat in companionable silence for several minutes. The snow of last month was gone. The river stretched dark into the distance in both directions bounded by riverbanks bursting with fresh spring growth. Ellen closed her eyes and listened to the birds. In another few weeks the dawn chorus would be in riotous full swing. For now, it was a quieter, calmer affair. Dan broke the silence.

"I heard the trial date has been set."

Jackie, you bigmouth!

Matt Jackson had been charged with taking bribes, passing on information, and intimidation of witnesses. Paul Benton had already been internally disciplined and had been demoted. Alastair Monroe had phoned Ellen himself the previous evening to give her the news. She had been with Jackie at the time. Jackie could never keep anything to herself for long. It wasn't that Ellen didn't want Dan to know, just that she didn't feel like talking about it yet.

"Yeah, twentieth of May, York Crown Court."

Ellen stood and picked up the two half-full mugs.

"How you feeling about it?" Dan asked.

Ellen turned and opened the door to the galley. She sighed. Dan meant well. He knew how she had been treated the last time by the press and by some of her colleagues. He was right to be worried. It had been a nightmare, and no doubt this trial would be just as bad.

"Can't wait, Dan," she said humourlessly.

While on leave from work, Ellen had felt insulated from reality, happy in her little bubble of decorating, moving onto the boat, spending time with Zoe. The decision ahead of her, about whether to go back to her job as a detective, had seemed a long way off. Alastair Monroe had burst that bubble. In six weeks' time she would have to stand up in court and relive everything that had happened. The question was, would she be standing in court as a serving detective or as a retired one?

Ellen put two slices of bread into the toaster. Tea and toast was her go-to comfort food. Day or night, a few slices of white toast, slathered in real butter with a lick of raspberry jam, had the power to calm her like nothing else. Dan appeared in the galley just as the toast popped up. Ellen buttered it in silence.

"Look, I know you don't want to talk about it, but . . ."

"You're right, Dan, I don't."

She opened the fridge and took out the jar of jam, opened it and proceeded to place a dollop on each slice of toast with the buttery knife. Dan tutted. It drove him mad when she left traces of butter in the jam. Well, to hell with him, it was her bloody jam. He took a teaspoon and carefully scooped out the offending trails of butter and flicked them into the bin.

"Now, come on, talk to me, Elly. I haven't pressed you to talk about it before now, but fair's fair."

Ellen carried the plate of toast back out on deck. Dan followed her and passed her a tweed blanket he had taken from the kitchen to wrap around herself. She unfolded the blanket and threw it around her shoulders. He deserved to know what going on.

"Fine. Here's what we know so far."

Dan sat down opposite her and lit another cigarette.

"After Vicky came into the station to report Gascoyne, Jackson set out to intimidate her and Connie. He wanted to make sure they never made any further allegations. He followed them, wrote them threatening notes, he even killed Vicky's dog."

Dan grunted. "And the guy on the CCTV, at the café Connie Taylor worked in, was that Jackson?"

"No, that was Samuels. Samuels befriended Connie, but because of Jackson's intimidation, Vicky was already in hiding. She was so terrified after her dog was killed that she wouldn't even tell Connie where she was staying from night to night. So when Samuels broke in and tried to extract that information from Connie, she didn't have it to give to him."

"So he killed her. But what I don't get is why he staged Connie's body?"

"He was looking for maximum publicity. He wanted the murder shown on every television screen in the country. He wanted Vicky to see it and make the connection with Lockton House. His plan was to terrify her, to get her to run to the police for protection, and out of hiding. And that's why he approached me. He wanted to create a friendly ally for Vicky to run to."

"Because he knew you were someone Vicky would trust. The press were all over the Ana Petrescu angle."

"Exactly. He used me. And I fell for it. Vicky trusted me, and I delivered her and Kallie to that psychopath."

The sound of footsteps on the stairs alerted Ellen that Zoe was up, and she mimicked zipping her mouth to alert Dan.

Zoe appeared on the deck. She gave a high five to Dan, then came and sat beside Ellen. She was wearing her dressing gown and slippers.

"What has you up so early, young lady?" Dan asked.

"We're making a cake," said Zoe.

"Maggie's coming for lunch," explained Ellen. "And before you ask, yes you're invited."

Ellen realised with surprise that she was feeling excited about Maggie coming. Her friendship with Maggie was something she had left behind all those years ago, and her life had been poorer for it. Rekindling that friendship was part of a fresh start. Maggie also had good news to report about Vicky. A solicitor friend had taken on Vicky's case. She had a good chance of getting substantial compensation from Harry Gascoyne's estate. A public enquiry was on the cards, which would look into the abuse that happened at Lockton House. At last Vicky would get justice. She was back at her job in the nursing home, and Kallie had settled back into her nursery.

Anthony had agreed to postpone the custody case on the advice of Zoe's therapist, which was a relief. But Ellen could see now that he had been right. The hours she had been working before her leave had been unfair on Zoe. The child deserved better. Ellen wasn't sure what the future held, but if she was certain of one thing, it was that she was not going to leave Zoe's side, not for a long time.

The sun had started to rise on the horizon, lighting up the riverbank as far as the eye could see.

"Look, Zoe, the sun is coming up," Ellen whispered and kissed her daughter's head.

Paddy had loved the sunrise, especially at this time of year. He had sat where they were now, year after year, looking down at the curve of the river. At that moment Ellen had a sudden epiphany. In spite of everything that had happened, in spite of all her regrets, right at this second she felt more at peace with the world than she had in a long time. Zoe reached over and took a slice of toast. Right now, on board her father's boat, with Dan and Zoe watching the sunrise, Ellen knew she was right where she was meant to be.

THE END

nailing list for free Kindle crime thriller,
.ry, romance books and new releases, as well
news on the next book by Caroline Bale!
www.joffebooks.com/contact/

Thank you for reading this book. If you enjoyed it please leave feedback on Amazon, and if there is anything we missed or you have a question about then please get in touch. The author and publishing team appreciate your feedback and time reading this book.

Our email is office@joffebooks.com

Follow us on facebook www.facebook.com/joffebooks

We hate typos but sometimes they slip through.
Please send any errors you find to
corrections@joffebooks.com
We'll get them fixed ASAP. We're very grateful to eagle-eyed readers who take the time to contact us.